RIPTIDES

Praise for Kirsten Alexander and *Half Moon Lake*

'An impressive historical fiction debut . . . A captivating tale that explores the bonds between mother and child, the power of money and the importance of truth.' *Herald Sun*

'A gripping, nervy tale of identity, class and race . . . A strong original narrative, with a central mystery and an intriguing plot.' *Sydney Morning Herald*

'By covering complex terrain, *Half Moon Lake* opens up an emotionally charged dialogue surrounding the choices we make and the lies we tell ourselves.' *The Age*

'This is why we read novels – to come across a story such as Kirsten Alexander's *Half Moon Lake* . . . In its craft and psychological subtlety, Alexander's story comes close to a masterpiece.' Robert Hillman, bestselling author of *The Bookshop of the Broken Hearted*

'An accomplished debut . . . The publisher's blurb says the novel is about "the parent–child bond, identity, and what it means to be part of a family". All true: but what the novel is really about is power.' *Australian Book Review*

'A thought-provoking tale of the lengths we go to in order to save those close to us – and ourselves. I was gripped throughout.' Natasha Lester, bestselling author of *The Paris Seamstress*

'An evocative, unputdownable story about every parent's worst nightmare – losing a child . . . I highly recommend this novel.' Sally Hepworth, bestselling author of *The Mother-in-Law*

'Alexander's thoughtful novel kept me engrossed and raised plenty of questions that had me thinking about the book long after I finished.' *Good Reading*

'This isn't simply the story of a missing boy . . . it's also a skilful exploration of multi-generational trauma, wrapped up in an engrossing mystery.' *Books+Publishing*

'A captivating novel . . . Transporting us to another time, [Alexander] takes readers to a world rife with injustice and prejudice, where the truth can be bought with gold and social appearances mean everything. For readers who enjoy both historical and thriller fiction, *Half Moon Lake* should be on your reading list.' *Better Reading*

'An incredibly strong debut that left me thinking about this book for weeks.' *Sam Still Reading*

'This book defies categorisation. Elements of mystery, true crime, family drama and social commentary are woven together seamlessly. *Half Moon Lake* should be read and re-read – devour it for the engrossing story, and return to it for the lyrical language.' Meg Keneally, bestselling author of *Fled*

'A truly mesmerising novel, beautifully written with such a strong sense of time and place.' *Theresa Smith Writes*

'On first appearance it can seem like *Half Moon Lake* is a cut-and-dry historical-based kidnapping story. I need to make it clear that *Half Moon Lake* is so much more than this.' *Mrs B's Book Reviews*

RIPTIDES

KIRSTEN ALEXANDER

BANTAM

SYDNEY AUCKLAND TORONTO NEW YORK LONDON

BANTAM

UK | USA | Canada | Ireland | Australia
India | New Zealand | South Africa | China

Bantam is part of the Penguin Random House group of companies whose addresses can
be found at global.penguinrandomhouse.com.

Penguin
Random House
Australia

First published by Bantam in 2020

Cover photography by Bo Le, SA from Above
Cover design by Christa Moffitt, Christabella Designs
Typeset in Adobe Garamond Pro by Midland Typesetters, Australia

Printed and bound in Australia by Griffin Press, part of Ovato, an accredited
ISO AS/NZS 14001 Environmental Management Systems printer

 A catalogue record for this
book is available from the
National Library of Australia

NATIONAL
LIBRARY
OF AUSTRALIA

ISBN 978 0 14379 208 6

penguin.com.au

To Milo

I want you to remember the perpetrator and I am going to ask you to remember the victims: not just tonight but tomorrow and the next day. I want you to find a way to include them – the perpetrators and the victims – in what you do, how you think, how you act, what you care about, what your life means to you.

Andrea Dworkin

PART ONE

CHAPTER ONE

Friday 6 December 1974

Charlie

I wake when Abby shouts. She reaches across me and grabs the steering wheel. A car horn brays. White beams flare at us then pitch to the right. For an instant, a rump of blue metal shines in our headlights. I elbow my sister out of the way and take the wheel, leaning back hard so I don't slam my head into it. Abby flattens her hands against the dashboard as I brake and strain to control our sideways skid. She screams my name. We sling to one side of the narrow dirt road and the other car slings the opposite way, like wrong ends of magnets made to meet. We slide to an angled stop, pointing into scrappy bushland.

Dust swirls in front of our headlights, the only movement in a frozen moment. My window is open but I don't hear a sound from the surrounding bush, the cicadas and creaky eucalypts dumbstruck. Abby and I stare through the windscreen at the dust, panting, coughing.

Neither of us moves until the cassette ejects with a clunk, having played its silent end, giving way to static. Abby hits the off button, fumbles to get out of the car and walks through the settling dust. I don't follow her straight away. I'm clocking what just happened. What the hell just happened? I turn off the engine, feel the thumping drum of my heart, the heat where my jeans sink into ridged vinyl, a breeze through the open door. I watch my sister walk away, her long hair splayed across the back of her singlet like a web.

Once I get out, I cross the road and stand on the thin verge, shaking my sore wrists. Down in the ditch, Abby stands next to the crumpled car. A blue Holden Premier, stopped on the cusp of a roll, one front wheel and one back not touching earth, the bonnet crunched against the trunk of a white gum, headlights still blazing. Abby's on her toes, yanking at the driver's-side doorhandle. I slide down to join her. 'Help me,' she says. Instead, I go to the front of the car, worried she'll pull it down onto all fours, onto us. But it's pushed so firmly into the tree, pug-faced, there's no chance of that.

I can see the driver, a woman, slumped across the steering wheel, glowing under the internal light. She has thick blonde locks shot through with caramel and gold. Blood oozes from her head. She's coated in shards of glass.

'Charlie, help me. We have to get her out.'

'You're not supposed to move –'

'It'll blow up! I've seen it on TV.'

We stand side by side and pull on the handle, yelling at the woman to come to, poking her limp arm through the open

4

window, until the door gives. I'm jammed into the join of door and car when she falls out onto Abby. They hit the ground together, a mess of bloodied skin and hair and glass. Abby screams. 'Get her off me. Get her *off*.'

I shove the car door away from my chest, then squat beside them and lift the woman so my sister can get out from underneath her. We lay the woman on the ground's coat of leaves, sticks and bark. She's honey-skinned, with a spray of freckles across her nose and cheeks, and her hair is incandescent even away from the light. She's beautiful, and heavily pregnant.

I look across at Abby. We're both open-mouthed, mirror images of shock.

'Charlie,' she whispers.

I nod.

'Wake up,' Abby says, kneeling closer to the woman. She shakes her by the shoulders.

'She's not sleeping.' I speak more loudly. 'Hey, lady, *hey*! Can you hear me?' I stare at her. I'm not sure but – 'Is this Stevie Nicks?'

'No, you idiot.' Abby places two fingers on the woman's wrist.

'It might be,' I say. 'You don't know.'

'No pulse.' I hear panic in her voice.

I put my hand on the warm skin of the woman's neck, pushing aside hair, but I'm shaking and can't be certain if I feel the throb of blood. I scan for movement under her closed eyelids, block song lyrics from filling my head.

'See if you can feel her heartbeat.'

'Why me?' Abby asks.

'I'm not touching her boob.'

'It's not a grope. We need to know if she's alive.' She rests her palm on the woman's chest while I wait in silence. 'Nothing.'

'Fuck,' I exhale. 'Holy fuck.'

Abby moves her hand to the woman's belly. The rolling lump lifts her fingers like a wave pushing a board up and over. A shoulder maybe, or a foot. She jerks her arm back.

'We need to get to a hospital. We'll drag her up to the road, move the car closer. Charlie?'

It occurs to me that we didn't check if there was anyone else in the car. I yank open the heavy door, haul myself up onto the front seat. There's a bag on the floor of the passenger's side but nothing and no one else.

'Charlie!' Abby shouts.

'It's not going to blow up. That doesn't happen,' I call back.

'Come here.'

I clamber out and go to her side. 'She's alive?'

Abby is holding up the woman's limp wrist. 'Mum's ring.'

'No way.' I frown at my sister. 'How?'

'I don't know. Obviously.'

'Obviously.' I mimic her, knowing this is stupid. Even now, in a disaster, I can't help myself.

Abby narrows her eyes at me. 'A cleaner, a neighbour.'

'Or Dad's . . . no.'

'We'd know if he was seeing someone.' Her voice quiets at the end of her sentence. Then, as if it's the next logical action, Abby tries to twist the ring off the woman's finger.

'Don't do that, Abby.'

'When you're pregnant, you swell up and –'

'Seriously, stop.'

'Why, you think I'm hurting her?' She starts to cry, and in her frustration tugs the ring hard enough to almost pull the finger out of its socket. I touch her arm but she shakes me off. 'Got it.'

When she's freed the ring she examines it, pushes it deep into her jeans pocket, and closes her eyes for a moment. 'Okay.' She wipes her cheeks with the back of her hand. 'Okay. Let's get her up to the car.'

'Hang on. I need to think.' I look away from her, into dark bushland dotted with anthill mounds. 'Where would we take her, Abby? There's nothing here, no hospital for miles.'

'We'll drive back to Chinchilla and find a doctor. Take her arm.'

'No.' I shake my head. 'I'm not doing that. I'm not driving into some strange country town with a dead body. That's a bad idea.'

'What's the alternative? You want to leave her here? Charlie, the baby's alive. We *can't* leave her!'

I scramble up to the road, drop into the driver's seat and close the car door. I wait for what seems like an eternity – radio on, immediately off, glove box open, closed, looking for any distraction – before giving in to the fact she's not following me.

By the time I walk back, she's decided to drag the woman up the slope by herself, making small gains then sliding again into the ditch.

'It wouldn't live,' I say. My voice sounds too loud, doesn't belong here.

'You don't know that. She's seven or eight months. The baby's still moving.' She persists a few minutes more then shouts up at me in exasperation. 'Get down here and help. What is wrong with you?'

7

'Let's go, Abby.'

'What the *hell*?' she yells, now standing upright. Her words cut through the silent night, ricochet between the trees. 'You are *not* serious.'

I am though. Usually Abby calls the shots. Older sister, younger brother. But I've never felt so sure in such a weird, dark situation. We need to leave. I watch her bend down once more with renewed determination. She holds the woman's arms and pulls. It's hopeless. I don't know why she's not seeing it. Even with my help we couldn't get the body to our car.

Abby flicks her head up when rain begins to tap onto the dirt around her. It's light at first, then quickly becomes insistent and heavy. I stand still, watching my sister. When she's so wet that her shirt hangs forward like a billowing sail and her hair forms a long slick, when I can smell the leather of my watchstrap, the grease on my scalp, and I can see the woman's dark nipples through her cheesecloth smock, I shout Abby's name again. This has to stop.

Abby sits on the wet earth, her head slumped forward. She folds the dead woman's arms low across her belly, removes a piece of glass from her hair and throws it into the bush.

The crashed car's headlights go out.

Abby hits the driver's-side window with her fist until I wind it down.

'A doctor could save the baby.' Her voice turns to a plea. 'We can't leave her.'

'Get in the car.'

'It was an accident. It's the worse thing not to help her. And what about the ring? Dad must know her somehow. Stop – what are you doing?'

I wind the window up while she presses her fingers down onto the glass, pulling out at the last second. I point to the passenger's seat but she yells insults at me to the effect that I should never drive again.

I slide over, then glance at the back seat, where I'd put our carton of beer. Crushed empties litter the floor. How many did I have? I resist the urge to open a fresh one.

Abby drops onto the seat, all wet air and fury. She's about to speak again when she sees where I'm looking.

'I said two, *two*. Is that what happened? I thought she'd – I thought she might've been asleep. *You* were asleep?'

'You were asleep, too.'

'I was the *passenger*. My God.' She rests her forehead on the steering wheel.

'I'm not that drunk. I haven't slept in days. It wasn't my fault.'

She jerks her head up. 'You can't possibly think this is anyone's fault *but* yours.'

'You let me drive.' Even to my ear this is bullshit. She punches me in the arm. I shove her off. She thumps me a few more times then takes a deep breath, stares out the rain-slashed window. 'How long was I asleep? How far are we from Chinchilla?'

I shrug, dig around in Abby's bag for the cigarettes she made such a big deal of buying for me at the bottleshop.

'Charlie, I'm driving us back there. We'll go to the police and they can come get her.'

'Where will you send them – third tree after the rock?'

We could be anywhere you'd call 'the bush', on a road to nowhere except Dad's farm. There's not a single thing in my sightline that makes this place different from the miles of other bushland we've passed through. And Abby knows it. It's not like it's a straightforward trip back to that couple of chopstick roads she's calling a town either. We took a lot of left then right then left to get on this road before she fell asleep, and that was when it was light. I think, though, we're about an hour and a bit from Dad's farm. I'd followed the few signs she'd said would take us close, planning to wake her up once her map let me down. The baby will be long gone before anyone gets to this place.

'How old do you think she is?' Abby asks.

'Mid-twenties maybe, our age.'

She hits the steering wheel. 'Damn it, *damn* it.' She climbs out of the car into the rain, back to the dead woman.

CHAPTER TWO

Sunday 27 January 1974

Abby

At sunrise, dark clouds gather like an angry mob and throw down thick rain onto Brisbane. Thunder lopes from the fringes to the centre of the city, building from a low growl to an unrestrained roar and snap. Currawongs and magpies shelter in the crooks of our ironbark tree, possums hide under our roof. Stocky banksias whip about in the wind as though they're made from hair. And we seal ourselves from the storm.

Mark puts beach towels along the bottom of the back and side doors. He checks windows for leaks. I make a pot of coffee and put a torch, a kerosene lamp, batteries for the radio, candles and matches on the kitchen bench in case we lose power. I straighten the towels when Mark isn't watching. And when we're done we stand, holding hands in the stifling heat behind our glass veranda doors, barely able to hear one another over the smash of water onto our tin roof. We watch the rain slash gravel, grass and concrete, and form quick rivers in the gutters. Woof sits alert beside me, his shaggy tail still.

The football fields at the bottom of our hill are four feet under within a few hours; the stately eucalyptus trees that ring them are cut off from one another, arms up, surrounded by a push of muddy water. By the time the kids wake up – hair plastered to sweaty heads, pillowcase wrinkles on doughy skin – our access roads have vanished. I've never seen anything like it. We heard on the radio last night that Cyclone Wanda would lose its puff before it reached the city, but the newsreader warned that another kind of trouble was on its way.

It's rained on and off since October. Three months. On TV, I watched Queen Elizabeth struggle to control her notes in the wild wind as she declared Sydney Opera House open. The air was manic but the sky was blue and dry. Here, that day heralded a seemingly endless wet patch. No matter how much I clean, our house smells dank. Mould spreads across the bathroom ceiling, magnified – after we shower – in hanging drips of water. Our canvas sandshoes, left by the back door, grow black spots, and clothes draped on the drying rack are wet for days.

The children sleep under gauzy white nets hung from ceiling hooks, to protect them from mosquitoes that thrive in our mushy garden. Fidgety swarms of midgies hover above my pot plants. The air lies like a clammy veil on my skin.

Outside, rain pools on the earth; the nearby creek bloats and heaves itself onto the surrounding ground.

Late morning, as we're cleaning the breakfast dishes, Mark says we need to cancel our barbecue, which we've had every Australia Day weekend for the past five years. 'I guess we should ring people. Or maybe it's obvious.'

'The water will go down, won't it? The roads will clear.' I wipe my tea towel this way and that across a smoky-grey glass plate. 'Can you see what the kids are up to? I get worried when they're quiet.'

'This will get worse before it gets better. Geoff says –'

'Geoff got himself into a knot over Cyclone Wanda, too. But nothing happened.'

He frowns. 'What do you mean nothing? That cyclone's the reason the city's underwater.'

'It's not underwater.' I move on to wiping the laminex bench-top, admiring the sparkle where the light strikes gold flecks.

'It will be by tonight.'

While I'm on the phone, apologising to our friends for cancelling the barbecue and talking about their kids, the weather, I scan a magazine article: 'Creative Ways with Pineapple'. I draw overlapping circles on the glossy paper. All the while, Mark comes in and out of the kitchen, opening drawers and pulling out scissors, string, rubber bands and pointing at his watch.

'Okay, enough,' he says, as I put the phone down. 'I need a hand. Anything we want to save has to come upstairs right now.'

'You need string for that?' Forever the boy scout.

'C'mon, we don't have much time.'

'One more call.'

After Lou and I agree we'll meet as soon as the rain lets up, I work with Mark to move our belongings from one floor to another. We haul boxes of old books and uni assignments, Mark's home-brewing supplies, and clothes in mothballs that Sarah has outgrown and the twins don't yet need. Mark lugs the lawn-mower up the muddy side path to the shelter of the back porch.

We listen to the news and watch large puddles joining up on the lawn. Our garden starts to resemble the Japanese rice paddies you see in documentaries, but in colour.

'Do we know anyone with a powerboat?' Mark asks, standing barefoot near the back door, a glass of ice water in his hand. 'I might need to get to work.'

'You'd leave us in a flooding house to go to work?'

He gestures for me to follow him. We walk through the living room, around the sprawling cushions-and-blanket cubbyhouse Sarah and the twins are building.

'Down there, past the Martins' place,' he says, once we're on the veranda. I smell his sweaty armpit as he lifts his hand to point. 'See that white pole? That marks the highest level the water reached during the 1893 flood. The worst flood Brisbane's had. So even if it's as bad as that, it'll only get partway up our stairs. We'll be fine.'

I scan our street. 'Our downstairs floor is higher than all the other houses.'

'Yes, it is.' He glares at the pole as though it's somehow responsible for this.

Despite my certainty that Mark is exaggerating, the rain doesn't stop. It grows heavier. When he tells me Lou's house is going under, I feel rattled for the first time.

'They're alone,' I say. Andrew is forever travelling to Bougain-ville, coming home to present Lou with more unwanted net bags, tins of cocoa, tales from the mine, another ugly wooden mask for their walls. He's gone for weeks at a time.

'Tell her I'm on my way,' Mark says.

I rush to the phone.

I'm a strong swimmer, stronger than Mark, and know I could help bring Lou and her kids here. First place in freestyle at school carnivals, always a ribbon in backstroke and butterfly. The current is calling to me as a challenge and I'm itching to pit myself against it, to steel my muscles and swim hard. But Mark says if we both leave the house the kids will try to follow or hurl themselves into what Sarah is calling our backyard sea. I know he's right. So I stand in our front doorway and watch Mark walk down our steep driveway, shirtless, head bowed against the rain, bare toes gripping the concrete, his beige shorts speckled by water then darkening to brown. He raises one arm as a wave, without looking back.

I feel a surge of love, and fierce pride. Why don't I feel like this when he goes to work? Some people think journalists are heroic. I've never thought that. But now, seeing my brawny husband calmly set forth to rescue our neighbours, I imagine myself running outside and throwing my arms around him, as if he were boarding a plane for a war zone. Instead, I watch. I worry that Lou won't think to bring useful things with her. I should have sent Mark with a list. A list in a plastic bag. Woof frets by my side, unnerved at being left behind but too scared to venture into the swill. We jog upstairs to continue watching from the veranda.

Mark is knee-deep within minutes, staying close to the edge of the water, pushing through even that with effort. He wipes wet hair from his forehead. Mark has a thick, curly mane, forever bleached by the sun. I spent countless hours in my teens lying in the backyard with lemon juice coating my own hair, trying for a blonde like that. My skin tanned, leaving satisfying triangles of white where my bikini covered it, but my hair stayed black. Even now, the brightest summer sun can't shift the darkness.

I stand with my hands on my hips and look over at Lou's house, where she's gathered her three kids by the front door, painted a glossy mission brown a month ago. The rain falls at an angle so from the knees up I'm sheltered by the roof, while my feet are shiny wet. In the living room behind me, under the slung blanket, Sarah presses the dome-shaped plastic popper on a board game, calling out the number that shows on the dice after each clack. The twins giggle.

Mark continues to stride forward, pushed and yanked, goaded by a current that strengthens before my eyes. The right choice, I think, to keep his feet on the ground as long as possible. On his side of the road, the water is surging towards Lou's house, but there's a strange current forming on the other side, heading in the opposite direction. A rip, in floodwater. I didn't think that was possible. I hope they see it.

Lou is wearing a sleeveless orange jersey dress I borrowed once, when it was new. She's top-heavy, full of milk, and the dress strains across her chest. She rests Jemima above her hip, as the baby, in only a cloth nappy, squirms to be free. Joe holds his treasured Paddington Bear in one hand, and a scrunch of Lou's hem in the other. Daniel, eleven months older than Joe, stands beside a cardboard box doubtless crammed with photographs and the kids' baby books. I wave at Lou and she waves back.

Mark swims the last thirty feet on a diagonal to navigate the current, keeping his head above the fast-flowing water, avoiding floating branches and furniture sucked out of smashed

16

windows. He pulls himself up onto what still shows of Lou's railway sleeper path, tan bark and leaves sticking to his back. She steps forward, and wraps her free arm around him. Mark places one hand on Jemima's back as he talks to Lou.

After a minute, he disappears into the garage and comes out with Andrew's surfboard, which he slides into the water, urging Daniel and Joe to straddle the board while he stops it with his foot from taking flight. He points at the box and says something. Lou runs inside the house and returns with a black garbage bag, into which she places the cardboard box. That makes me smile because it's what I would do, and because I know Mark not only wants to rescue Lou, he wants to do it well.

Lou lifts the plastic-wrapped box onto Mark's shoulder, where he balances it with one arm. Then she stands beside the board with Jemima held so high on her chest that the baby's top half flops onto her mother's shoulderblades as though she's about to go headfirst down a slide. Mark stands on the other side of the board, his free arm across it, and they walk forward into the wild floodwater, the hammering rain. When the muddy flow rises above Lou's chest, she puts Jemima on the surfboard, nestling her in front of Joe. Mark has seen the rip, which would pull them towards the football fields, and steers the board the way one would a ship, adjusting and readjusting to stay on course.

I stay fixed to my wet spot, until they are where our front garden used to be, which is close enough for me to see the fear on Daniel's face, the determination on Mark's, to hear Lou shout, 'Almost there.' I run inside, grab a stack of towels and barrel down the stairs. Sarah and the twins run down with me, despite me telling them to stay where they are.

I open the door to a gush of wind and rain, shouts of relief. As Lou's children tumble inside, sliding on the glazed tiles, pushing Woof away as he jumps about and licks their faces, Mark places the surfboard against the wall and drops the box onto the closest stair. I hold his face in my hands and give him a kiss, Lou a hug, and then strip the children, creating a mound of sodden clothing in the entryway. Once the children are wrapped in towels and have scuttled upstairs together, and Lou has gone to our bedroom to change – 'Anything you want,' I say – I search for Mark. He's standing at the kitchen sink, guzzling water.

'Go have the first shower. The kids can wait.' I pick twigs off his back.

'Not done yet. Everything they own is in that house.'

This time I go, too, despite Mark and Lou's objections, which are half-hearted at best. They both know I can outlast anyone in the water.

'But if it gets too dangerous, turn around. They're just things,' Lou says. She holds me and whispers, 'Thank you, friend.'

The flood is a living beast now, large and throbbing, a serpent. It could dumbly drown us in an instant, and while logic says that Mark and I should stay inside with our children and tell Lou that whatever she loses can be replaced, I feel a shiver of pleasure as I put my feet in the strong flow. With Mark behind me, I wade in slowly, assessing the currents, then feel the tug of the water and think, go on, try me. Like Mark, I don't look back.

Together, we make two trips to retrieve bags of clothing and records, a box of paperwork and a typewriter, treasures from the kitchen and bedroom, a sack of masks.

'Why does he collect these?' I ask Mark. 'Uglier than *Blue Poles*.'

'And worth less.'

The second time we head back, the water is higher and the journey more arduous. I am panting when we return to our house, excited, unconscionably pleased with myself.

'That's it,' Mark says as he drops a heavy plastic bag onto the kitchen floor. 'No more.' I have one more trip left in me but I can see he doesn't, so I agree.

While we've ferried her belongings to our house, Lou has allowed the kids to run riot. The living room is a chaotic mess, but for once I don't care. All six kids seem happy – a miracle in its own right – and I can see from the empty bags of chips and browning apple cores that they've eaten. Woof lies on the carpet, gnawing a wet branch into splinters. Lou isn't in the room. She's in the kitchen, on the phone, wearing one of my kaftans.

'Thank you, thank you,' she says to us once she's done speaking with her mother. 'You're my heroes.'

Once Mark and I are in dry clothes, the children in pyjamas, we three sit on the couch, drink cold beer and eat potato salad and ham. There's enough barbecue food for a week. We watch lightning crackle across the leaden sky, hear thunder rumble and boom. We flick through magazines, scan Friday's news-paper for anything interesting we might have missed. The rain has softened, but none of us trusts it to stay that way. Mark urges Lou to stop checking what is left of her house. 'There's nothing you can do,' he reasons. I top up Lou's glass, grimace in sympathy, then flop back and rest my head on Mark's shoulder. Jemima and the twins are in the playpen in front of us; Sarah,

Daniel and Joe muddle through a sloppy, argumentative game of Go Fish.

Despite the drama, I could fall asleep here on the couch. Last night was punctured by the yipping of our neighbour's terrier, Jock, and by remembrance of tasks undone, my restless body, children. The twins had alternated their cries for attention as if on a secret schedule. In one of the quiet hours, Sarah climbed into bed beside me – apple-shampoo-scented hair, small toenails scratching my leg – and whispered fearful questions that kept coming as we plodded back to her room: *How do people find each other in Heaven? Do ghosts get hungry?* And her questions – which I couldn't answer in a way that satisfied either of us – rolled in my head as I drifted in and out of sleep until the storm woke me at five, followed by the gushing overflow of water from the leaf-clogged gutter onto our window ledge.

I don't sleep, though, because the phone rings nonstop: Gavin Martin from number sixteen says they've made it to his sister's house; Caroline from twenty-two asks if we've seen her cat; Dad tells us to switch off appliances so they don't short. There are many variations on the question 'Mark around?', asked with the assumption he'll know something they don't.

It's true that Mark has been in touch with his news mates, and keeps the TV and radio blaring so he doesn't miss any details of the escalating horrors: whole suburbs are without electricity; clean drinking water is running out; elderly people are trapped in their homes, alone; a child drowned when the torrent pulled her from her father's arms. Occasionally we hear upbeat news. On TV we watch two burly men in a dinghy rescue a fretful terrier from a rooftop, and another, who looks like Santa in a blue singlet, hand out cans of beer from his boat with shouts of 'we'll be right'.

'You battening down the hatches?' Charlie's voice echoes and lags across the long-distance line. 'I met a guy who's sailing from Perth to the Philippines. Says there's a cyclone headed your way, a real roof-lifter.'

'We're past that. The cyclone's been and gone. The whole city is flooded. They're using schools and churches as evacuation centres. You should see it, Charlie. There are *cars* floating down our street.' Through our kitchen window I watch water rushing from our backyard towards the side of the house, as if chased. Mark had predicted that the slope of our block would create this river to the road, sparing us from a sodden upstairs.

'Whoa. It was a couple of days ago I talked to him so, yeah, old news it seems. I've been meaning to call but the restaurant's crazy busy. People coming through before they head to Goa for Shigmo.'

'What? Never mind. The news says the river's broken its banks, and we're –'

'Broken its banks?' I can see him grinning, bare feet on a table, around his neck a thin strip of leather anchored by a shark's tooth. 'My sister the weather girl.'

'It isn't funny.'

'Poetic turn of phrase.' He pauses; smoking, I'd guess.

'You should call Dad, too, Charlie. He's alone.'

'Isn't he with you guys for your Australia Day shindig?'

'He can't get here. It's *flooding*. Are you listening?'

'Sure I'm listening.'

21

'Anyway, he wouldn't want to come here. He's busy with his . . . I don't know, chickens or something.' Mark walks into the room to fetch another longneck from the fridge. I click my fingers to get his attention, then point outside. 'But he's better off at his farm. It's at the top of a hill.'

Mark assesses the backyard water situation. He nods at the phone.

'Charlie,' I say.

'So, I don't have the readies to call Dad as well. But tell him hi. And hey, leave a message for me at the post office if there are developments, weather-wise.'

'Wait, don't go yet. I haven't heard from you in weeks. Are you all right? Is everything –?'

'I'm good, restaurant's good, everything's good.'

'When are you coming back, Charlie? Say you'll be here before Christmas, please.'

He sighs.

'You promised not to miss another one.'

'I'll be there. Early December, most likely, but for a month max. I don't see why it's so important for me to be part of the carnival though.'

'You're family. Anyway, Dad's upset you've been away so long.'

'We both know upset is not a word Dad would ever use.'

'The kids barely remember you.'

'Low blow, Abby.'

'So you'll definitely be here.' At the top of the back door, rainwater has gathered into thick threads that are leaking down onto the towel.

'Almost totally definite.'

'Charlie, you're killing me.'

He laughs. 'I'll be there. Enough with the guilt trip. Stay dry.'

I return to the living room and tell Mark about the leak. While he goes to check it, I recite my conversation with Charlie for Lou. I miss him.

She shares a story about her younger brother – a playboy pilot who shuttles holidaymakers between Cairns and islands in the Great Barrier Reef. 'Hate to think what goes on in that cockpit. He'd do anything for a screw. Probably lets the wives fly the plane.' She picks up her glass and puts her free hand on my thigh. 'Take a squiz down the road and tell me if my house is fully under. Wait, don't. You have more beer, don't you?'

I smile. 'Plenty.'

'Okay, let's have another one.' She pauses. 'But then I need to know.'

Mark is on the phone, the twins are napping, Sarah is watching Mr Squiggle. Lou and I sit together, spent. I try to think of tasks, but there's truly nothing to do. That's the thing about floods. You move your belongings, help your friends if you can, and then you wait. And wait. Wait to see what will survive, what's changed, what's destroyed.

Our power's gone out, so I can't run the washing machine, but the linen cupboard would benefit from attention. Perhaps I can work on folding the troublesome fitted sheets that look like cotton boulders no matter how I tackle them. That would be something.

23

I turn to ask Lou what she thinks and see she's crying without sound. Tear trails mark her face, and her chin has scrunched up into a hill of dimples and pores.

'Oh, Lou.' I reach for her hand and hold it in mine. Our skin, tacky from the heat, melds. 'It'll be okay. We'll fix your house. And you can stay here as long as you need to.'

She wails. Mark comes into the living room, sits on the other side of Lou and puts his arm around her – warm and hairy from the elbow down, powder-dry white cotton above – on top of mine. I smell his musky deodorant, notice that he's shaved. He's antsy. I can see from his face he's as frustrated as I am by being trapped here.

'Did you find someone with a boat?' I ask.

'Not yet.' He pats Lou's shoulder. 'Don't worry. The rain will stop before the end of the week.'

Lou's wail rises.

'The end of the week?' I glare at him. He mouths, 'What?'

Lou will not be soothed. She sobs loudly, lists things that will have been destroyed by the water – the dining table given to her by her grandmother, the kids' beds. 'The car!' She shrieks at the realisation. I murmur vague reassurances.

'How about you lie down for a while?' Mark says. 'Get some rest.'

She takes a jerky breath. 'Okay, yeah.'

He stands, helps Lou up, and walks her down the hallway.

Mark is working on a story about the Whiskey Au Go Go. He was convinced, when the nightclub was firebombed in March last year, killing fifteen people, that the case against the two men arrested was shaky and, after seeing the way they reacted at their

24

trial in October, he's sure they're innocent. Mark has hushed, urgent phone conversations with his producer, and disappears for hours to interview sources. When he tells me about his story he jigs his knee. Last week he told me he's convinced that the police fabricated evidence against Finch and Stuart.

'Don't they have real evidence?'

'Not enough to convict. But the lead detective is sure they're guilty, and needs to make that appear credible while he gets some solid evidence.'

'But they admitted they did it.'

'False confessions. Both of them say they were verballed, beaten at the watch house until they signed.'

On Wednesday, he'd come into the kitchen and kissed me goodbye so early I wasn't even dressed.

'We're doing a final edit today, showing it to Reid. I reckon we can get it to air this week.'

'That soon?'

'What do you mean? I've been working on this for months.'

'I know that. We all know that.'

'Try to be happy for me, will you?'

'Sorry. Just, I dunno.' I shrugged. 'I'll be stuck at the pool all day with the kids.'

He'd reached over, taken a piece of my toast. 'Stuart's sewn his lips together with paperclips.'

'My God, why?'

'To protest.'

'Is this the same one who swallows chunks of metal and wire? Is hospital that much better than jail?'

'Everywhere's better than Boggo Road.' He rubbed the top of Petey's head. 'See you tonight, champ. Where are your sisters?'

'They're dumbheads.' Petey had a milk moustache, and a smear of Vegemite on his nose.

'Girls,' I called out. 'Come say goodbye to Dad.'

They ran down the hallway. Mark hugged our smiling, dishevelled girls then turned back to me. 'Hope your day's not too terrible.'

'I didn't mean – That's awful about the paperclips.'

'Don't feel sorry for him. He's nuts. They'd both kill you in your sleep. But they didn't bomb that nightclub.' We kissed goodbye.

I'd stared out the window to calm myself so I didn't snap at the children – their inane bickering, their tugs for attention. None of it warranted my rising fury. I wasn't that angry at them, nor was I angry at Mark. I liked to swim. But some days felt so incredibly pointless, so driven by other people's needs and desires, that the steam built inside me until I wanted to shout. I didn't. Instead, I wiped a scatter of breadcrumbs from the benchtop into my scooped palm while I listened to the radio. Last year, Mark's colleague Caroline reported a story called *Housewife*, in which she'd calculated what household tasks would be worth if we were paid for them in the working world. She'd only included the obvious: cooking, buying food, dishes, laundry, mending, ironing, vacuuming, making beds, taking care of kids, feeding pets. And sex. It'd caused a stir at the time. And nothing changed.

Paperclips. What a strange thing to use.

Life had once felt expansive – large and elastic enough to hold the things Mark and I loved to do, our Saturday tennis matches, pub lunches with friends at Caloundra overlooking the beach, drives to Mt Glorious, watching bands,

26

seeing movies, sex in the afternoon, eating dinner in bed and then more sex, with space left for dreams about the future. Life was smaller now. Somewhere along the way I'd lost myself, and my life with Mark had become tethered to this house, governed by so many rules and such a different set of activities.

I'd turned back to my children. Sarah spotted her opening, told me Petey was kicking her, then yelped for dramatic effect. I laughed and raised my coffee mug at her, confusing them both.

Joanne, ignored by her siblings, quietly drew stick figures on the bench with a finger dipped in strawberry jam. Woof vomited something plastic on the kitchen floor.

After five days the clouds clear, and the opposing forces of earth and sky begin to reclaim the water. The ground absorbs the lakes that cover it. The sun inhales triumphantly. Hard surfaces are coated in wispy columns of steam as water rises back to the heavens.

We try to revert to life as it was before the flood. It's not easy. Three-quarters of the state has been underwater. Grown men are stoic in front of Mark's camera but become emotional when tripped up by a kind question. Our neighbours find solace in exchanging platitudes: 'We're better off than some', 'Won't forget that in a hurry'. We stand on the scorching footpath and talk over the warbling magpies about our shared experience, like soldiers after war, women after birth.

We help Lou and Andrew, since returned, clear the mud from their home. They don't need us since Lou's whole family is there – her solid, mulish parents, two muscly older brothers, her younger brother who's not as hardy but good at directing the family workforce, two uncles, an aunt who brought ham-and-cheese sandwiches, honey for the children. I watch Lou's family as they weave in and out of one another, touching a shoulder, working in pairs, the uncle and father in close conference about how best to move the fridge, the mother and aunt sharing a look at this or that ruined memento. Such a sad reason to come together, and yet . . . I regard them longingly, their relaxed warmth with one another.

Lou walks along her squelchy hallway carpet, running her hand through her hair, holding up one dripping, dirty belonging after another. 'We can't fix this,' she says. 'Everything's wrecked.'

I don't tell her that I agree. I'd always thought of rain as cleansing, encouraging growth, only temporarily the cause of mould and puddles, but this ferocious destruction is something different. This rain was violent. And mud coats everything, like the remnant drool of a subterranean creature that's sunk back underground.

Lou and Andrew hold one another while Mark and I work on, guilt at our good fortune energising us. We pile destroyed wooden chairs, waterlogged books, soiled curtains and shoes onto the footpath. There are similar bundles of ruined personal treasures dotted along the street, waiting to be collected by rubbish trucks. The children find dinted spoons and filthy underwear in the gutter. Mark finds a plastic flea collar and we wonder what happened to the dog who should be wearing it. We wonder if it belonged to Jock next door.

The flood wasn't part of my plan, not part of anyone's. These few days will derail us for months. I know now that I should have recognised the flood as a warning, a caution. Everything I thought I could control was uncontrollable. Life, insistent, persistent, was about to take on new shapes, shimmery and unpredictable as petrol on a wave.

CHAPTER THREE

Friday 6 December 1974

Charlie

I'm on the plane at 2 am Bali time. Denpasar to Darwin, Darwin to Brisbane. Every part of me is crumpled, from my shorts to my face. I thought I'd sleep on the plane but that's going to be challenging. The girl in the window seat next to me is a chain-smoking chatterbox, a toothy whippet-like thing who fills the first hour with rambling tales of tripping in Koh Samui and meditating by the Tjampuhan River – she might've said *in* the Tjampuhan River – and rants about people who don't get it. Evidently I do get it. She's flirting with me, and going about it in the most awkward way, twirling her hair into rope, watching my mouth as I suck on her cigarette. I'll need a few more fags for the trip, but not from her.

'Long flight ahead.' She winks at me. It's kind of endearing, but I couldn't be less interested.

'I need some shut-eye,' I say. 'Last few days have been intense.'

That's swear-on-the-Bible true. Wednesday was the busiest day and night we've had – a taste of the future, Ryan said, now that travellers are spreading their wings past Denpasar, 'finding their balls'.

'Manning up,' I said. 'Sal, what's the chick version of manning up?'

'Manning up.' She gave me the finger. I smiled but it'd been a serious question, as serious as they ever get with us anyway.

We'd cleaned the restaurant by eleven o'clock, and joined Ketut, Made and our mob of local mates at the beach for a farewell bonfire in my honour. I would only be gone a month, but these people love to celebrate. I drank my body weight in Bintang and fell asleep on the cool sand to the sounds of party murmurs, a settling fire and Ketut strumming a Dylan song on his guitar.

Ryan prodded me awake at sunrise. 'I've got your board.'

I sat up and ran one hand across my matted hair while I surveyed the beach: bodies arranged around a pit of charred logs, and stray dogs wandering between them, sniffing at tossed beer bottles and strewn clothing.

'We had fun, right?'

Ryan smiled. 'Yes we did.'

'Cool. I look forward to remembering it at some point.'

I stripped off my t-shirt, getting a whiff of smoke and sweat as I pulled it over my head. I walked with Ryan towards the sea, squinting into the rising sun, achy and parched, my surfboard under one arm. The salty breeze was strong at the ocean's edge, pushing the board against my body. I spread my legs to keep my balance and felt cold, frothy water pour over my toes. Looking at the blue sea, rising and falling, filling its lungs and exhaling a roll of clean water, a gust of fresh air, made me feel better. By the time I stood on the board, my top layer of grime and the sludge in my head had been sloughed away, gone.

Between waves we lay on our boards, bare chests on slippery plastic, paddling to keep ourselves facing the shore, waiting. Salt water dripped into my mouth. Ryan flicked a lump of hair off his face. On the beach, our friends were waking up and moving into the shade of palm trees.

'Paradise,' Ryan said.

'Let's never leave this place.'

I wasn't so upbeat by the time we got to the market. The sellers have no respect for hungover customers, and I'm sure they called out to us louder than usual for fun. My head thumped, and everything smelled terrible: a cocktail of fruit baking in the sun, petrol fumes and dog piss.

'Keep it down, dude,' I said to Komang, our go-to man for noodles and greens. 'I'm right here.'

'You want a beer?' He grinned and banged a stick of bamboo on the bars of the cage at his feet, making his monkey scream. Next to him, an elderly woman squatted on the ground, arranging flowers on a woven tray. Without pausing in her work, she shouted in rapid-fire Balinese. From her tone, I figured she said something like, 'Charge the foreigners double.' A young girl stood beside her, as poised as a ballerina, holding a basket of bananas on her head, smiling at us. We were the morning's entertainment, not for the first time.

After the beach, the market and the sweaty drive home, we opened up the restaurant and got back to work. I stumbled through Thursday, serving more fish and sambal than you'd think could come out of a shoebox kitchen. We set to drinking again after we closed. I don't know why I thought that was a good idea. Maybe because I was stoned.

Just after midnight, Sal drove me on the scooter to Denpasar airport, winding and beeping through the usual puzzle of motorbikes, overloaded trucks churning out black smoke and beaten-up cars driven by toothless men. I'd rested my aching head between her shoulderblades and closed my eyes.

The plane was shutting its doors as I ran across the tarmac, shouting at the hostie to wait.

I'll be in Brisbane for almost four weeks, the result of being nagged, repeatedly, by Abby to 'come home'. Except Brisbane isn't home anymore.

When I went to Bali I didn't plan to stay for so long, but it turned out there was no compelling reason for me to rush back. I think if Abby visited Kuta she'd understand.

After I graduated from Queensland Uni I'd spent a lot of time reading about different parts of Asia. Abby said I should channel my interest into a job, so I dropped down to part-time work at the student union and enrolled in postgrad studies in Mandarin, not to please my unpleasable sister, but because I figured a second language might get me a job as a translator. Mostly, though, it offered another stream of girls to date. Not a terrible result.

When Ryan and Sal came back from Kuta for a month-long visit to appease their families (a great Australian tradition), we hung out. I stopped going to classes. I lost my job. The morning I got fired, I called Ryan. He said that there were other jobs and

I shouldn't stress out. But he and Sal are both from rich families, and the whole idea of working felt a bit optional for them back then. It still does. At some point Ryan will be expected to do something in law and Sal will do whatever it is she'll do. But I went with them to our friend Jason's house anyway. That day set me on the road to Bali.

Jason lived on a steep hill, his house sitting on poles like a rangy mountain climber hanging on for dear life. I parked my VW outside his place with angled wheels, the way Dad taught me, and we walked up a broken concrete path through waist-high grass and scraggly lantana. At the bottom of the paint-chipped stairs I heard happy noises coming from the veranda, which was shaded and hidden from view, enveloped by lush tropical greenery.

We slouched about in Jason's living room on couches draped in saris. The windows were covered with matchstick-thin bamboo blinds; the walls were decorated with movie posters – *The Godfather*, *A Clockwork Orange*, *Klute*. The smell of weed and seagrass matting wafted through the house. We kept our drinks in a bathtub filled with ice. The day drifted past, steamy and loose.

Late afternoon, when Ryan and Jason had driven to the local pub on a beer-and-ice run and the others were strumming guitars out the front, Sal curled beside me on a sagging couch, her long arms wrapped around her knees.

'Do you remember that day after our Victorian Lit final,' she said, 'when we were sitting on the lawn, and I said one day we'd do something meaningful?'

Meaningful. She locked her almond eyes on mine, a smile lifting rose-painted lips, and I thought, 'Finally.' I'd adored Sal since we met. In truth, I'd lusted after her even before we met. I'd stood behind her in a smoky night-time crowd, watching Railroad Gin at Cloudland. A tight t-shirt, a glimpse of upturned nose, feather earrings brushing her neck. We almost touched when she'd lifted her arms up, twirled her wrists – I felt the heat of her, inhaled patchouli – but I stood back a bit to watch. It took all my willpower not to reach out and pull her towards me. At the end of the night, as Ryan and I were heading for the exit, she called out hello to him (a shared class, how great to see you here). She recalls that moment as the start of their romance. I don't think she noticed, or remembers, that I was there.

After that, and all through uni, we three hung out, sometimes alone and sometimes with friends. We spent Friday nights at the Red and Black, Saturdays at parties. Sundays were for FOCO, the club in Trades Hall where we'd watch bands or the DJ, hear poetry readings and political talks, buy month-old copies of the Cuban Communist Party newspaper. You know you're part of something cool when a federal pollie calls your club 'Australia's most repugnant nightspot'. That'd been a five-star review as far as we were concerned. Naturally, it spelled the beginning of the end.

We found other places to go, went to a bunch of protest marches, racked up a million hours together. Whenever Sal's parents went overseas, we'd have pool parties at their house, and I'd wonder why Sal was slumming it with us. But now, sitting on Jason's couch on a summer's day, alone, I felt sure this was the time to make my move. I touched Sal's tanned thigh and she said, 'A sanctuary. Do you remember?' She gently lifted my hand back towards my lap. I felt my cheeks burn while she continued talking like nothing had happened. How had I got that so wrong?

'Organic food, handmade soaps, homeopathics, Ayurvedics, oils. Hemp clothing. We'd make vegetarian meals, grow our own vegetables and herbs. It'd be a place with authenticity and soul.'

Jason's cross-eyed Siamese cat padded into the room, stretched out on the floor in front of us in a rectangle of white sunlight. Sal kept talking. I willed my heart to slow down, my cheeks to cool.

'We've talked about how great it'd be if you joined us there,' Sal said. 'Will you come?'

The cat had offered me a distraction while I calmed down, and I'd stopped listening. But I heard Sal say she wanted me to come to Bali. It wasn't the move I'd had in mind, but as soon as she said it my bags were as good as packed.

By the time I arrived in Kuta, Ryan and Sal had decided to set up a restaurant that would serve noodles, juice and cheap beer. Not the vibe we'd originally talked about but there was a garden behind the kitchen and the food was right for the location. Ryan made an offer to rent a place on the beachfront. I wasn't convinced there'd be customers for what they wanted to do; there were already two restaurants on the main road. But life in Bali was intoxicating – no other word for it. My days were filled with sun, surfing and getting high with my friends.

Work did kick in. People showed up to eat and drink, but we'd chosen this work so we didn't mind – we enjoyed it. Our surfer mates came by late morning, ravenous, along with their girlfriends, the people we knew from beach parties, random travellers. Ryan cooked, Sal waited tables and I washed dishes and spruiked for business. We went to the market in the morning and spent the night figuring out what would make the place even better: floor cushions in the back corner, more potted plants. We hammered up a noticeboard and left paper and pencils on the tables, made nice with anyone who had good drugs to sell. Sal put candles around the room. She wanted to call the place Kuta Dreaming, inspired by her favourite Mama Cass song, KD for short. Ryan painted a sign on a piece of driftwood and we hung it above the front door.

Our first big purchase was a fridge. We rented a rust-bucket truck – one day for two dollars – and headed up to Kerobokan, the three of us squashed on the cracked vinyl bench seat, Sal in the middle. We drove on a narrow track through jungle, keeping the ocean on our left, for lack of any other marker. It was rugged driving. Twice we had to stop to move logs off the road, and Ryan rested one hand on the horn to beep at monkeys when they wouldn't get out of our way. It must've been forty degrees. Sal sang 'A Horse with No Name' and passed around a joint to keep our spirits up – from Ryan to her to me, so each time I put the wet end to my lips I tasted her, smelled her.

The mood changed on the way home. The combination of heat and dope and the beer we'd drunk to recover from lifting the fridge onto the truck left us wasted. A couple of miles into the return trip we stopped talking. We listened to a whirr of cicadas, the wind, breaking waves, our tyres on loose dirt. We rocked from side to side as the truck hit every bump in the road. Ryan put his hand on Sal's leg, high up where the frayed edges of her cut-off jeans dipped into the V between her legs. He ran his hand up and down her brown thigh. Sal in turn put her hand on my leg. She kissed my neck. It felt good, but Ryan was right there, feeling her up, staring straight ahead. I pushed Sal off.

'Pull over,' I said.

'Why?' Ryan asked.

'I need to take a leak.'

He stopped in the middle of the track.

'Take your time, man,' he said. When I was about ten feet away he leaned out the window. 'Charlie, give us a few, yeah. Go for a swim.'

For the rest of the trip home I sat in the back of the truck with the fridge. My suggestion. Nobody objected.

When we got to KD we hauled our fridge inside, washed the chicken muck off, and gave it the only power point in the kitchen. None of us said anything about the ride home, but I felt bad about it.

A few mornings after the trip to Kerobokan, Sal and I were in the kitchen together, peeling and chopping bowlfuls of fruit for the juices we'd make throughout the day. We were listening to a Joni Mitchell tape, and Sal sang as she worked, playing vamp. I wasn't rude to her but I wasn't chummy either.

'You're getting strong.' She ran a finger wet with watermelon juice down my upper arm. I said nothing. She went outside to get more fruit.

'Help a girl out, will you?' she said when she passed by on her way back to the bench. She had her arms around a full basket, and tilted her head in the direction of a sleeve that had fallen off her shoulder. I lifted the sleeve back into place and she winked at me. 'Thanks, babe.'

I recognised her moves because I'd used them, or their equivalents, for years. But never with Sal. She seemed to enjoy our newly charged cat-and-mouse game. I found my days becoming increasingly tense.

*

The girl on the plane rocks my shoulder. 'Hey, Bali boy.' I open my eyes. In my dream, Sal had her arms around my naked waist as I drove our bike along the track to Uluwatu. It takes me a second to realise it's not her speaking. The hostie lifts a bag out from overhead. I stretch my arms and yawn. The man in the seat in front of me tells no one in particular that it'll be a scorcher.

'We're here,' the girl says, smiling. 'God save us.'

'Yeah, I reckon God gave up on Queensland a long time ago.' I stand up. 'We're on our own.'

We're only past hugs and 'how was the flight?' before Abby announces we're driving straight to Dad's.

'It's five hours, give or take, and by the time your luggage is unloaded . . .' She looks at her watch.

'You've got to be kidding. I need a shower and a bed.'

She frowns. 'We won't make it if we go home. The car's packed.'

'Oh, c'mon.' I feel sure Dad could wait one more day to see me. 'We can go tomorrow. What's the rush?'

'We're going today and coming back Sunday. Wash up. I'll meet you at the baggage carousel.'

I splash water on my face in the airport bathroom then go find Abby.

'Every one of these hippy backpacks is the same,' she says.

I see my pack (not the same, no Thailand or India scarves or ties decorating it), haul it off and put it on the floor next to me. 'Let's stop for beer before we leave the city. Need to flush the Bintang out of my system.'

'We don't have time.'

'At a drive-through.' I nudge her. 'C'mon, you know you want to. Kids are at home, free woman on the road.'

She smiles. 'Yes, okay. But we're not going inside.'

We leave the airport through sliding glass doors. The air outside is humid and dense.

'Hey, give me the keys. Haven't driven a decent car in a year.'

CHAPTER FOUR

Wednesday 4 December 1974

Abby

Lou and I sit next to one another on the wet tiled edge of the pool and dangle our legs in water so warm it's as though nothing is touching our skin at all. Water circles my calves, like a cuff where the surface, rising and falling, meets the air. The sun sparkles on the small waves.

Lou is wearing white-framed sunglasses, her strawberry-blonde hair is pulled into a ponytail and a crescent of deodorant marks the armpit of her lime-green bikini top. She has freckles on her chest and shoulders – three half-circles of darker skin, like a theatre curtain ready to rise. She lifts one leg out of the water and admires it, droplets sliding off her oiled skin.

'Gorgeous day,' she says, then adds, 'You seem edgy. Everything okay?'

My life is about to change and I should be preparing for that rather than hanging about at the pool, toggling between annoyance and boredom. 'Sorry. Weird mood.'

'Tell me,' she says, peering over the top of her sunglasses.

'Just feeling anxious.'

She nods. 'Bound to, but you'll be great. Anyway, it's months away. Don't let worry wreck your whole summer. Go swim. I'll watch the kids.'

I squint at the sky. Maybe I should swim. I like to start slowly, tighten my goggles after a lap or two, then get my pace up. By the third lap I'm timing myself. My heart beats fast, my breath is rapid, all pistons firing. For a few minutes, I'm at the Olympics and hear the roar of the crowd. Stopping is the problem. Once I stand in the shallow end, goggles off, I'm back in Jindalee: a little boy yells at his brother, a hairy man in red Speedos waddles by. And there's a bandaid floating on the water in front of me.

The pool occupies the centre of this fenced-off rectangular block of land. Close-cut green grass rings it on three sides. On the fourth side are bleachers that stay empty except during school swimming carnivals. The one building – low, red brick, tin roof – has a metal turnstile through which to enter, and another through which to exit, as well as a canteen and change rooms. The canteen has its roller door up for the day. Here, on the other side of an orange countertop, children line up in their bathers to buy Redskin lollies, cans of lemonade, and iceblocks that stain their tongues orange. The change room stinks of urine and chlorine.

A boy wearing a headband and tie-dyed singlet is watering the grass so that within the boundary of the wire fence everything is wet, while everything outside it is bone dry. The deep end of the pool is empty of people; serious swimmers come early. Later in the day, teenagers will commandeer the back corner to sunbake and flirt. But right now, the water belongs to mothers, children and retirees. Toddlers leap from the edge, launching themselves at one another's heads. Inflatable balls go up and down in the air as if the pool itself is juggling them. A yellow frisbee spins across the lawn.

Petey paddles close and grabs my ankle. He spits water at me in an arc, makes a gappy smile and wriggles away like a tadpole. The family clown, from the moment he was born. Joanne plays with Daniel, both of them in blow-up rings, bumping off one another. She'll drift away soon, having forgotten what the game was. Sarah, always on duty, is showing Joe how to hold his breath underwater, pinching her nose between her forefinger and thumb, blowing her cheeks out like a pufferfish and dropping to the bottom of the pool while he stands on the step and looks down at her, making no move to follow. Meanwhile Jemima sleeps peacefully in her pram behind us, next to the half-dozen towels we've thrown on the grass like a bad hand of cards and the esky packed with honey sandwiches, celery sticks, cubes of rockmelon and lamingtons layered between sheets of greaseproof paper.

'Go,' Lou says. She reaches forward and splashes water at my legs. 'Swim it off.'

'A walk maybe?'

'Walk where?' She frowns. 'But sure, go ahead.'

I walk across the puddled concrete and sit on a wooden bench outside the entrance to the toilets for lack of idea about what else I could do. Lou is right: the day is gorgeous. And

43

there is nowhere to go. Wisps of fairy-floss cloud decorate the sky. A breeze cools my feet.

I'm an inch away from a new beginning, counting the days, ignoring news stories that warn the prime minister is on shaky ground, making changes too quickly, unnerving the business community and ordinary Australians. He isn't unnerving me. I'm glad he brought the rest of the troops home from Vietnam. Ten years was ten years too long. And who has a problem with using tax money to keep Australians healthy? Maybe changing the national anthem was too much for some people. Not me. He's giving me exactly what I need: free uni will change my life.

I watch as a straw-haired woman and a stick-thin boy head towards the toilets. The woman, his mother I suppose, seems annoyed. The boy is hurrying as if to get away from her. I can see from her face that there's more she wants to say to him before he flees. She reaches forward and gives the boy a smack, making a sound like a pop gun. He jumps, shoots me a look of surprise mixed with fear and embarrassment, and runs away on his toes.

'I told you not to,' she barks at him, as he escapes her reach. 'I warned you.'

She makes eye contact with me. Shock must show on my face.

'Like you'd never,' she mutters.

But I have. I know her expression because I've made it, and I understand her anger because I've felt it. And yet . . . What if I end up with people like her as my clients? Years of study, followed by a fancy wardrobe and a city office, only to defend the woman who hit a kid at the pool? I've invested in work before, and it hasn't gone the way I wanted. The times I counted to one hundred when I brushed my hair, the

44

assignments on American pre-war poetry reworked late into the night, forever in terror I might get a B, the nappies folded perfectly, for what? I was vice-captain at high school, head of the swim team. On my last day, Principal Thomas presented me with a hardback dictionary and said that whether I decided to pursue teaching or nursing, he was certain a good vocabulary would come in useful.

'Oh Mum, don't be a goose. I'll pay.' I look towards the entrance as Lou's cousin Eliza removes a folded one-dollar note from a coin purse and gives it to the pool attendant. Eliza and her mother are similarly dressed in sorbet-coloured cotton frocks and white sandals, both women pale and scrubbed. Eliza wears coral lipstick and a hat that would suit a fifty-year-old librarian. She strikes me as someone who's spent her entire life preparing to be middle-aged.

Eliza's mother rests one hand on the enormous pram by her side, its kittens-and-balls-patterned fabric unbleached by the sun.

There's no one lined up behind them so the man takes his time unhooking the waist-high door that separates him from the public and walking the few steps needed to open the gate next to the turnstile. Eliza's mother wheels the pram through and Eliza follows in her wake, leaning to one side then the other as she peers past her mother to ensure there's room. Eliza dips her head in the direction of the attendant, as though his act of chivalry warrants notice, but not much since it is the least a woman with a baby – one who paid for her mother's entry – deserves.

Eliza stares at me for a moment before recognition shows on her face. Which is fair enough: we've met once. She smiles, says something to her mother, then takes the pram.

'How nice to see you. This is my mother, Barbara. And, oh, I can't remember a thing right now.'

'Abby.' I am being eyed off by two generations of prim.

'Abby, yes. I was pregnant last time we met, wasn't I?'

As I stand up, I feel the squelch of my wet bather bottoms ungluing from the bench. I fold one arm across my body as I look into the pram. It's lined in pink satin, and the baby is lying on a pink sheet and wearing a pink dress. The little girl's skin is flushed from the heat. The cavern smells of sour milk and laundry detergent. I pull my head out as fast as politeness allows.

'She's lovely,' I say. 'What's her name?'

'Ellen. Ellen Barbara Wilson,' Eliza replies. 'The middle name is to honour her grandmother.'

'You're friends with Lou, dear? I'm her aunt.'

I smile at Barbara, wishing I had a towel to cover all this flesh I'm baring. 'We came here together. She's over there.' I gesture with the hand that's not draped across my stomach.

'Ah, and your children?' Eliza asks.

'They're swimming.'

'Abby has three,' Eliza says to her mother.

'In good time,' Barbara replies, patting Eliza's arm. And then, to even the score, 'Eliza and Ted had good news this morning. He's been made state divisional manager. Isn't that wonderful? It's an early Christmas present for us all.'

I can't put a face to the name Ted, but Eliza and her mother are staring at me, beaming, waiting for me to respond.

'That's great. Congratulations.'

'He's been working so hard,' Eliza says. 'He's earned this. And more.'

'More, yes,' her mother says. 'We're making a roast for dinner, to celebrate. All the trimmings.'

I feel a pain in my gut. I never think to do that when Mark's stories go to air, even though he works on them for months. I could do it tonight – say in front of the kids how important his work is.

'So,' says Eliza. 'We best say a quick hello to Lou.' They offer synchronised smiles of farewell and walk away. Eliza pushes the pram while her mother carries a large canvas bag. From behind they could be the elephants from *Fantasia*, bulbous bottoms perched on comely legs.

Lou rises and meets them halfway. Unlike me, she is unself-conscious about wearing what is essentially underwear. I stay in the shade and watch them talk. The little boy who'd been smacked runs past me and dive-bombs into the pool.

'Mum!' Sarah stands in the shallows. Even from this distance I hear her exasperation. Someone has behaved unacceptably. 'Make him stop.'

Petey's head pops to the surface. He spits water at Sarah, and she shrieks. I can't believe he still finds this funny. Unbeck-oned, I remember myself and Charlie at Noosa when we were young: Charlie mucking about on the sand, the waves breaking far behind him, swivelling his hips and pretending to be a hula dancer while I worked – *worked* – at making a sandcastle, digging a perfectly square moat, matching the height of my turrets to one another.

I wait until Eliza and her mother head to the baby pool before I make my way back. Both Lou and Sarah start talk-ing when I'm ten feet away, my mind still at a beach nearly twenty years ago.

'My lot are hungry. Should we eat now?' Lou asks.

'Petey spat. He's spitting.' Sarah has her hands on her hips.

I glance across at the baby pool as I walk. Eliza and her mother, both still dressed, stand in water only deep enough to cover their ankles. Eliza is holding baby whatever-she's-called and dipping her tiny toes into the water. The baby curls her legs up at each touch, making it look like Eliza is lifting a large egg up and down.

I walk onto the first step of the bigger pool to cool my feet. Lou stands beside me. 'That baby reminds me of Andrew's retarded uncle Frank. Have you met Frank?'

I laugh with such a burst that my lips vibrate. She guffaws at my noise and we lean into one another and laugh together. Our children – stern Sarah, grinning Petey, goggle-eyed Joanne, little Joe and Daniel – fan out at our feet and regard us as though we are an exhibition at the zoo. Lou lifts one foot and splashes the children. 'Hey,' shouts Sarah, but the others giggle and swim away, like a pod of happy dolphins.

'Funny buggers, aren't they?' Lou says. I wipe tears of laughter off my cheeks.

As Petey swims away I notice his bandaid has peeled off, showing the gaping sore beneath. Yesterday, when I'd cleaned his wound, the result of the neighbourhood bully Tom Sullivan knocking him onto the asphalt, he'd been so brave. He'd clutched my arm and bitten his lip when I'd dabbed disinfectant on his raw skin, stayed sombre and uncomplaining as I'd applied a cotton pad, watching my face the entire time. When I'd finished, he put his other arm around my neck and hugged me.

This should be enough. To be loved. To stand in the sun with a friend and a gaggle of children. To feel water lap against my skin, to walk across cut grass and lie on a warm towel. To plan birthdays, cook dinners, clean the house, take care of the people around me. To know my brother will be home in two days. To know a new adventure is on the horizon, planned and prepared for. But I turn to Lou and see her smile has dropped and she's looking at me with an expression I don't recognise, sadness and love together. I hear my daughter shouting at her brother. I feel the skin on my back suddenly too hot, burning.

CHAPTER FIVE

Friday 6 December 1974

Charlie

The rain falls harder, hitting the car like a shower of rocks. Abby turns on the engine, then the headlights, does a slow U-turn and points us towards Chinchilla. We drive away, abandoning the woman in the ditch; we leave the baby to die.

For the next hour, we alternate between deafening argument and steely silence. Abby hits me in the arm again, smacks my ear. I kick her dashboard with my muddy sandshoes.

'Do you *understand* what you've done?' she shouts.

'How many times do I have to tell you it was an accident? Do you think I wanted this to happen? There's no point going to the police. And no matter where we took that woman she'd still be dead – and her baby would be as well, if it isn't already.'

Abby gasps at this and the car slows. I shouldn't have said that. It's too much even for the words to be in the air.

'Listen.' I lower my voice. 'If we went to the police I'd end up in jail because I *have* had a few beers. Which I will regret for the rest of my life. I'd be locked up for years, never get out of this shithole country. My whole life would be wrecked and you know what – nothing I do and no amount of jail time will change *anything*.' I pause. 'I'll make my amends some other way.'

'Amends, Charlie? *Amends?*'

'Stop, okay?'

'You're not the only one in trouble, you know. I was in the car, too. It's my car. And what about the ring? Either she's a thief or Dad knows her.'

'Or a thief *and* Dad knows her.'

She scowls at me. 'Yes, this is the time for semantics.'

'That's not – never mind.' I watch our headlight beams on the rainy road, the light seeming to move both forward and back. 'Are you sure you know how to get us to that town?'

'Yes. And it's called Chinchilla.'

'But why? Drive us to Dad's. We'll sort it out.'

'We're wet, and covered in mud and blood. How would we explain that?'

And right then I know my sister won't turn me – us – in, or tell Dad the truth. She's angry at me, and scared and upset. But she'll fix this, somehow. It's what she does.

I stay awake. Rumbling thunder threatens us from all sides. From time to time, a gust of wind shakes the car, or lightning cuts a jagged gash into the sky. The rain keeps coming. The first sign I see, where dirt changes to bitumen, says five miles till Chinchilla. Abby pulls the car to the side of the road.

'We need to change our clothes.' Bum-up like a duck, she climbs over the seat to reach into the rear of the station wagon. The styrofoam esky makes mouse-like squeaks each time she bangs against it. She pulls a towel from her bag and throws it at me. 'Here.'

I wind down the window and let rain soak the towel till it's heavy and my arm is wet to the elbow. I rub the towel across my arms and face. Abby finds two more towels and clothes for both of us and gets dressed in the back seat, while I do the same in the front, pulling jeans and a tight t-shirt over clammy skin.

'We'll stay at the pub,' she says, whacking my shoulder with her elbow as she clambers back into the driver's seat. 'I'll call Dad and tell him we'll be at his in the morning.'

'If you were okay to scrub up in the car, why didn't we do that and go to Dad's?'

'I can't face him tonight.' She holds out her hand to show me how badly she's shaking.

I hold up my own hand so it's level with hers. I'm shaking, too. We stay that way for an instant, her left hand and my right twitching like wounded moths, thumb and finger almost touching, dirt under our nails, her wedding ring glistening, and not a drop of blood between us despite what we've done. Will I think of this moment every time I look at my hand? I already know I won't. Life will go on, and I'll forgive myself. I'm not so sure about Abby.

We drive to Chinchilla, a town that's no more than a lick of buildings either side of a skinny road, a strip of runway lights back to the highway, a patchy receiving line at a shotgun wedding. The first building we see as we drive over the plank bridge, across the rising creek, is the Chinchilla Pub. It towers over everything around it. At two storeys, it would, in the daylight, cast a shadow over the corner shop, haberdashery shop and the few surrounding weatherboard houses. Painted white, dark trim, white verandas. Lights shine through the red, green and clear cut-glass windows downstairs.

We park on the dirt lot next to the pub, grab our bags and run, shake the water off ourselves, and open the double doors into a wide hallway. The Ladies Lounge, signed to the left, is dark; from the room to the right we hear muffled sound through an ornate panelled door. The three men perched on stools at the bar, each one nursing a sweating pot of beer, stare at us as we enter the room. Whorls of smoke rise from ashtrays. A radio calls out the results of the night's greyhound races.

The men wear checked flannel shirts with rolled-up sleeves, left open to show singlets of white or slate blue, with work shorts or jeans. Two of the men are in their fifties and one is about half that age, but they all sport the same hairstyle: slicked back with a wide-toothed comb so the neat lines of hair resemble a ploughed field. The only man wearing long pants is running a carpet-sweeper across the floor. He nods to us, and we nod in reply, drop our bags near the wall.

'Wet enough?' he asks.

I offer an awkward smile.

'I'm about to close up,' he says. 'But I could pour you a drink.'

'We're after a room, two rooms, for tonight,' Abby says.

The man pushes his sweeper upright. 'Reckon we can squeeze you in.'

The men at the bar chuckle.

'And a beer,' I say.

The woman we've left behind has a boyfriend or husband waiting for her. Maybe he's bragging to his mates about how he's going to be a dad, but she's lying in a ditch, with mud in her hair and a baby inside who'll keep kicking until it runs out of oxygen. Surely it has by now.

'You all right, mate?' the bartender asks.

'Yeah, everything's cool. Just need a beer. And a packet of Marlboros.' I open my wet leather wallet.

'Not a good night to be on the road,' he says. 'Bridge'll be underwater in an hour.'

The men mutter agreement.

'It's almost covered already. Didn't think we'd make it across. Your bridge might float away before the night's over.' It's an effort to speak normally. I sit on the nearest stool and the bartender places a cold pot in front of me. He looks at Abby, who's still standing, and asks if she'd like a shandy. She shakes her head at both the offer of a drink and a seat. I gulp my beer down, the drink of a Bali summer night, the possibility of oblivion.

A grey-haired, wide-jawed man at the far end of the bar speaks up. 'That bridge'll outlast you, son. My great-grandfather helped build it. Solid as a bloody rock.'

I raise my hand as if to tip an invisible hat. 'No disrespect. That's some real rain out there.'

He lifts his glass and takes a deep slug, putting it down empty. 'Seen worse.'

'Next round's on me.' I light a cigarette, a Bali cigarette.

'What do you reckon, Mick?' the man says to the bartender. 'One more?'

He shakes his head. 'All right, but this is your last. Marion'll rouse on us both, you know that.'

The man shoos away bartender Mick's worries then beckons him to get a move on. He turns to me. 'What's your name anyway?'

'Charlie. This is my sister, Abby.'

'I'm Reg.' He dips his head in Abby's direction. Abby has only moved a few steps inside the doorway. 'That's Benny, Troy. You've met Mick, saviour of every man in town.' He lifts his glass and the bartender smiles.

'Where were you headed?' Benny asks.

'My dad's place,' I say. 'Somewhere . . . thataway.' I gesture towards the windows.

'I'd appreciate the key to the room,' Abby says to Mick. 'If you don't mind.'

'Like some help with your bags?' he asks.

'I'm fine. There's only the two.'

Benny straightens in his seat. 'Give your sister a hand, son. Show some manners.'

'I don't need help.' Abby hasn't made eye contact with me since we came inside. 'Oh! But can I use your phone before I go up?'

Mick inclines his head in the direction of the phone, which is sitting on the bar on its own terry-towelling square, and waves away her offer of money. Abby stands as far from us as she can, stretching the pigtail cord till it's almost straight while Mick holds the base of the phone so it doesn't fly off and hit her. When she finishes her call, he says he'll show her to her room. She leaves the bar with him, and my whole body relaxes.

'Where you coming from?' Reg asks.

'Brisbane.'

He grins at my idiocy. 'Why'd you go over the bridge? Bridge leads north out of town. You don't go over the bridge on the Brisbane road.'

'Overshot the pub and turned around.'

'How'd you overshoot this place?' Benny asks. 'There's nothing else here. And it's lit up like the bloody *Titanic*.'

'You drove across the bridge and then drove back again?' Reg asks. 'That's daft.'

'Another round?' I say, when Mick returns. 'Last one, I promise. Actually, pour me two.'

'Suppose I may as well join you. We're all in trouble now anyway.'

Dad would love it here, would enjoy the company of these men. Maybe I'll bring him down for a drink. Even though he's proud of his uni education (first in his family), my father is most at ease around the type of men he grew up with – straight-talking, unpretentious. I'm struggling, can see in their faces they're regarding me with amusement, as a lightweight from the city who doesn't even know which way's north. Then, with a shudder, I picture sitting here with my dad without Reg, Benny and Troy as buffers. What would we talk about? How incredible it is to surf the endless left break at Uluwatu, mind-altering after mushrooms? What he feeds his chickens? We've reached the ages where he wants my approval more than I want his, which makes me feel kind of bad for him, and can make him boring company. Abby says he's worried about me being 'directionless', but I reckon when I talk about my life in Bali he's out of his depth, maybe even jealous. Makes me tired to think about it.

'There's still time,' Troy says.

'Time to what?' I realise I'd tuned out.

'For Troy to get married,' Benny says.

'Count yourself lucky,' Reg says.

'Don't listen to him,' Mick says. 'Nothing wrong with being married.'

'Early days for you,' Reg says. 'You'll see. Before you know it you won't be able to do a thing right.'

Reg, Benny and Troy complain about the weather, which seems to cause them grief, summer and winter. Mick tells me he's doing a correspondence course in hospitality. These are men who know how to handle their drink. They ask more than they answer. I need to watch myself. One of them might know her. One of them might be her father or her husband. Christ.

Benny leans back to get a better look at me. 'You don't know where your dad lives?'

'Haven't seen him in a few years.' I tap my cigarette on the edge of a glass ashtray, beg another beer.

'What's that smell?' Reg asks. 'Are you smoking marijuana?'

'Cloves.' I hold the cigarette out to him. 'Want to try?'

'You must be bloody joking.' He chortles.

'Is he up near Hanson's place, maybe?' asks Benny.

I smile. 'Man, I know you want a better answer but I honestly have no idea. He bought a farm a while back and this is the first time I've been there. Home for Christmas.'

'Cattle?' asks Benny.

'I don't know, Benny. Swear to God.'

Could Dad have some reason I haven't thought of for wanting to see Abby and me at his place? Maybe it's to show off the farm, but what if it's something else? What if he's run out of money? What if he needs to sell up and live with one of us? I'd sooner kill myself.

A wave of nausea comes over me. I'm too harsh on him. What if my father is sick? What if he's lonely and that woman with Mum's ring has been taking advantage of that? That *dead* woman. Sweat beads form on my forehead, nose, and under my moustache.

'I run a restaurant in Bali,' I say. I have to think about something else, anything. No dead women, trapped babies, sick fathers, shitty sons.

Reg raises his eyebrows. 'Do you now?'

I swivel so my back is against the bar. I watch slashes of rain hit the stained-glass windows. The world on the other side of the glass is black. By day, the coloured glass will make everything easier on the eye, tolerable for the mind. Rose-coloured.

'Where's Bali anyway?' Reg asks, as he rolls off his stool and yanks up his shorts. 'Are you a wog? You look like a wog.'

'Bali Hai, Reg,' says Mick. 'From the movie.'

'Don't you ever watch the news, Reg? They had a plane crash there, in Bali,' adds Troy. 'Plane crashed into a mountain. It was on the news.'

'Why would I be worrying about Bali?' Reg says. 'Some of us have work to do,' and they laugh phlegmy, smoky laughs.

'I'm calling it a night,' Mick says. 'Clear off, all of you. I want to go to bed.'

After the three regulars bid their farewells, Mick guides me up the stairs. We walk to the end of the hall, where he opens the last door to the left. 'The royal suite,' he says and walks away.

The room is large and spartan, with a high pressed-metal ceiling, painted the same dusty white as the wood-panelled walls. The light bulb is so far up it's of little use. None of the furniture holds its own: a skinny bed covered with a khaki blanket stands dead centre, next to a spindly side table gussied up with a crocheted doily and an empty vase. A lumbering brown wardrobe leans lopsided in a corner. A scrap of rug lies on the floorboards next to the bed, like a flea-bitten stray.

I left a baby to die.

I left a woman lying in mud.

I repeat the words to remind myself of what I've done. But I'm too drunk to make sense of it, to feel it. I sway as I stand in front of the toilet (the bathroom blessedly close), thinking about how I'll see Sal in a few weeks, and realising I'm hungry. When did I last eat?

I think about how bizarre it is that Troy knows about the plane crash, all the way out here. After that crash there'd been a group of distraught American backpackers in KD who'd had friends on board. As people had milled around them, offering condolences, they'd lurched from highly strung to morose, unsure what to do with their grief other than pass it around in words until they'd worked the edges off it.

Sal had summoned Ryan and me out the back and said we shouldn't charge the backpackers for their meals. 'Tea and sympathy. That's what they need.'

Ryan, never keen on Americans, had disagreed. 'We bought that food they're eating. Why should we pay for something that has nothing to do with us?'

'Karma,' Sal said.

He scowled. 'Karma's about cause and effect. We didn't cause this. It's nothing to do with us. And free food won't bring anyone back.'

'Babe.' She stepped closer. 'Karma is about good deeds in this life guaranteeing you don't come back as a flea. A kind act now will shape the lives we have to come. We need to help these people.'

Ryan thinks Sal's newfound dabbling with Buddhism is bullshit. But when she described karma it sounded selfish, doing things for later payback, and that does seem like a Sal way of thinking. Not sure I've seen her do anything that didn't in some way or another benefit her. It's messed up how attracted I am to her. Nothing dims it.

I'd watched, hoped he'd get angry or scoff so I could step in and side with Sal. That's what I'd hoped for. But true to form, Ryan had melted to Sal's will, and the Americans had eaten at our expense.

In my dreams I stand on the white sand at Kuta, my back to the sea, and watch as a falling plane smashes into the side of a mountain and bursts into flames. I'm not sure if I believe in karma. But even if I did, I don't have a clue how to make up for what I've done.

CHAPTER SIX

Saturday 7 December 1974

Abby

I bolt to the bathroom as soon as I wake, my bowels about to explode. I'd been dreaming I was leaking from every hole in my body, one part of my brain trying to stay alert while another part slept. Not that I had more than a minute's sleep.

The bathroom floor is cold underfoot, which is good since I start sweating as soon as I sit on the toilet. I pull my nightie out of the way and hang my head over my knees. It's like the first day of a bad period. My arms are heavy as stone. My head is foggy. I slump until the sweat cools me and I begin to come clear.

I sit up, shiver, and assess the small room: there's a rack of half-open louvre windows high on the wall behind me, rows of green rectangular tiles, a ball of white glass covering a dangling light bulb, a dark silt of dead moths at the bottom of the glass. Shiny toilet paper hangs from a wire loop to my right – waxy, see-through paper, not at all what I need. A calendar is thumbtacked to the back of the bathroom door, courtesy of the local petrol station. A lippy blonde, naked save for a pair of red knickers, sits on a windswept beach pushing her breasts forward like an indignant cockatoo. We stare at one another, we two birds.

I don't knock on Charlie's door on my way back from the bathroom since waking him has always been a job and a half, and I want to get myself ready before I worry about him. I put on a yellow blouse and denim skirt, and pull my hair back. Once I've packed my nightie I go to Charlie's room and knock for as long as expected, until he opens the door, still in the jeans and t-shirt he had on when we arrived.

'What time is it?' he asks, yawning.

'You're wearing a watch. Didn't you even take your watch off?'

He ignores me and starts to close the door until I put my hand on it.

'I'll tidy the room while you do whatever it is you do when you're already dressed.' I point to the bathroom. 'You can brush your teeth.'

'Yeah, okay.' He stretches his arms above his head, interlacing his fingers and cracking his knuckles. 'How are you holding up?'

'I didn't sleep.'

He drops his arms. 'Me either.'

'I can't understand why a woman wearing Mum's ring would be driving away from Dad's house.'

'I thought we agreed she stole it,' he says.

'No we didn't. And why would a pregnant woman steal a ring from a farm in the middle of nowhere at night?'

'Maybe she's had it for months. Maybe she wasn't coming from his –'

'There's nothing else out there, Charlie.'

'Maybe he sold it and wanted her to leave before we showed up.'

'Why would he do that the night we're coming? Or ever?'

'Or gave it –'

'You said yourself, she was *our age*.' I rub my eyes. 'I can't even – We need to get out of here.'

There's nothing to pack, so I sit on his bed and assess the state of my body. I have a headache and my empty stomach is turning somersaults. Through the window, I watch a skinny girl push a stroller on the concrete footpath that stretches a few metres in front of a tacky shopfront. She can't be much younger than I was when I wheeled Sarah around the streets.

The woman's head hit the steering wheel. She would've felt a moment's panic, a painful blow, then nothing. I need to convince myself this is true. But the baby . . . How long does it take for a baby to die once its mother is gone? Was the roll and shudder that I felt through her smock the baby's dying moment, or did it lie alive in its dark space while we drove away?

Next year Sarah will be six. The twins will start four-year-old kindergarten. No more strollers for me. They'll sleep better as they get older. I'll have the energy to apply myself. This is the time: my time.

I almost didn't enrol. I was nervous about whether I could fit study into my life again and, later, how I could work as a lawyer with children, a husband and a house to run. Then I met

Lou's cousin Eliza. We were at Clancy's for a last-hurrah lunch for Eliza, due to have her first baby in a few weeks. There were five of us there, all of whom knew Eliza except me. I was introduced as Lou's friend and a mother of three, to sounds that made it clear I had more children than anyone else at the table.

'Are you ready for the baby?' I asked Eliza.

'Oh yes,' she said, smoothing down her blue-and-white seersucker dress.

'Do you have family around? It'd be so much easier with family.'

'You don't have a family?' she asked.

'My dad's in the country, my brother's overseas and my husband's family are interstate. But we manage.'

I could see from her expression she found this puzzling, jarring. 'My parents live in the same street as us. They've put a nursery in their house. Mum says the baby can stay there when we need a night off.'

I should've felt strong, hearing this. I raise my children without any help aside from Mark. When Dad visits, he's only another person to feed. I manage the long nights. I learned from books what my babies should eat and how to settle them when they cried. There's no time off.

Eliza gazed around the table. I pictured her walking the halls of her spotless house, with her husband at work, her baby being rocked by her mother, and realising her life would be a line of same-same days, like a panda in a cage. I made a face at Lou to make it clear she'd cop it if we didn't leave soon.

I filled in my enrolment forms when I got home. Twenty-five, a mature-aged student and mother. I felt sick at the idea of it, but I did it anyway.

Did the woman beep her horn? I think that's what woke me. She'd been wide awake, assessing her options. Deep gullies on both sides, our car taking the whole middle of the road, coming right at her. She must have been terrified. I think about why she was on the road, alone, at night. Was someone waiting for her at the other end?

I force myself to focus on something else. I've bought my textbooks. I have Mrs Lewis lined up for babysitting. The Christmas presents are wrapped. The trip to Dad's farm was the last thing to tick off before the end of the year. I can get it back on track. I can't – I won't – throw away my life because of an accident that's not of my making. But I know I'm an accessory. I let Charlie drive. I sit still so I don't vomit.

'What's the plan?' Charlie is standing in the doorway, toothbrush in hand, his hair wet and finger-combed. The drips from his head have made a dark cowl on his shirt.

'We get some food. They serve breakfast downstairs. You'll need to put shoes on . . . Let's eat fast though.'

We pad down the hallway on plush floral carpet that seems strangely grand given the boarding-house decor in the bedrooms. All the doors are closed. I wonder if other people slept here or if we'd had the building to ourselves. Maybe the men in the bar live here. Maybe they know the woman in the car.

I shouldn't have left Charlie alone last night. God knows what he said.

To get from Chinchilla to Dad's farm we need to travel past the crashed car. We've only been driving for a short while, though, when we see a tow truck coming towards us. I pull over to the edge of the road so it can pass while Charlie twists around to watch the wreckage of the Holden dragging behind the truck. I listen to the gravel being flicked up by the truck wheels. It's the sound dry rice makes when it hits the bottom of a saucepan, plastic peas churning inside Sarah's favourite toy dog as she drags it across the floor, grit going into the vacuum cleaner near the kitchen door.

'What are you doing? Abby?'

I pull the car back onto the road, roll down the window to a blast of hot wind.

We don't speak again until we get to the bottom of Dad's driveway. My mind is racing as I park in front of the metal milk can Dad has painted lime green and nailed onto a post as his letterbox. Charlie opens the gate. The driveway winds a few times and goes up a steep incline before the gum trees lining it on both sides give way to a cleared expanse and we can see the house.

'Okay, we need to be normal, talk about Bali and Christmas and the kids. Make sure you say something nice about his garden. You could mention the chicken pen. And the new water tank. He'll have installed that by now.'

'Cool it, Abby. You sound like you're on speed.'

'Charlie, look.'

A police car is parked near Dad's open front door. I pull up behind it and turn off the engine.

'Do you think they're asking locals about the accident?'

My nerves are on high alert. 'That makes sense. Or else they're here because of the robbery, the stolen ring.'

He stares at the house. 'What if the police being here is nothing to do with her? What if Dad had a heart attack?'

'A heart attack? What are you talking about?'

Charlie leaves the car, slams the door. I hurry out, too, and rush after him. We stand in the doorway calling out 'Dad' and 'We're here', and jostling to get inside first.

'Living room,' Dad replies. His voice is small. He is standing next to a policeman and looks scared and deflated, a soft balloon of himself. He's wearing such a long frown it's as though the edges of his mouth are pulling his whole body towards the ground.

The policeman is schoolboy young. He nods in our direction. No one speaks until Dad sees Charlie, whose presence jolts him from his trance. 'Son.' He lurches forward and hugs Charlie in an unusually large show of affection. The policeman turns to me.

'Constable Roberts.'

'Abigail Campbell. That's our dad.'

I touch my father's wiry arm. 'Dad, what's happening? Are you okay?'

Charlie seems unable to extricate himself, so I unhook Dad and lead him to the couch. Dad loves this couch, this knobbly mess of orange, beige and green stripes, with big buttons and wide arms. There's a copy of a Frederick Forsyth novel on the carpet next to the chair; maybe he was reading when the police showed up. I sit beside him and hold his hand.

'What's going on?' Charlie asks.

'There was a car accident last night,' Constable Roberts says. 'Your father's fiancée was caught in some bad weather and ran off the road. I'm afraid the accident was fatal.'

'Fiancée.' *No, no, no.*

Constable Roberts studies me.

Charlie drops into an armchair with a thud. 'Dad,' he whispers.

Dad lets his head fall back onto the couch.

'Fiancée?' I say.

Constable Roberts frowns, picks his hat up off the coffee table. 'I'm sorry for your loss, sir. We'll be in touch again soon.'

The policeman leaves the room, closes the front door behind him. Dad doesn't move. I hold him as best as I can sitting sideways, and he briefly rests his face on my shoulder before pulling back and wiping his hand briskly across his mouth. Charlie stares at Dad, says nothing.

'I'll make us a pot of tea.' My voice cracks; my throat is clenching. 'Do you want tea? Charlie?' No one responds. And then, like a punch that's made its way across the room, gathering force as it travels, the horror of the moment hits me. I try to stand but my legs won't hold me. I crumble onto the couch, next to my father.

CHAPTER SEVEN

Saturday 7 December 1974

Charlie

'What was her name?'

'Skye,' he says.

Abby's banging around in Dad's kitchen. She's making sandwiches but there's enough ruckus it could be a four-course meal.

'Need some help in there?' I call out. I can see her: the kitchen and living room are only nominally separated by the kitchen bench and the fact that lino covers one floor, shag carpet the other.

'I'm fine.'

I look in Dad's direction, hoping for a moment's bonding, but there's no shared understanding between us. He's staring at the leg of my chair, not at me.

'She would have called,' he says, 'or asked Mal to. When she hadn't come back by sunrise I phoned him to see how it was going. He didn't know about Skye coming round, said Carol wasn't in labour. It doesn't make sense. It was a woman's voice. I should've asked her name. I can't figure it.'

'What can't you figure?' Abby sets down a tray with food, plates and paper towels on the coffee table.

'It'd been a good day. She sang in the bath.' I don't know why he's telling us that but I can see it matters to him. 'The house smelled of her bathwater, lavender and rose. She left the door open and when I put my head in, the room was warm and she was singing. She was happy.'

'She lived here?' Abby asks. 'How long had you been living together?'

I turn around to glare at her.

Dad ignores us both. 'She was excited you were coming. We'd put sheets on the beds, tidied up. She made a carrot cake while I trimmed my beard.' He grimaces. 'Tried to remember all the things I'd told her you two don't eat.'

'I eat everything,' I say.

'Condensed milk.'

'Yeah, that's not food. What meal would use that?'

Abby walks to Dad's side and places a small plate of sandwiches on the wide pine arm of the couch, touching his fingers to alert him to its presence.

'A cheesecake,' Abby says quietly. 'If she was making a cheesecake, maybe.'

'She stood there, dripping onto the carpet. The towel was too small to wrap around her, belly pushed it out.' He turns his face away from us. 'If I'd known it was the last time, I would've got in the bath like she asked.'

'You should rest, Dad,' Abby says.

'Her cheeks were pink, hair piled on her head in a bundle, stray bits.' He points to the side of his head. 'She splashed water towards me. I could see her footprints pressed into the mat. If I'd known I wouldn't see her again . . .'

'You loved her,' Abby murmurs.

He lifts his chin up and regards her sternly. 'Yes. I loved her.'

My heart is pounding in my chest, it must be audible.

'I don't understand why she was out driving,' Abby says. She crosses her arms, stays standing. 'You said your friend wasn't expecting her. Where was she going?'

Dad shakes his head. 'I don't know.'

'But there was a phone call?' I ask.

He looks at me as if I'm a simpleton. He must have made his students quake with those glowering expressions. 'Yes, that's what I said. And she was flustered by it. I thought it was the timing, a few hours before you were due.' His bottom lip shakes. 'We'd come inside from a walk around the property, checked on her tomato plants.'

'So the phone rang when you came back from your walk?' I ask.

'It was a woman, but it wasn't Carol. Spoke in an almighty rush. Said she had to talk to Skye right away. And Skye listens then says to her —' he shakes his head in distressed confusion — 'says, "Will you help me?" I thought it must be a complicated birth for her to ask the person on the phone for help. Then "Tell him I'm coming," she says. The father, I assumed. She was in a flap after that, didn't sound happy like she usually does heading to a birth. I followed her to the kitchen. We keep the keys on a . . .' He points towards the kitchen. 'She was so bothered she forgot her birthing bag. Rushed to the door without it until I called her back. I could see a storm was coming. But babies don't wait, and she wouldn't let me drive her.'

'Why didn't you tell me you were engaged, Dad?' Abby says. 'I've never heard her name before and now you're engaged and she was about to meet us.'

'Abby, not now,' I say.

'How did you meet her?'

'Abby, c'mon.'

She ignores me. 'I don't really understand why you'd keep this from us. Did you think she might not like us?' She has tears in her eyes.

This is beyond belief. 'Abby, I need to talk to you in the other room.'

'Not like you?' Dad raises his voice, a bear poked with a stick. 'Not *like* you? That woman didn't have an unkind bone in her body, wouldn't have known *how* to not like you, wouldn't have dreamt of it as a possibility. Do you know what she said?'

'I'm sorry, forget it,' Abby says.

'She asked me if you'd like *her*. She was worried about you not *approving*, judging her. Which you would have.' He slumps back into the couch, his energy spent.

I will Abby to stay silent.

Dad gets up with a grunt. As he stands, Abby steps back. Mum always said Dad's temper was a war wound. He's a tough nut. He likes to tell me how easy my life is, as if it'd be good for it to be otherwise. Abby's out of line but Dad doesn't say any more, just walks out of the room.

'Why didn't he tell us about her?' Abby asks me.

'More importantly, why is that the thing you're fixing on?'

I crane around to be sure Dad has left the room. 'He hasn't mentioned she was pregnant. He said something about her stomach being big but he never said she was pregnant. So don't bring it up.' I lower my voice. 'If the baby's his, that means it was our –'

'Don't,' she says. 'I can't take any more in, Charlie. Please.'

I hate when she does this, tries to dominate me.

'And that's on you,' she says in a hurried whisper. 'You said "let's go". I wanted to take her to a doctor. I wanted to help that baby.'

'Stop.' I frown at her. 'It's done.'

She leans forward. 'How does this not bother you? How are you –'

'What are you talking about? Of course it bothers me. Fuck, Abby, I'm just trying to survive this.'

She makes a low moan, then covers her face with her hands and sobs.

There's nothing I can do to comfort her. So I go outside, walk a lap around the house, past the chicken pen, an impressive vegetable patch that holds more food than two people could ever eat – staked tomato plants in careful rows, interspersed with basil, some flowers – and a locked-up corrugated-iron shed I know will be as orderly as a library. The ground is spongy under my sandshoes. I take a slow drag on my cigarette. I wonder if the baby was a boy or girl, then push away the thought.

The afternoon is quiet. The birds make a few warbles and peeps but are chill compared to the free-for-all I wake to in Bali. A magpie perches in silence on the arm of a nearby spotted gum. The hum of bees and crickets is set to lull; possums and wallabies snooze. I see a dozen cows milling together at the bottom of the hill, near the dam, chewing grass and swishing away flies.

The heat here is wet. It's the heat I grew up with and it's what I live with in Kuta. Sal grew up in Melbourne so she struggles with humidity. At KD, I tell her to do her running around early then to slow down in the afternoon if business slacks off, sit in the shade at the end of the day rather than throw herself straight into the clean-up. In this kind of heat you need to seek out shade, be around water, and stop when it's too much.

I rest against the coarse brick wall by the front door. Abby's car is parked nearby, mud-splattered, but unmarked by the accident. The rain will have washed away our tyre tracks and footprints. There'll be nothing to show we were there, which is a relief but a hollow one. Something huge has happened but there's no one I can talk to about it except my sister. And that's the last thing I want to do right now.

Late afternoon, I sit in the white wicker chair next to Dad's bed. I figure what I need to do is keep him company and listen.

Dad lies on his back with his hands by his sides. He's black-eyed, and his skin has taken on a yellowy-grey colour, as though he's the one heading for the funeral home. He snorts in disbelief. 'She was here yesterday, wearing that dress I bought her in Montville, stringing beads into a necklace, taking a bath.' He lifts his head up and looks at me. 'We walked around the garden.'

'I know, Dad.'

He drops his head back onto the pillow. 'There isn't much of her here,' he says. 'She left that place in a rush so whatever belongings she has are there, but I suspect she never had much. Only him.'

'Him?' I sit forward.

'I would've judged Skye if I'd met her ten or twenty years ago. I didn't know Adam from Eve when I was young. It's true that you get wiser with age, Charlie, learn to forgive people their mistakes, their bad choices, learn to hear what they're telling you.' He faces me. 'You should know that.'

'Sure.'

'I didn't judge her. I could see she was an angel, couldn't think about anything but her for days, weeks, jiggered around the house like a teenager, got a whole lot of nothing done. You wouldn't understand.'

'I've been in love, Dad.'

He ignores me. 'When I was with her, I felt hopeful. I hadn't felt that way in years. I used to laugh with joy when I'd see her, and she'd be hurt, and I couldn't explain, so I'd say I couldn't believe my luck she'd want to be with an old bloke. Fifty-four to her twenty-six. You may as well know.' I resist the urge to tell him I had sex with my grade twelve geography teacher. 'Some of the women in town didn't approve. I don't care much anymore what people think, but I didn't want Skye to be uncomfortable.' He pauses, frowns. 'I was shocked when she told me what she'd done. I did ask a lot of questions.'

'What had she done?'

'Broke my heart when she told me about the times she'd gone back before she met me. Kept making the same mistakes as far as I could tell. And no one to help her, because how could they? And don't say she should've called the police! Ha! She was up against them, too. But I'd had enough of it, the pain it was causing her. Wish she'd told me earlier. I'm not young but my noggin still works. I had a plan. She knew that. Even drew me a map.'

'Dad, what?' I try not to sound annoyed, but his ramblings and half-stories are getting on my nerves. That, and the fact I don't want to be here, and my sister, and my gut-wrenching guilt. 'You've lost me.'

'That young cop who came around, Roberts. He doesn't know. I can tell. But there are others who do. World's gone to hell, Charlie.'

'Dad, what's the "go back" bit, the map? Do you know where she was going?'

'Maybe. But no, it doesn't make sense. Why would she run off and do it the night I'd arranged for you to meet her, the night after I'd asked her to marry me? I said I had a plan, and she knew that.' He sighs. 'I worry about him. I never told her how much I worry about him.'

'Who?'

'Dad.'

Abby taps on the door. Taps. Timid and bossy at once.

'Not now,' I call out. 'Dad.' I reach out and touch his shoulder. 'Who's "him"?'

Abby opens the door. 'Everything all right?' She walks in and stands next to the bed, arms wrapped around her like a straitjacket.

'I said "not now". I know you heard me.'

She furrows her brow. 'Would you like something to eat or drink, Dad?' She lets her eyes wander around the room.

76

'I don't want anything.'

'Should I put fresh sheets on the bed? Tidy the room?'

I silently curse her for coming in before he finished his story.

'I'm sorry she's gone, I am.' Her voice quavers. 'Do you have a picture? A photograph of Skye?'

'What are you doing?' I scowl.

'No,' Dad says. 'For someone so beautiful, she didn't like having her picture taken. Maybe she's in the background of a house shot, but I doubt it.'

'Oh, your camera's here, on the dressing table. I can get the film developed if that would be helpful. I'll go to the chemist.'

'No.' He sits bolt upright. 'Don't touch anything. Leave it alone.'

And then I hear my father let go of a sob, like a child. I sit in my chair, paralysed, and watch as Abby perches on the edge of the bed by his side and places her arm around him with a touch so light it's as though her arms are hollow.

CHAPTER EIGHT

Monday 9 December 1974

Charlie

'Dad.' I stand in his bedroom doorway. It's early in the morning but I see that Abby has already left him a tray of breakfast to ignore. 'Cops are here. They want to talk to you.'

'I didn't hear anybody knock.'

'Yeah, well, they're here anyway.'

'They?'

'Guy from the other day and another one. Country cavalry.'

'I need to put on a shirt. My shoes, I don't know where my shoes are.'

'Dad, it's okay. I don't think they'll care what you're wearing.'

'Is Abigail here?'

'She's gone to get the newspaper, but I can handle a couple minutes' small talk by myself. Do whatever you need to.'

'Go on then. Don't leave them waiting.'

Roberts stands in the middle of the living room, not doing anything in particular, like a soldier at ease, straight-backed, hands folded over his crotch. Despite his muscle-man arms, there's something almost girlish about him. The other cop, Roberts' superior, Sergeant Doyle, has his back to me, and is staring out the window at the bush. He's a different story from Roberts. Meaty, wide, speckles of white in nut-brown hair, in his late forties, at a guess. First thing I'd noticed about him at the front door were his cattle-dog ice-blue eyes and beer gut. I hear him belch. He's the type of cop who arrested us at uni demonstrations, who twisted arms, gouged skin with hard fingernails, who kicked the door in at parties. I know his type. Fuck.

'He won't be long,' I say to Roberts.

The sergeant turns around, eyes me up and down more carefully than he had at the front door. I reckon now we both have one another's number. 'Your sister about?' he asks.

'Went into town. She'll be back soon. So . . .'

I feel like I'm being interrogated already and try to make my face and stance seem as relaxed as possible.

'Do you want some coffee?' I can't be much younger than Roberts but I feel like a child about to be busted, awkward and as transparent as glass.

Roberts shakes his head, takes a small Spirax notebook and biro from his shirt pocket.

'You been out of the country recently?' Doyle asks.

How could he know that? Did Dad say something to Roberts? 'Bali,' I say.

'Thought so.' Doyle looks at my shirt. 'Don't see that type of get-up around here. Not on blokes anyway.'

Prick. I don't have a snappy comeback and even if I did I couldn't say it. It's irrelevant anyway, since Dad walks into the room, dressed as inoffensively bland as I guess cops prefer.

'Gentlemen,' he says. There's name-exchanging, condolences, trouser-adjusting to sit down in chairs; I want them gone already but they're just starting. I watch Doyle. He has a slow toad-like demeanour but I reckon he's taking everything in, watching me, Dad, the house. I wish I could talk to Abby before she walks in. She doesn't have much of a poker face at the best of times.

Roberts clears his throat, pulls back his shoulders.

There's no way they could know. Is there? Are fingerprints washed away by rain, and would a country cop even have fingerprint equipment? Did one of us drop something? Did the car leak oil?

Dad studies the empty coffee table. 'Charlie, do I have to –'

'It's cool, Dad, no one wants a drink.'

'I do. Make me a cup of tea.'

I stand in the kitchen, fill the white plastic kettle and rinse limp tea leaves from Dad's tin pot, hearing the water hit the steel sink and the ping of bellbirds and gentle whoosh of wind through the open window. My hands are shaking. I'm getting water everywhere.

'I'll be brief. I'm sure you're –' Roberts starts. Dad waves away the rest of the sentence. He clearly has no desire to be comforted by a stranger. 'I have some concerns about your fiancée's accident. Her body was –' He registers the pain on my father's face. 'Your fiancée was lying a short distance away from the car, the door was closed, and the way she was placed –'

'Placed?'

'Well, that's the problem, sir. It seems someone took the body out of the car. She couldn't have fallen out at that angle, in that position. The door was closed but the window was open, and the rain damage indicates the water came in through the window.'

'Slow down, son. What does the window have to do with anything? She fell out the window?'

'No, sir. The window was open when the car crashed, which means the rain started after the accident. She'd have had her window up in a storm.'

Dad nods.

'And she couldn't have closed the door herself after the accident,' Roberts says.

'Why not? There's your answer. She left the car before the rain started, and tried to walk for help.'

'The medical examiner says she died of a blow to the skull from the steering wheel. And –' Roberts hesitates – 'even if that hadn't been the case, she'd smashed her left kneecap on impact, so she wouldn't have been able to walk. I'm sorry.'

I put Dad's teacup on the coffee table. He makes no move for it, sits like a Pompeii statue.

Roberts stands up and walks to the window. 'It's a strange position to find a body in, laid out on the ground like that, with her arms folded across her. The others think –' He turns back to face Dad. 'What we're considering is if there's a chance someone was in the vehicle with her. And if you'd have any ideas about who that might be.'

When there's no response, Roberts looks to me.

'Dad?'

'No.' He speaks in a whisper. 'She left here alone.'

'Has she ever picked up hitchhikers, sir?'

'She knows better.'

'Then is it possible she drove in the other direction first, up to the national park?'

Dad seems baffled. 'You know there's nothing up there.'

'Not normally. But if she'd arranged a liaison, or . . .'

'Please tell me, Constable,' Dad says, riled now, 'that you have some theory not based on random speculation.'

'Sir, someone moved her. We need to talk to that person. So if you have any idea of who that might be, it would help our investigation.'

Doyle has stayed silent throughout. He's sitting back in his chair like he owns the place, watching my father.

'Was she robbed?' Dad asks.

'Her belongings are in the police-station safe. Her bag was untouched, and there's money in her wallet.'

'And there's absolutely no chance she could've fallen out of the car in this exact position?'

'None at all, sir. It's impossible.'

'Rain got rid of any footprints, I suppose?'

Roberts nods.

'So you're saying someone moved her onto the ground, took nothing, then left her there?' Dad moves forward, elbows on his knees.

'Are you all right, sir?'

I stand up. 'I'll get some water.'

'Sit down, Charlie.' We wait for him to continue speaking. 'Do you know the work of C. S. Lewis, Constable Roberts?'

He reaches for his notebook. 'Does he live locally?'

I shouldn't laugh but I do. It's an icebreaker. Roberts blushes slightly but otherwise ignores me.

Dad glares at me then turns his attention back to Roberts. 'To the best of my knowledge he never visited these parts. But he was a wise man and he knew about grief. He said, "The pain I feel now is the happiness I had before." I have to go through this, Constable, whether I want to or not. I think you might be holding back some details. But I need to hear what you know, no matter how unpleasant.'

'He was a writer,' I say to Roberts. 'C. S. Lewis. Wrote kids' books.'

'I see.' He brushes invisible dust from his shirtfront and locks eyes with me. 'There's one other thing. Skye's brother has arranged for the body to be transported to Darwin for burial once the medical examiner has finished his work.'

He's sharper than I gave him credit for. Such a quick return to power.

'A brother,' I say.

Dad sinks back, deep into the curve of the couch. 'She'll be buried up there? Of course.'

I feel a rise of fury that my father is in a position that is so emasculating, so humiliating. And then I remember I've caused it.

'Do you have *any* idea where she was going?' Doyle seems impatient with the conversation, is taking over to move things along. It seems no one is going to address my father's comment that they aren't telling us everything. But they're cops. They ask the questions.

'Thought she was going to a birth,' Dad says, and explains the phone call minus yesterday's strange ramblings.

Doyle waits a moment then asks, 'Do you know much about your fiancée's life before you met her?'

'Not much,' Dad says. 'She was a private person.'

Doyle heaves himself to standing, hoicks up his pants, his black belt almost entirely hidden beneath his lump of a stomach. 'Mind showing us where she stored her keepsakes, letters and so on?'

Roberts has kept a fairly neutral expression until now, but I can see from the quick dart of his eyes that he didn't expect this question. Neither did Dad.

After Dad and Doyle to and fro over whether this is necessary and what point it serves, it's clear that Doyle is going to search the house anyway. So it's best if we at least watch while he does. Dad leads the two cops to his bedroom, where they rifle through the bedside drawers, the dressing table. Doyle tells Roberts to check under the bed.

They search the bathroom drawers after this. 'You want to know what brand of shampoo she used?' Dad asks. 'That'll help your investigation, will it?'

They don't answer. Doyle heads back to the kitchen, muttering to Roberts then more loudly directing him to open drawers, search behind tins, reach into the back of cupboards. Whatever they're looking for, they don't find it.

When they're done they offer cursory nods, the cop sign-off – 'we'll be in touch soon' – and leave. After the door closes, Dad goes to his room.

The same morning the cops visit, there's another knock on the door. Abby's still out; Dad and I arrive at the door simultaneously though we've come from different parts of the house. A plump woman who's maybe a handful of years younger than Dad stands on the threshold. Dad introduces her as Donna McCarthy.

Donna puts a warm hand on my cheek and gives me a gentle pat. 'You're the spitting image of your father.' She turns to Dad and tilts her head to one side. 'John. Come here.' She folds her fleshy arms around him and then pushes him away so she can examine his face. 'How are you holding up? You look peaky.' She turns to me. 'Have you been taking care of him?'

I don't recall either of us inviting her in, and I'm not sure how she's managed to carry in a wicker basket full of food without me noticing while also steering Dad to the couch, and yet, here we are.

'Now.' She lifts her basket onto the bench. 'Skye's going north to her family, which is as it should be.'

'How could you know that?' Dad says. 'I only just heard it myself.'

'Never mind. The poor family, my heart goes out. Can you imagine?' She makes a disapproving face at her own question. 'But we need to say goodbye. She was special to me, John. She was a lovely girl. Milk?'

'Black, with one.'

'Oh, I know that.'

Donna seems like a woman who's inclined to cheerfulness but she goes about her business with quiet gravitas. I can see she's trying to behave in what she thinks is an appropriately sedate manner. Dad notices this, too.

'Go on, say it.'

'Say what, John?' She wipes the chopping board energetically.

'Donna, you don't have to stop being yourself. I say, black with one. You say, like my men. It's what you say.'

She tilts her face down, adding another chin. 'I don't think it's suitable to be making jokes at a time like this, John.'

'No, you're probably right.'

She places a tray in front of us – white-bread sandwiches (sliced cheese, tinned beetroot, tomato), chopped apple, tumblers of Coke – and sits, the cushion issuing a loud puff as she relaxes into the chair.

'I want to be mindful of your loss, of what we've all lost.' Donna takes a sip of her drink then speaks directly to me. 'It's only a thing I say, a bit of fun. About the black men.'

'Why don't you tell me what you have in mind, Donna? I can almost hear your brain ticking.'

It turns out other people have a stake in Skye's death. Her mates from the chemist, where she worked with Donna, as well as the women she'd acted as midwife for, and their husbands, and all the rest of the people she knew around here want some commemoration of her passing from their lives, regardless of where her body is ending up.

Donna places her drink on a coaster. 'A ceremonial rose-planting is what I had in mind. Before you head to Brisbane with Charlie and Abby. If you give the nod I'll ring around for a gathering tomorrow afternoon. Kathy and I can get together a slice, some melon, scones. The boys will plant the bush. We'll need a table.' She peers out the window. 'That one will do. We could play some songs she liked.' She turns to me. 'Linda Ronstadt. Quite fond of her.'

I smile.

'Funny name isn't it? Ronstadt,' she says.

Dad takes a slow breath. 'Do we have to do this, Donna?'

'We do, John.'

Donna opens her mouth a few times to speak and then stops. There's something else she wants to say but she's second-guessing herself, or having trouble finding the words. She gulps like a goldfish a few more times then says, 'Was she unhappy that night, John? She did get down in the dumps sometimes, go silent on us. Was she out of sorts when she got in the car?'

'Not especially,' Dad says.

'And there's some confusion about where she was going, I gather?'

'How, Donna? How do you know these things?'

She tilts her head. 'Well I don't know why she crashed into a tree, I'll tell you that for free. We've been on that road a hundred times together. John –' She opens and closes her mouth again, then speaks in a rush. 'Is there any chance she did this on purpose?'

It's obvious Dad feels some affection towards Donna, but he looks daggers at her. 'No,' he says.

'With the hormones, and Christmas coming – Christmas is a difficult time for some people. And I thought if the phone call upset her or you'd had a blue – I'm not saying that doesn't happen to every couple. Rod and I have our moments. It's just hard to understand how she ended up in that ditch unless she wanted to be there.'

Dad stands up, and Donna, mercifully, recognises this as a signal it's time to leave. I wish I could tell her Skye didn't commit suicide, that she can put that worry to rest, and that I'm sorry.

CHAPTER NINE

Tuesday 10 December 1974

Charlie

A funeral without a body seems supremely weird to me, but
Donna says the ceremony will be a farewell, not a funeral.
I don't know how Dad will cope with being around other
people. He barely has the energy to shower, and stands in the
hallway in his pyjamas, confused about why he's there.

'She's with me in the morning,' he tells me. 'When I wake
up, I wait before I open my eyes because Skye is here. I smell
her rosewater spray, see her moving around the room, casting a
shadow on my lids. I feel her sitting on the bed.'

He moves from reverie to lists of chores, telling me straight
after this that I need to call Ed. 'Tell him not to drop the other
chickens over after New Year like we'd said. I don't want them
now.' I say I'm sure Ed will understand.

But Donna is adamant there will be a send-off here, so early Tuesday morning, two weeks before Christmas, thirty odd people gather in Dad's backyard to farewell Skye.

I do mean thirty odd people, too. There are craggy farmers dressed in their best who'd sought Skye's advice on painful corns and cuts, teary pregnant women sad she won't be in the room on their big day, a quiet and spotty teenage boy. There are tanned men in polyester paisley shirts and wide ties, women in kaftans, and kids in all kinds of garb, from ironed shirts to tutus. It's a motley crew. Donna and her friends are wearing nondescript dresses of apricot, turquoise and beige, with hats that seem, to my untrained eye, relics from the Second World War. Maybe the first one.

'You look nice, dear.' Donna squints in the bright sunshine, adjusts my collar. I've borrowed a short-sleeved mustard-brown shirt from Dad and combed my hair. 'Not a cloud, is there? It's weather for a wedding.'

And then she heads into the kitchen, where I know Abby will be, doing whatever it is that needs to be done. I'm sure my sister is feeling as churned up as I am today but we don't discuss it.

'Donna,' Dad says, walking towards the house. She stands a few feet away from me now, accepting a plate of lamingtons from a recently arrived mourner. 'I can't. You'll have to do it.'

She hands me the plate, takes my father's hands and holds them in her own. 'No one expects you to have prepared a speech. Say what's in your heart.'

He shakes his head.

'You listen to me, John. If you stay silent today you'll regret it forever more. You don't need to use fancy words or important quotes. You need to say goodbye.'

She leads him by the crook of his arm to a clearing under a gum tree, where she's set up an altar of sorts: a fold-out picnic table covered by a white cloth and topped with a vase of lilies, a silver pen and an open book in which some guests have written their memories of Skye.

'Excuse me.' Donna claps her hands. 'If I could have your attention. Before we plant the rosebush – thank you, Ned Darmody – John will offer a few words. If anyone would like to speak after him, come to the front.'

'Is he all right?' Abby whispers. She's standing next to me now.

'How could he be?' I say.

'Why are you –?' She points at the lamingtons, frowns as she takes them from me and puts them on the food table. A currawong trills in the branches above us. Leaves crunch under Dad's leather soles as he rocks from one foot to the other. A child burps and the people nearby laugh. Dad clears his throat. Donna stands by his side, her wrists folded across the pleats in her skirt.

'Off you go,' she whispers.

'Thank you for coming,' Dad says. He straightens his hat, and the crowd relaxes its stiff stance once he speaks. 'I don't know all of you, but I know you're here because you cared about Skye. And I'm sure she cared about every one of you.' He stops. 'Skye loved working at the chemist and helping people. She loved bringing babies into the world. She was, you'd all know, about to have a baby of her own, our baby.' He bends over as though he's about to pick something up off the ground, then stays like that. He lets out a long awful howl.

Donna reaches down for his arm as Abby pushes through the crowd and takes Dad's other side. I follow them as they right Dad and guide him into the house.

'Stay with him,' Donna says to me when we reach his bedroom.

'I couldn't do it.' He drops facedown onto his bed and sobs.

'It's okay, Dad,' Abby says. She is crying, too. I stand with my back to both of them, resting my forehead on the closed bedroom door.

At eight o'clock the next morning, once Dad has done the rounds of his house and property, and made phone calls to check that his animals and vegetable patch (and rosebush) will be properly cared for in his absence, I carry our gear out to the car. Abby says it'll be recuperative for Dad to be in Brisbane, with the kids, out of this house. The truth is, she needs to be home, preparing for Christmas, and far away from where we abandoned Skye.

Maybe having Mark around will help Abby get herself together – she's more terrible at dealing with Dad's pain than I would've expected. I've told her to stop patronising him, to stop talking like she's a nurse in a retirement home. But she can't hit the right note, and I can see it's irritating both of them. She flips between pity, compassion and disinterest, though I know her weirdness is coming partly from the sheer effort of keeping our secret locked behind her lips.

Partly.

She's bruised. It's understandable Dad wouldn't clock how the news of his engagement has affected Abby. But marriage is a big deal to my sister. And Dad not only committed to a woman who's not our mother, he also didn't talk to his family about it. I don't care too much if I ever get married, and I figure after fifteen years Dad must be keen for some female company. Abby doesn't see it that way.

'He's known her for *two years*,' she'd whispered to me when we were in the kitchen at night after dinner, when Dad was in the bathroom.

'Yeah, but they probably weren't an item that whole time. Maybe he was waiting to see where it would go.'

'She lived here.'

I gave her that. Skye is everywhere in this house. There's no way Dad put dried flowers in the vase on the dining table, or hung the bamboo wind chime that sounds when the breeze blows through the laundry window. Skye's name is on the water-colour of a sunrise that hangs above Dad's bedroom chest of drawers. And the wooden slats in a pile next to his wardrobe – a cot waiting to be assembled. Skye's past and future are right in front of us. She probably chose the plates Abby was washing, the bowl I was drying.

'He proposed to her the night of – It's not like he'd kept that a secret, Abby. He'd wanted us to meet her. Cut him a bit of slack.'

She'd frowned in confusion. 'What do you mean?' Then she lifted one wet hand up and gestured to the stove. 'Have you not noticed all the things I'm doing?'

Like housework was the point. While my sister knows what it is to grieve, she's in denial about the extent of Dad's suffering, seems annoyed at him, somehow convinced this loss isn't as serious as it was with Mum. As if there's a scale of grief. As if time spent is related to pain felt. She wants to tell herself he's mourning for a slip of smoke or a silhouette. Which we can both see is far from the truth.

I drop the last box into the boot of Abby's car.

'Be careful, there are breakables in there.'

'I know, Abby. You know *how* I know? Because you've told me twice already.' But I can't get too cocky. I'd forgotten to call Ed, who only learned from Dad a few minutes ago that his poultry are no longer wanted. So now there's a whole chicken thing for me to hear about on the drive.

'When will you two grow up?' Dad says before walking back inside, but there's nothing left in there for him to check on or do. It's all done – generator off, appliances unplugged, beds made. After Donna and Abby's competitive cleaning yesterday afternoon, the house is in better order than before the funeral crowd arrived.

As I carry Dad's suitcase to the car I offer a small salute to Lenny, the brush turkey I've been keeping an eye on. He's strutting backwards across the driveway, using his long claws to flick bush litter behind him towards his huge nesting mound. His neck wattle wobbles as he increases his efforts. He's the hardest worker I've ever seen. Yesterday, I tried to help him by raking a few leaves in the direction of his nest, but he scattered them across the earth in an outraged frenzy. Turkeys aren't smart birds, but I respect Lenny's insistence on doing things his own way.

Dad walks out of the house carrying a book that he hands to me, a copy of C. S. Lewis's *The Problem of Pain*. 'Kids' books.' He snorts.

'Narnia is for kids,' I say in my defence.

'Read it,' he says, then takes the front seat.

As we pull away, I watch Lenny through the back window, running after another turkey. Dude owns the place.

Once we're on the road to Brisbane, Dad says he wants to see where Skye's car ran off the road. 'Keep an eye out for the police ropes. They've cordoned off the area.'

'Are you sure that's a good idea?' Abby asks.

'Yeah, Dad, probably not.' If it was up to me, Abby would drop the accelerator to the floor on that stretch of road. 'I think we should head straight to Abby's place.'

'You'll pull over when we see the ropes.'

When we arrive at the site of the accident, Abby stops as instructed. Dad climbs out and stands on the edge of the road, staring down into the ditch. I walk over and stand beside my father, feeling a rush of nausea and fear.

There are ragged wounds in the bark of the tree where the metal cut into the wood, and flecks of glass near the trunk, but the scrub is already closing in, obscuring the skid that led from the road to the tree. If not for the ropes and scarred tree I wouldn't know this was the place. I wonder if the animals who live nearby remember that night? Do bandicoots and kangaroos stay clear, or is every day a fresh start for them?

I scan the surrounding bushland. There's nowhere Skye could've pointed the car that would've left her unharmed. Had she hit a smaller tree or come towards this one at a different angle, she might've walked away with a head injury. Maybe.

I watch my father as he looks from the tree to the road and back again, pushes his hat a bit higher off his forehead. I pray he doesn't go down there, into the ditch, down where Abby sat in the mud beside Skye, where the baby tumbled and died. I owe Dad this moment, but I can't wait to get away from here.

'She was a safe driver,' he says. 'Car was in good nick. Road's not wide but she was on a straight. It hadn't started raining if

94

her window was down, so the road wouldn't have been slippery. And she was used to watching for kangaroos.' He frowns. 'I don't understand what went wrong.'

I shove my hands deep into my pockets. 'Guess we'll never know.'

CHAPTER TEN

Wednesday 11 December 1974

Abby

The mechanic checks the water and oil and fills the tank. Dad wanders off in search of the toilet. He's even more gaunt than usual. During the past week I've offered him every type of food, but he regards my meals as a sick animal would: with suspicion or indifference. None of us is eating much right now though.

Charlie and I stand a few feet away from the car, in the shade offered by the half-roof of plasterboard and tin above the petrol bowsers. He smokes. I lean against one of the poles holding up the roof and feel the hot metal through my rayon dress.

Not far from the garage, two skinny brown dogs lie in the dappled shade of a stringy tree. One lifts his head to bite at the flies hovering around his nose, and then flops back onto the dirt. I move myself off the pole and peel my dress from the back of my thighs.

'Eight bucks'll do it.' The mechanic drops the hood of the car with a bang. 'Keep an eye on the oil,' he says to Charlie.

I give him the exact money and he heads back to the garage. Dad strides the length of the building, still searching for the toilets, not having asked.

'Have you told Mark yet?' Charlie asks, dropping the stub of his cigarette onto the ground.

'I don't know why you think Mark will have some magic solution I haven't thought of.'

'Have you told him?'

'Please stop asking me that.' I wipe away the sweat from under my eyes then let my sunglasses drop back down.

'Don't you want to talk to him about what we've done?'

'What *you've* done. And no, I *don't* want to.'

That's a lie. It would be a relief to tell Mark, to have him hold me and stroke my hair, say he'll take care of it. But that won't happen. When I let Charlie drive I put everything – both of our futures – at risk. This is not Mark's problem to fix.

I walk away from Charlie. Our looping conversations don't help anything. Even with endless hours awake every night to think, I can't find a way to make this situation better. I need to protect Charlie from the police, and Mark, my children, my father from the truth. I need a way to assuage my guilt. And telling Mark won't solve any of that.

'Band on the Run' blares from the garage, where two other mechanics are working on a raised ute. One of them is set to slide himself under the chassis, lying face-up on what I think is a door with wheels; the other one, shirtless, is standing beside him holding a can of soft drink, sweat on his bare chest.

I pace a small circle back to the car and see that Charlie has taken the front seat, though I'd told him that was Dad's spot for the whole trip. 'You don't think you owe him at least –' I point at the seat.

'He doesn't care.'

I sit down behind the wheel.

'Dad's not an idiot, Abby. He's going to work this out. We need to tell Mark. We need advice from someone who's not involved, someone we can trust.'

'Dad's not going to work it out.'

'Well, aren't you supposed to tell your husband things – isn't that the deal?'

'Dear God, stop. And don't lecture me about relationships. You've mooned over your best friend's wife for years.'

He slumps. 'They're not married. And I don't *moon* over her.'

'I thought they were married.'

'You're glad to hear that, aren't you? Moon happy.'

'Don't be ridiculous.'

Charlie looks out the window at the garage. Dad's inside, squatting down to speak to the man underneath the ute. 'Dad!' He shouts for him to come to the car. 'Good to go? It's an oven in here.'

'People are asking Mark about this, Charlie; he *is* involved, it's his father-in-law for God's sake. It was in the newspaper. Can you imagine if he knew the truth, what problems it would cause him?'

I speak quickly and watch Dad walk back to the car. Behind him, the mechanic blows me a kiss. Dad sits in the back without commenting on Charlie's seat coup.

'Bloke in there tells me this road was once a droving trail.' His voice is flat. 'Says there used to be a river that ran past here but over the years the cattle drank the life out of it.'

'Cheery,' Charlie says.

I check for oncoming trucks then pull onto the highway.

'Do you two remember that first Christmas after your mother passed away?'

Charlie shakes his head.

'How can you not remember that?' I ask.

'I was nine.' He stares out the window, away from me.

'I should've said yes to one of your mother's friends,' Dad says. 'One with kids. They all offered to let us join their Christmas lunches, dinners. June only asked out of obligation. Christian charity.'

At that, Charlie and I exchange an eye roll. Aunt June never offered so much as a raisin without an air of martyrdom. I'd hated visiting her as a child, her spinster house sterile as a hospital ward, with begrudging, tight-fisted nods to hominess by way of framed prints – frigid flowers and vacuumed land- scapes – and pert couch cushions made of some material that could catch fire from a warm body.

'*Endures* life, June does. She's always been that way.' Dad sighs. 'A few days before Christmas, before I dragged you to her door, she called to *reiterate* she was in no position to waste money on gifts. Can you credit that? "I've bought them some- thing," she said, "since I know you'll want that. Tell them not to expect much."'

'The kids whose mother had died,' Charlie says.

'Maybe it's good you don't remember it,' I say. 'Maybe not remembering is a way of protecting yourself.'

'You think?' He reaches into his shirt pocket for his cigarettes.

The gift-giving hadn't been the only bothersome part of Christmas as far as June was concerned. The possibility we'd sully her house was raised with us as soon as we arrived. 'I'm not saying you're grubby but I like to keep the place neat. It's the way I am. I've gone to the trouble of having the carpet shampooed. I'd appreciate it if you'd take your shoes off.' Which we did, Charlie and I so cut up and raw. Even now I can hardly stand to think of that day. It fuels me if ever I find myself resenting the work I do to make our own Christmases so perfect.

I glance at Charlie. 'The table was set as though she thought a horde of animals was about to descend on her: a tiny Santa Claus centrepiece wrapped in plastic, vinyl covering the table. And she wouldn't let us open the crackers. We ate in silence like it was some unseemly activity to be done with as fast as possible – no music, no talk, just the clang of cutlery on her horrible beige plates.'

Charlie blows smoke towards his cracked-open window.

Dad huffs. 'Merry bloody Christmas.'

I look in the rear-vision mirror. 'So why did you take us there?'

He meets my eye, sighs again. 'Christmas was something your mother did. How would I know? Anyhow, she's my sister.'

Charlie shifts in his seat. 'Let's listen to some music.'

'There are tapes in the glove box. Grab the Helen Reddy one.'

He groans. 'Seriously?'

'What? The driver picks the music. That's the rule.' But it takes one verse of 'I Am Woman' for me to realise my poor choice.

'How much of this claptrap do we have to listen to?'

'It's not claptrap, Dad.'

Charlie forms a gun with his fingers and makes as though to shoot himself in the head.

'Whining about nothing. There are people in the world with no food or water. Why isn't she singing about that?'

'How about something less controversial?' Charlie says, pressing the stop button.

'Only if it's by a woman,' Dad says. 'No good has ever been done by a man, Charlie.'

'Nobody said that, Dad.'

'That's what your sister thinks. Isn't it?' We lock eyes in the rear-vision mirror once more. 'Thinks it's beneath her to be a mother.'

'I absolutely don't,' I say. He's in pain, lashing out. I should let this go.

'It was enough for your mother, nothing to scoff at. It's dignified work to take care of your home, husband, raise a family.'

I focus on the road, keep my mouth shut though there are a thousand things I want to say, though I feel stung and enraged.

'Don't think I've ever heard her say otherwise, Dad. Hey, do you remember my friend Jason from –'

'Well, why do you want to be a lawyer then? What are you trying to prove? Mark earns a good salary. You'll make his life harder by being at university now you have kids to look after. Who'll be doing that? I suppose you expect him to. As well as his job. So you can go off and do what you want. Which, by the way –' he flicks his hand angrily in my direction – 'plenty of lawyers in the world without you.'

Breathe in, breathe out.

Charlie glares at Dad now. 'You're talking like a guy from the fifties.'

'The fifties weren't so terrible,' Dad says.

'You know what I mean. Abby's a great mother. What's your beef with her working? Sounds like your baggage, Dad, not hers.'

'I'm well aware that women work. Skye worked. Donna works. But I don't see why your sister, why young women now, are so hell-bent on creating division, making a big statement about it. It doesn't need to be so bloody . . . pious.' He sits forward so his head is closer to mine. 'You should think twice about this, Abigail. You have a good husband and those kids deserve a mother. You don't need to show off.'

'Jesus, Dad,' Charlie says. 'Harsh.'

'And wrong,' I say. 'It's not showing off. It's studying, to pursue a profession. Not grounds for personal insult. I'm not going back to uni to further the cause of women, though it'd be *fine* if I was. I want to be a lawyer because I care that people who are vulnerable, poor, wrongly accused, have an advocate, Dad. You might not have noticed, but I'm good at helping people. I've had a lot of practice.' I look at Charlie. 'I meant –'

'It's okay,' he says. 'I get it.'

'So you'll turn your back on Mark and your kids? Leave them to fend for themselves so you can help some strangers, puff yourself up?'

'That is *not* what I'm doing.' *Breathe in, out.* 'Why does this annoy you so much anyway? Mark's proud of me. Why can't you be?'

He pauses. 'Mark's a good man. You did well there. I was impressed with the piece he did on the National Hotel commission. Very thorough. *He'd* make a good lawyer.'

Charlie offers me an expression that combines sympathy with the unspoken advice to drop the topic.

'Some people want to be mothers, you know,' Dad says, sitting back in his seat with a thump. 'They get a bit crazy if they can't.'

I wonder if Charlie hears this the same way I do. Is Dad telling us something about Skye?

'June had a baby but it died,' he says. 'She never got to see it, doesn't know if it was a boy or girl.'

'That's terrible,' I say. And absolutely not where I thought this was going. 'What happened?'

'Things were different then,' he says. 'None of this giving birth in a bathtub. When she came to on the hospital bed she wasn't pregnant anymore and they'd taken the baby away. Doctor told her it had been born dead and it would upset her to see it.' He pauses. 'She mentioned it over the years, wished she at least knew where they'd buried it. She worried about whether they'd baptised it . . . And then Hal running off on her.' He becomes brisk and admonishing without warning. 'You two should have shown her a little more understanding.'

'How could we have been sympathetic about something we didn't know?' I ask.

He huffs. 'When did you become so argumentative?'

We sit in silence after that. Charlie never does put on another tape; he and Dad fall asleep instead. I drive the long bleached bitumen road, wide open land spreading out on either side of it, passing wheat-coloured fields speckled with eucalypts, granite boulders, depleted dams and glassy-eyed Hereford cattle, in lots divided by strings of barbed-wire fencing: a landscape low and predictable. Small insects slam against my windscreen. Squashed cane toads spot the road. The road lies like a ribbon on the earth, heat rising from its mirage of an end, making it appear that just up ahead everything solid becomes quivering gas.

There are no houses here, no signs, no overhead cables or telephone poles. This is the land my mother spent her life trying to escape and for which my father pined. From the moment Dad bought the farm he was happy and energetic, as he'd been when Mum was alive.

When construction on the house began we went out to help, without giving any thought of what that entailed. Mark's not much of a handyman, and I spent my time making sure the kids didn't stand on nails or fall into trenches, so it was more of a show-and-tell event. We followed Dad around the site as he pointed out where the bathroom would be, the kitchen and doors, and described the merits of the septic system and generator he'd chosen. He tried to interest Sarah in the local topography – the mountains in the near east are shaped a lot like people's heads – the Dreamtime story about the lizard and the lake, and his latest readings about raising cattle and poultry. We'd eaten dinner around an open fire, slept in tents. We visited once after that.

Mum wouldn't have liked the farm one bit. She'd wanted us to be in Brisbane, so we could go to decent schools and she could enjoy the bustle and social life of a city. My parents were forever 'going out' or 'having guests in'. I can only imagine how desperately lonely she would've been if Dad had insisted they live in the country.

I come up behind a truck with cartoon drawings of dope leaves and Varga girls decorating its mudflaps. Its fat wheels send out a spray of pebbles. I hold my left hand against the windscreen to stop the rocks shattering the glass. I recall my mother doing this from the passenger's seat when Dad was driving, her long fingers decorated with gold rings, some with diamonds, some with gems of blue or green, the one-off ruby engagement ring she loved the most, the one that's wrapped in tissues in my coin purse.

Mum said she was glad she had a daughter to leave her rings to, but they never came to me. At first because I was too young, and then later, when I tentatively asked for them, because my father simply said no. He didn't want to give over any part of my mother to me, to anyone.

I knew how special the ruby ring was, not in a dollar sense, because the ruby wasn't that big and the gold band was thin, but in sentimental value. Mum was impressed Dad had chosen it without help from her, and had chosen so well. She'd admired his initiative, a quality she said many men lacked. When he'd decided to propose to her, Dad had taken an opportunity (how, who knew, for the story was hers to tell) to remove a ring from Mum's jewellery box, place it on a piece of paper, carefully draw a circle around the inside of the ring – not once but several times, for good measure – and then find a ring that was the perfect size, with a gemstone in her favourite colour, made in Paris, the city of her dreams. He'd applied calm, manly logic to the task of buying women's jewellery then had the word 'love' inscribed in cursive where the gold touched her skin. 'How,' our mother would say, arm stretched in front of her, her eyes on the ruby ring, 'could I have said no?' Her wedding ring, while larger and more traditional, seemed almost an afterthought.

I grip the wheel tightly as I overtake the truck. The driver waves and honks.

And then I hold the car steady on an endless straight. I know the road will get more complicated later on, but for now only my arm muscles are tested. My mind is free to wander, which, today, is not good. But, lacking the energy to stop it, I stare at the road and give in to memory.

The end of my first day in grade one. I'd walked out of the classroom into a mass of mothers waiting for their sons and daughters. There was my mother: standing to one side of the other women, wearing cat-eye sunglasses, dark hair in a perfect dome, a patent-leather purse hanging off her angled forearm, a dress of blue shot silk. My mother, who never left the house without 'eyes on and a perfect lip', as advised by Amy Vanderbilt's *Complete Book of Etiquette*. My mother, who bought expensive overseas fashion magazines. My mother, who asked my father to haul her sewing machine onto the dining-room table almost nightly, so that I became accustomed to falling asleep to the sound of whirring machinery and shaking wood. On my first day of school, and each day thereafter, she picked me up dressed like Elizabeth Taylor in a crowd of Julie Andrews, and her loveliness filled me with pride.

Even on our twice-yearly obligatory family stays at our grandparents' farm near Kingaroy – which we knew she loathed – my mother dressed like a *Vogue* cover girl. I'm sure I disappointed her as a daughter. I liked to play outside and didn't care much what I wore back then. She persisted with me, gently. I'd sit on her lap, both of us facing forward, her arms wrapped around me to show me how to thread a needle, sew a button. I had no interest in sewing but enjoyed the warmth of her enveloping me, her powdered cheek an inch from mine, the waxy smell of her lipstick.

The last time we went to Nan and Pop's farm before Mum died, I found the courage to swim in the murky dam at the bottom of the hill. I dropped my dress in the grass and ran across the dried-earth rim that led to the water, wearing only my undies, trying not to think about what might be underfoot. I squelched in mud then dove into the warm water and swam, blissful, to the middle of the dam. Afterwards, I pulled my dress on and ran to the house to boast, but everyone had gone to see the new calves except for Mum. Before I could explain myself she bundled me off to the bathroom, asking why I insisted on ruining the pretty things she made me.

Once I'd washed, and my grandparents, Dad and Charlie had returned from the calving pens, we ate warm scones in the crowded kitchen while Pop's cattle dog, Girl, sat by the open back door, watching me with anxious eyes. Charlie and I weren't allowed to feed Girl but my grandparents – ancient, cranky – were so dismissive of her, yapping instructions at her all day, that I took it as my mission to sneak rewards to her. I went out to the shady porch and sat beside her, whispering advice, counselling her to run away while we slept, to head north, being sure to stay clear of the elephantine trucks that stormed the road throughout the night.

But the next morning she stared at me vacantly, as if we'd never spoken.

I thought it would be nice for Girl to swim in the dam, too, so that afternoon I'd tried to coax her in. But she wouldn't get in the water no matter how many times I called, and Dad came down and told me to stop yelling at the dog.

'You're turning her into a nervous wreck. Don't ask her to do something she's been forbidden to. She knows better.' He took a half-dozen steps away before remembering I was now also forbidden to swim in the dam. 'And get yourself up to the house quick smart.'

After dinner, when Nan sent me to the kitchen to fetch her a glass of sherry, I caught Mum feeding Girl pieces of ham. I smiled, and Mum put a manicured finger to her red lips.

I pull the car onto the weedy verge to empty my bladder. I squat down and urinate, Dad and Charlie both still out like lights. Twenty feet away, a wallaby stands, balanced on its thick tail, watching and chewing.

I dig in my handbag for tissues to use in lieu of toilet paper. My fingertips feel the bulge of the ring in my coin purse. How could he have given it away? I drop my wet tissues onto the dirt, stand and pull up my undies. Neither Dad nor Charlie wakes when I open the car door and start the engine.

I stare at my father. His head is drooping to one side, spit drying white in the corner of his mouth. I love him. He enrages me. I am gutted at the grief we've caused him. I want to wake him and tell him I am sorry and cry. And shout at him, too, for the years of pain he's caused. Cry and shout.

On the day Mum died, Charlie and I left her side only to use the toilet or eat in the hospital canteen. I wanted to help make my mother better but there was so much going on that made no sense. None of the nurses would give me a proper explanation about what went through the tubes and into her arms. None of them was sure if Mum could hear me when

I asked her if she'd like me to tidy her hair. I tried to decipher the words on the chart that hung on the bar at the foot of her bed. I refolded her nightgowns.

Throughout her illness, Dad had whispered conversations with neighbours, drove us to and from the hospital, and moved around the house like a zombie. The day before she died he went to Kenmore High and taught his history and English classes. If I'd been in Dad's shoes – an adult – I would've fought like a beast to save her, berated the doctor or demanded new techniques or fought for the attention of an outside specialist – *something*. But when it most mattered to speak up, Dad was quiet, still. And after a while I became quiet, too, because I didn't know what else to do.

Not far outside Brisbane's city limits, bushland gives way to sprawling trucking yards and rubbish tips before it turns to outer suburbia. Here, the land begins to hold more houses, all dropped on sharply defined plots, houses hunched low, neat and apologetic with boundary walls only four bricks high, plants cut back hard and ringed by small rocks so as not to take space they don't deserve. Then come corner shops, schools and public swimming pools. Then suburbs with hills and valleys where wooden Queenslanders rise up on stilts like flamingos, with air flowing all around them, and lush gardens allowed to unfurl, their arms draped across fences and raised up to the sky. Telegraph poles, light poles and traffic lights stick up from the ground haphazardly, like tree trunks after a bushfire. In the distance, a clump of skyscrapers marks the city centre.

And the heat. Always, everywhere, the relentless garish heat.

I drive alongside the Brisbane River. Near the city it's brown and indecisive, lumbering out to sea with thin swirling gyres covering its surface, as though the skin is reacting to some twitchy internal doubts. It's tricky to tell which way the water is flowing. Dredging barges work the river, making it deep for cargo ships and for mining sand and gravel. I pass one bridge after another: the Story Bridge, the Captain Cook Bridge, the William Jolly Bridge. As we approach the Arnott's factory I roll down the window to breathe in sweet, biscuit-scented air.

CHAPTER ELEVEN

Wednesday 11 December 1974

Charlie

Abby and Mark's house sits in a cul-de-sac in a suburb where the streets twist and bend as though designed by someone who'd dropped a bowl of spaghetti on the floor and thought, 'Yes, that is how people can best get from A to B.' Streets have been added on as the council cut lines around weirdly shaped parcels of bushland and sold them to developers; there doesn't seem to have been much consideration given to how this mess would be navigated by residents. It's kind of funny.

To drive into her carport, Abby makes a tight left turn off Woondarra Street, then holds left to veer into the cul-de-sac off Jamison and whips the car up a steep driveway, hitting the brakes the instant she's at the top to avoid slamming into the brick retaining wall. The driveway was Mark's handiwork, and for the life of me I can't figure out why he'd make a situation that's already difficult even harder.

'Another triumph for Evel Knievel,' I say as Abby pulls to a stop. 'Fans are on their feet, the cheers are deafening.'

'How about thanking me for driving for five and a half hours?'

'I told you I'd drive. Say the word, I said.'

She glares at me. 'Are you insane?' Which, sure.

'Dad then,' I say.

'I do quite enough driving,' he says. I hadn't realised he was awake.

Dad and I stand in the carport and stretch towards the low ceiling, both of us moaning and cracking as though we'd spent a week in a box. Abby moves straight to the task of unloading. She places bags, cartons, Dad's suitcase in a line on the concrete floor and calls out, 'We're here.'

Woof scrambles down to the car first and jumps up to greet Abby. He shrinks down under Dad's too-hard pat.

Sarah comes clomping out of the house to greet us, long hair swinging loose, wearing a t-shirt, undies, knee-high white socks and Abby's clogs. Abby bends down and hugs her, and by the time she gets up, Mark's standing before her, arms out for his own hug.

'Hi. Why is Sarah wearing her pyjama top?' She wraps her arms around his waist.

'We missed you.' Mark kisses her. He slaps my back. 'Welcome home. I'm keen to hear about life in paradise.' Then he looks to Dad. 'John, how are you holding up? I wish we could've met her.'

Dad gives a small nod of acknowledgement, turns his

attention to Sarah. 'Who is this young lady? And what have you done with my granddaughter?'

'Ha, ha.' Sarah reaches for his hand.

'And where are your sister and brother?'

She seems disappointed by his ignorance. 'They're asleep, of course. Little kids sleep all the time.'

'How was the drive?' Mark asks Abby.

'Long. And it's leaking oil again. But, hon, why is she in her pyjamas? It's two o'clock.'

'She's in a t-shirt,' he says, pulling my backpack onto his shoulder. 'A shirt is a shirt. John, go on inside and pour yourself a drink. Charlie and I've got this.'

'It's says Time for Bed on the front.'

'Abby.' Mark puts a hand on her shoulder. 'Relax. It's all good.'

Ignoring Mark's offer, Dad carries his suitcase and pillow out of the carport across the wooden-sleeper pathway to the front door, with Sarah *clop-clopping* behind him. Mark and Abby follow behind me till we're all standing around a pile of belongings in the hallway.

'I've set up the camp bed in the spare room,' Mark says. 'You and Charlie can sleep in there, if that's okay with you, John. Real bed's yours.'

Dad and I haven't shared a room since Christmas before last, and I'm sure he'd prefer some space of his own. I would've been happy on the couch. It occurs to me that he knew Skye back then, and didn't say a word, didn't bring her here.

'So, Miss Sarah,' Dad says. 'What've you asked Santa to bring you?'

'A unicorn,' Sarah replies.

'They're hard to come by, even for Santa Claus.'

'He can get anything.'

Dad and I look at one another.

'Christmas morning's going to be interesting,' I say.

'Show me the tree,' Dad says to Sarah. 'I hear you've made it extra special this year.'

Sarah leads the three of us to the sunny living room, Mark and Abby having wandered off somewhere. Dad and I sit on an L-shaped brown couch – 'New,' Sarah says, 'no shoes allowed.' The couch shares the room with a lacquered pine coffee table, pottery vases and cane baskets all from the same sliver of the colour wheel. Sarah stands beside the tree – a vision of disco glitz – points out various decorations, and moves a couple around. When she's done with the tree, she clambers onto Dad's lap with a paper star she's fancied up with lumpy glue and glitter.

'Fourteen sleeps till Christmas.' She holds up four fingers.

'You might need a few more fingers,' Dad says. 'You'll want this fellow to join in, for a start.' He uncurls her thumb.

It would've been a more touching scene if it weren't for the muffled arguing we could hear coming from the kitchen. I reckon Abby is being snarky on purpose, dreaming up a reason to fight with Mark so she can keep him at arm's length, make him a minor but distracting villain, in order to not spill the beans. Maybe she doesn't even see what she's doing, but to me it's plain as day. And I think she's making a mistake. We need him.

For Sarah's sake, Dad and I keep up a stream of banter until Dad can tolerate it no longer. He lifts Sarah off his lap and onto the couch, and walks out of the room. I can't hear what he says but it does the job, because a few minutes later Abby,

Mark and Dad are in the room with us, all jutting chins and dark expressions.

In times of stress – Mum dying, Grandma and Grandpa dying, Abby's school formal, me getting into trouble (shop-lifting, age thirteen; straight Cs, fourteen; smoking at school, fifteen), best-dog-ever Sooty running away – we revert to type. Abby becomes efficient and terse, the controller. Dad becomes morose, cross and, finally, the take-charge guy – which is when he and Abby lock horns. Mark's all cool facts and debate, except when he's charming people, in which case he's slick as a seal. You've never met a man who's calmer under pressure – shame he wasn't in the car with us. My choice is to loosen things up and take the heat out of the room.

I ask Abby for a pack of cards.

'I'll get them,' Mark says.

'I will.' Abby walks out of the room.

'You've gotta make her pull her weight, man,' I say. 'The woman doesn't lift a finger around here.' Mark and Dad laugh.

Abby returns with the cards and a plate of crackers, cheese cubes and pickles. On her next entry, she carries a box of wine, cups, and some orange cordial for Sarah.

'Okay.' I stand in the centre of the room and fan the cards out. 'Prepare to witness some mind-blowing magic. Young lady,' I say to Sarah, 'pick a card, any card.'

She does, and shows it to me.

'My fault.' I whisper a few instructions to her. 'Here we go. Pick a card.'

She doesn't show me her card this time, but announces it's the number five, which is how old she is until February, when she'll be six, and says I've done a good trick.

'Sarah, sweetheart,' Abby says.

I hold up my hand. 'Sarah's shown she's beyond card selection. She's ready to be a magician's assistant. Wait here. Don't move.'

I grab a tea towel from the kitchen and tie it around her waist, explaining that something more than undies and a t-shirt is called for on stage, and a lairy display of Flags of the World around her middle is just the ticket.

We're launching into our third attempt, getting Mark to pick out cards, the tension in the room eased, when the twins wake up, screaming. Not sure why kids do that – wake up unhappy with the whole situation of being in a bed. It's not exactly a hardship. Anyway, you'd think Abby would be pleased to hear them after so long an absence, but she startles at the noise. Maybe she forgot they were in the house. She and Mark both stand up to go to them. I've read about this, the uneasy handover of responsibility when a soldier comes back from the front.

Dad lifts the newspaper off the coffee table. Sarah and I have lost the spotlight. We wander out to the backyard.

Sarah wants to play in the sprinkler with Woof so I attach the metal ring to the hose, place it on the lawn and turn it up. I sit in the red canvas butterfly chair in the shade of the porch and close my eyes. I hear Sarah squeal with happiness as she leaps in and out of the flying beads of water, calling Woof back each time he wanders away.

If I could guarantee the month would be like this, I could handle it. I could come to terms with what happened, focus on how it'll all be when I'm back in Bali. But already I can tell there'll be ongoing tension between Abby and Mark.

I open my eyes in response to Sarah's shout for attention. I give her a wave and shut my lids again. I think about Bali.

The kids in Kuta aren't like Abby's kids. At sunrise, while Ketut and I sit on the sand talking wave strategy, we regularly see kids cleaning up food scraps and offerings left behind after the ceremony the evening before, and sweeping the sand with homemade brooms. If I'd been told to clean a beach before going to school, or at any other time for that matter, I'd have protested so loud and long I would've worn my parents down, and I know Sarah would, too. But Balinese kids don't do that. They muck around, but they get the job done. They mind little brothers and sisters, cook dinner, sell junk to backpackers.

Sometimes, when they don't have chores, kids hang around the front of KD, playing with balls they've made out of leaves. In fact, given the amount of stuff they have to do, it's strange how often we see kids hanging out. Whenever I go to Ketut's house there are kids milling around the front, sitting on the steps. I don't know why they're there, but they're probably asking the same about me. I spend a lot of time at Ketut's house, which probably annoys his mother, Wayan.

Whenever I see Wayan I ask her how old she is, and every time she gives me a different answer. For a while I thought we had a game going so I played along, making jokes about whatever number she threw my way. One day, while I sat on a wooden stool at the table in her kitchen, having moved aside bananas, incense sticks and woven leaves to make room for my arms on the cool slab, waiting while Ketut gathered his stuff for our bike ride to Sanur, she stopped chopping chicken, seemed genuinely annoyed at me.

'Same question over and over. Twenty-one, ninety-one, what's the matter? You thinking about the wrong things. Do some work. Find a wife.'

'What're you bugging my mother about?' Ketut asked, reaching across the table to steal a jackfruit. She slapped him away.

'How old is this table? How old is Wayan?' she said, and resumed her chopping with fresh energy. 'Go fishing.'

Ketut laughed and flicked me with the t-shirt he'd slung across his shoulder. 'Why would she need to know that? She's been around for one childhood, one marriage, four kids and a million dinners. Right, ma?' Ketut kissed his mother on the cheek. 'Let's go, Charlie.'

We walked down the path to where Ketut had left his motor-bike, dense low-lying shrubs brushing against our legs. The day was quiet but for the gurgle of chickens and the swoosh of brooms on stone.

'So how old are you?' I asked Ketut, sitting behind him on the bike.

'Twenty-nine or thirty. Ma says the war ended when I was a baby, but her handle on current affairs is slippery.' He turned on the rattly engine. 'I'm healthy and strong, that's what matters. I'm going to have babies with Made, raise a family and drive tourists around. When my teeth fall out I'll go fishing all day.'

We puttered along the skinny road, dodging potholes. The wind pushed back my hair. I remembered that feeling from when I was a kid, in the family car with Abby, coming home from a dinner party we'd been dragged to by Mum and Dad. We'd fallen asleep on the couch under crocheted rugs that smelled like cat to the sound of adults whooping it up, singing to Frank Sinatra records. At the end of the night my dad carried me to the car and placed me on the cold leather bench seat. The man of the house – Mr Wilson, maybe? – carried Abby out, placing her so that each of us had our head near opposite car doors, our legs parallel. As Dad drove, windows open, I'd made a pillow of my hands, watched the back of my parents' heads and shoulders, listened to them talk in low voices. Mum laughed and put her hand on my Dad's cheek, and he leaned in to her touch. I'd kneeled, and put my head into the rushing wind. The feeling had been bliss – the freedom of movement, the thrill of being awake so late at night – until hot ash from Mum's cigarette had hit me on the chin and I'd yelled.

Ketut and I rode through Pedungan and Sidakarya towards Sanur, heading to the house of Ketut's friend Nyoman. We cut through rice paddies, past a cow tethered to a tree, then stopped near a stone wall.

'You want to see old, wait till you meet Nyoman's mother. Older than the island.' He lifted the bull's-head doorknocker and let it fall. We waited. Ketut knocked on the door again. 'I don't think Nyoman's home.'

We walked to the back of the building to see if we could find anyone out there. A string of scrawny dogs trailed us. Roosters scuttled out of our way. We heard no sounds from behind the wall.

'We'll wait around the front. He'll come,' Ketut said.

We sat on the long, wide stone steps, dips worn into them from years of feet padding to and from the carved wooden door. I rubbed my hands up and down my legs to get rid of the mud, now dry, sprayed on my shins by the bike, noticing how dark my skin had become, and how the bleached and brown leg hairs together formed a salt-and-pepper field on my shins.

'The main thing,' I said, 'is that if your age doesn't matter, if people don't know how old they are, then everyone quits telling you to grow up.'

Ketut cocked his head at me. 'That's exactly what Ma was telling you to do.'

'Nah, man. She was messing with me. At home my sister and father actually tell me to grow up, as if rushing to old age is somehow life's goal. I don't feel that here.'

'So you don't want to grow up?'

'Sure I do. But in my own time, or Bali time. I'll be a boring old man when I'm ready. Until then, I'm going to be young and free, ride bikes and surf. And not feel guilty about that.'

Ketut laughed. 'Never seen you feel guilty about anything.'

I gazed across paddies spiked with palm trees, the green of the rice crops and blue of the sky insanely bright. 'My mother was thirty-two when she died.'

Ketut faced me, his arm up to block the sun. 'Sorry to hear that, man. That's young no matter where you are.'

We saw a bike in the distance. The driver had one hand on the handlebar and one on the side of a large bundle of fruit he balanced on his head.

'Nyoman,' Ketut shouted. We stood up and waved.

'Maybe you want to stay the same person you were when your mother died,' Ketut said. 'But she probably wouldn't want that.'

I told him I'd think about that, knowing I wouldn't.

Nyoman stopped in front of us, dropped his bundle to the ground, and rested his bike against a tree. Nyoman and Ketut hugged one another as if it had been years, though I'd seen them together a few weeks before, in Wayan's kitchen. Then he hugged me, too. We walked up the stairs, Nyoman promising durian and glasses of arak.

'I gather you messed up with the chickens.' Mark plops himself into the chair beside me. I open my eyes. 'Ed's not happy.'

'You know Ed?'

'First I've ever heard of him.' He smiles, hands me a cold can of beer. 'Think you're going to get an earful when you go inside though.'

'I'm growing grass on me.' Sarah, naked and wet, has bits of cut lawn splattered across her torso, arms and legs.

'Good job, Sar,' he says, as we both crack open our beers.

She returns to the sprinkler.

Mark lifts his can to his lips. 'Might get a pool out here, one of those plastic jobs.'

'Grand idea. You mean for Christmas?'

'I'm not brave enough to throw a wildcard into the Christmas plan.'

Sarah tires quickly of her play and sits on the concrete in front of us, water darkening the slab. Woof lies like a stringy wet mop beside her.

'No work today? The world's all good?' I ask. I could tell him now. Right now. But I scan his face and am suddenly unsure if that's a good idea. Maybe he wouldn't think of anything Abby hasn't. Maybe he wouldn't feel her obligation to cover for me. I'm not one-hundred-per-cent sure of what he thinks of me. It's a risk.

'I've taken leave until tomorrow,' Mark says. 'I won't abuse the privilege, but after my last story they'd let me write my own ticket. Did Abby tell you I'm being made executive producer next year?'

I clink cans with him. I try to act interested while Mark talks about his job. And then sport.

'Are you able to keep up with the cricket over there?' he asks. 'Rained for weeks before, then they dried the wicket too fast. Even Lillee and Thomson struggled with it. Mostly I reckon we won the first Test because they left Boycott at home.'

'We don't have a TV.' I don't ask if boycott is a person or a style of play.

'You'd have radio though.'

'Sometimes. Most days, the outside world isn't a pressing concern. Anything else been going on I should know about?'

He laughs. 'Skylab came back in February, Nixon resigned in August, and we have the most dazzling cricketing side in decades. Ashes to ashes, dust to dust. Ringing any bells?'

'Nope. I'm up to speed with music though. Sal's sister sends us tapes. And I'm keen to see a few movies while I'm here.'

'Great,' he says, watching as Sarah sits her wet self in the sandpit. 'You can take Sarah to see *Herbie Rides Again* so I don't have to.'

I have no idea who Herbie is or what he's riding but I'm up for distractions. I should feel bad all the time, guilt-ridden twenty-four hours a day. But I'm too superficial to sustain that. Or else I have great coping mechanisms. I catch myself laughing at a joke on TV or something one of the kids says, hate myself, and then move on. It's hard to hold any feeling nonstop, no matter how strong it is. I get waves of fear and guilt. But they pass. And I'm not sure who or what it would help if they didn't.

I turn my head at the sound of the sliding door. Abby stands in the opening. She's wearing a purple dress with gold stitching. 'Charlie, can I talk to you?'

'What's up?' Mark asks.

'Dad stuff,' she says.

I follow her into the kitchen, where she beckons me to come deeper into the house. In the hallway, with instantly forgettable landscape paintings either side of her head, she says, 'Constable Roberts called to say none of us should go anywhere.'

'How'd he get your number?'

'Dad gave it to him. That's not the point. The point is we can't leave because Dad's a suspect and we might be . . . accessories or something.'

'Where were you going to go?'

'*You*, you idiot. You need to stay in Brisbane until they say you can leave.'

'No way. I have a return ticket. I can't just cancel it.'

'Did you hear me? Dad's a suspect. Constable Roberts asked if I thought Dad could've been in the car and then walked home. I told him that was the craziest thing I'd ever heard, and hugely insensitive.'

'Why would he ask if you thought your father committed a crime?'

'To hear how I'd react, I guess.'

'Abby, this is getting out of control. We have to give them an alternative to Dad, to us.'

'Like who? Mick Fleetwood?'

'Okay, I'm going to find an album and show you. She's the spitting image of Stevie Nicks.'

'She's not, but it doesn't matter.'

Why do we do this? 'Whatever. What if we say the car was smashed into the tree when we found it.'

'And we left her there and never said a word until now?'

'Okay, yeah, so, what if we say we drove past and didn't see it?'

'What? How does that prove anything, or get Dad off the hook? Also, who took her out of the car?'

'Well, we need to think of something to say to the cops. Dad *can't* be a suspect.' I push my greasy hair off my forehead. 'Where is he anyway?'

'He went for a walk.' She makes a loud exhale. 'Charlie, I'm not going to say any more to the police. I'll . . . stall. And you should stay silent, too. You'll only make it worse.'

CHAPTER TWELVE

Thursday 12 December 1974

Abby

Mark is snoring, though it sounds like a purr. I watch him for a while, admiring the smooth skin on his cheek, the line of his nose. Would he leave me if I tell him about this? He'd definitely be angry. He likes Charlie in small doses, but he's told me a million times to stop mothering him. Even though he knows that's what I've had to do since we were kids. If he knew how far I'd gone this time to protect him – and myself . . .

While Mark sleeps, I play out in my head the most likely chain of events if I told the truth. Dad would disown me. Charlie and I would be involved in a legal case in which our best outcome would be a short jail term for a hit and run. The fact the victim was pregnant would make our crime seem all the worse, though the fact we stopped, took her out of the car and at least checked if she was alive might go in our favour. That shows good character, surely? Perhaps our lawyer would argue we'd tried to move the woman's body up to the car, but that Charlie had . . . an arm injury? But we didn't ask anyone in Chinchilla to drive out and get her, or fess up the next day. How could we explain that?

Mark would rail at my stupidity in staying silent and then lying to the police, and for effectively choosing my brother over my husband. He might divorce me. He loves me, no question, but his job means the world to him. How could he continue working as a journalist with a wife who'd committed such a serious crime, a wife in jail? People would assume I'd told him and he'd helped cover it up. How, then, would he care for our children, with no job and a wife in jail? And once I was out of jail, what would my life be?

I turn my head to the other side and stare out the window. Telling the truth is a terrible idea.

I forgot to close the curtains last night and I can see the sky is still black. The fuzzy red numbers on the clock radio say it's 3.40 am. The birds are still asleep.

Once my eyes fine-tune I can make out the elegant shapes of branches against the sky. In the dark they look flat, like rivers drawn onto a map. I watch a possum walk gingerly along the power line. I hear the wind swishing the leaves.

At five o'clock I'm still awake. I could get up, but the days are long as it is. I lie in bed and listen to the warbling magpies and admire the sight of my books and stationery piled along the wall near the door. I scan the pile, as I have a hundred times before, to see if there's anything I've missed, but there isn't. It's perfect. I've bought my textbooks, ring-bound folders, notepads, packets of loose paper inserts, dividers, pencil case and Bic pens – black, blue and red – a stapler, hole puncher and a sticky-tape dispenser.

I want to put these things on the desk in the spare bedroom, which will be my study area. I picture the desk with my belongings on it, books upright, held in place at one end by the statue of Nefertiti that Mark gave me on our last anniversary and at the other by a glazed vase I made in the pottery class Lou and I took in August. In front of the vase, I'll put the mug I bought to use as a pen holder.

Yesterday morning, when I went into the spare room to collect Dad's and Charlie's laundry, the only thing on my desk was Dad's watch. His dirty clothes were in a turtle-sized lump next to the bedside table. Meanwhile, Charlie's jocks, socks and shirts were draped across every surface except the light fitting and my desk – after two nights. Dad carries himself like the soldier he was, and there's a symmetry to him; Charlie wears his clothes like they've been flung onto a twisted wire frame.

Not knowing how long my book pile will be in limbo is unsettling. In bed, I pull the sheet up to my chin, close my eyes, and imagine I'm lying on a cloud. I'm wearing a blue dress, cinched at the waist by a satin bow, one end of which is held in the beak of a robin. I'm surrounded by clouds on which sit porcelain-skinned children with twinkling eyes – girls and boys dressed by loving mothers who turn their minds to nothing more than joyful domesticity. This is not an image I've fashioned myself but the cover of a book of poems I treasured when I was little, a gift from my mother. The book is gone, lost in the confusion of a house move, but the cover is locked in my memory.

After Mum died I wanted to climb inside that book and live there. I could almost smell her perfume, see the touch of her fingertip where she'd turned the pages the first time we'd looked through the book together. We'd admired the prettiness of the drawings. She'd read to me.

Then she got sick. Then she was gone. I didn't want to make my own school lunch, wipe my brother's wee off the toilet seat or spend my nights in a bleak house. I wanted to walk in a meadow of wildflowers, play with button-nosed kittens, and wake to the smell of hairspray, not burned toast and Brut. I wanted my mother to come back. She would've known that the box of supersize tampons, asked for in a humiliated quaver, having been left unopened for six months, might've indicated some other product was required to address this new and frightening problem. She would've noticed when my shorts pulled uncomfortably across my hips. She would have taken me to a hairdresser rather than Mrs Robinson's down the road when my fringe grew shaggy. She would've noticed how I tried to make life normal, how abruptly my childhood came to a stop.

Mark has added porky snorts to his snores, and I can hear Dad clattering about in the kitchen. I get up. It will make my life worse, and possibly destroy the lives of everyone around me, if I tell the truth. Better to hold it in and manage the pain.

CHAPTER THIRTEEN

Friday 13 December 1974

Charlie

When the doorbell rings I'm thinking about lunch. Mark is at work, Abby is out the back, and Dad is walking with Woof. That dog's never had it so good. The cricket's on the radio, and I'm glad I've heard enough to have a conversation with Mark about it tonight. I feel good for the first time in a week. I roll off the couch and drop my copy of *Zen and the Art of Motorcycle Maintenance* to the floor.

I open the door to Sergeant Doyle. He's bigger than I remember. Seeing him here makes my stomach clench.

'Hey, hello. Didn't know you were coming. Is Abby expecting you?' As if she wouldn't have mentioned that or rushed to the door instead of me.

'I need to ask you and your sister a few more questions. Mind if I come inside?'

'Sure, yeah.' I move so he can come into the house. 'The living room's upstairs.' He waits for me to start up the stairs then follows.

'Take a seat,' I say, pointing to the couch. 'I'll get her.' I walk through the kitchen out to the backyard, trying to keep a steady gait, but speeding up the closer I get to Abby.

'Now? Here?' she asks. She places the wooden peg she's holding onto Mark's shirt, straightens it so it hangs right and, seeming reluctant to do so, turns away from the clothesline.

When we come into the living room Doyle is still standing, examining the framed photograph on top of the television.

He greets Abby with a nod. 'Nice-looking family. Twins?'

'Yes, they're quite a handful. Please.' She sweeps her arm towards the couch like a game-show host showing off a prize.

He sits, and the couch I'd thought of as large and long appears doll-sized.

Abby asks Doyle in an unnecessarily loud voice if he'd like a cold drink. He does not, so she perches on the edge of her armchair seat. I sit on the corner of the coffee table and reach for the packet of Marlboros I'd left there earlier, before the door rang, which already feels like hours ago.

'You're a long way off your beat,' I say.

He smirks at me. But he's hours away from Chinchilla and I know that's where he works. Could be that beat is a word they only use on TV shows.

'I hope you didn't drive all this way for us,' Abby says.

'I have business down here.' He looks from Abby to me and back again. 'And we have a problem we're hoping you can help us with.'

130

At that moment Dad enters the room.

'Sergeant,' he says, stopping on the spot when he sees Doyle. 'Didn't expect to see you in Brisbane.'

'Duty calls, sir.'

'Carry on then.' Dad speaks to the cop as if he's still in the army, sits in the one empty chair. He has no idea he's regarded as a suspect.

Doyle turns to Abby. 'We've been informed that on the night of the accident you and your brother stayed at the Chinchilla Hotel.' My heart skips a beat. I'm guessing Abby's does, too. 'Now, given you said you left Brisbane at approximately two in the afternoon —'

'You stayed in the pub?' Dad interrupts.

I strike a match too hard against the box. The wood snaps. I hold my cigarette between dry lips.

'It was raining,' Abby says. 'There was a storm so we stopped at the pub. I didn't want to trouble you with the details, Dad. It didn't seem important. We stayed there and came to yours after breakfast. It's nothing.'

'Why didn't you drive through to the farm? The rain wasn't that bad,' Dad says.

'Yes it was.' I manage to light my cigarette. Small victories. 'Totally was. The guy at the pub said we were lucky to even make it over the bridge. We were worried it'd be underwater by morning.'

Doyle furrows his brow. 'You don't cross the bridge coming into Chinchilla from Brisbane. You'd only cross it heading north out of town.'

'That's right, yeah.' I don't look at Abby, hope to God she's not reacting. 'We were going to drive over the bridge and they said it was good we didn't.'

'Because it might flood later on?' Dad says. 'You're talking rubbish.'

'Did you drive across the bridge that night, Mrs Campbell?' Doyle asks.

'No,' says Abby. 'We came into town off the main road and I decided we'd stop for the night. Charlie was asleep. He didn't properly see where we were. He doesn't know the roads around there anyway.'

'And you do?' Doyle stares at Abby. 'What time did you arrive at the hotel, ma'am?'

Abby knows this is a trap and I can see she's stalling. Numbers aren't her strong point so I quickly work back in my head. I can't get it to add up in any convincing way: whatever we say, there will be hours unaccounted for.

'I was sick,' I blurt out. 'Chucking up. We stopped, some-place. I'd come into Brisbane that day, on the early morning flight from Denpasar, and I was rooted. Flight takes, like, eight hours and I'd hardly slept in days so –'

'What time did you arrive at the hotel?' Doyle doesn't acknowledge I've spoken. He's locked on Abby.

'I guess it was nine or ten? Would that be about right, Charlie?'

'Yep, I reckon.' I sit back with one hand on the coffee table in an effort to seem relaxed, hoping she'll register the need to do this herself.

Out of the corner of my eye I watch Dad. He's figuring it out.

'So to be clear,' Doyle says, 'you left Brisbane Airport around two after collecting the luggage from a flight that arrived on time at one o'clock, having changed planes after an hour's wait at Darwin Airport, according to TAA staff.'

'Yes, that's about when we left,' Abby says.

'You drove till you got to . . .? You'd know where you stopped for your brother.'

'Outside Dalby, maybe? I didn't pay a lot of attention. I mostly didn't want him to vomit in my car.'

'You stopped there for an unspecified time before driving on to Chinchilla, where you arrived at approximately ten at night according to the publican.' He pauses. 'Is there anything you'd like to tell me, ma'am? Because those numbers don't work for me. That would mean a four-and-a-half-hour drive to Chinchilla, five at worst, took you eight.'

She bites her lip as if thinking. 'Well, I'm afraid the publican is wrong. We arrived in town at about seven o'clock, had a walk around, Charlie was sick again and then we decided he was too ill to keep going. So we went to the pub for the rest of the night. It was definitely before ten.'

'It was after ten o'clock when you called me,' Dad says.

'Yes, Dad, but calling you wasn't the first thing I did when we got there.' Weirdly, her sharp annoyance feels useful and right this time. It makes her seem more solid, and her voice has lost any trace of a shake.

'I see,' Doyle says, obviously unconvinced by what he's heard. He turns to me. 'When did you first learn your father was engaged?'

The out-of-nowhere question seems to be his preferred tactic for throwing us off-guard. 'Same time Abby did, the morning we showed up at the farm.'

'And had you met his fiancée? Socially? She's about your age.'

'No. There's a lot of people my age. And I've never lived in the country.'

133

'She didn't always live there,' Doyle says, then he turns to Dad. 'How was it you met her, Mr Scott?'

'I don't see how that's important,' Dad says.

'It's important if I say it is. As important as searching your house.'

They stare at one another in silence. Dad wants to be top dog, but everyone knows better than to mess with a Queensland cop. Even if you're drunk or stoned or in a rage, that awareness is something we have in our state DNA. You don't swim against a rip or drive in a hailstorm or play chicken with a pig.

'At the chemist,' Dad says finally. 'She was working there.'

'I see. Ever make any day trips with her? Sunday drives up Eumundi way?'

'Eumundi?' Abby exclaims. I catch her eye and see she's as confused as I am. Doyle notices this, too.

'Not familiar with that area, no,' Dad says.

None of these questions seems to surprise Dad, or if they do he's doing a good job of hiding that.

Doyle slaps his thighs and stands up. 'I'll show myself out.'

When Dad hears the front door closing, he rises from his chair and glowers at Abby and me as he did when we were children.

'What are you two playing at? Charlie's never been carsick in his life.'

'The jet lag –' I begin.

'Bullshit. What's going on? You didn't stop near Dalby and you –' he points at Abby – 'you told me you drove through floodwaters in January to stock up on food, so don't tell me rain put you off. What happened that night?'

Abby leaps in to answer, having regained her confidence now Doyle is gone. 'Charlie and I had a fight and I left him in

134

some tinpot town. For hours. I didn't want to tell the police. It's embarrassing.'

Dad regards Abby, deciding whether to buy her explanation.

'You're bloody right it's embarrassing,' he says at last. 'When are you going to learn to get on?' Then he walks out of the room.

When we're alone, I swivel around on the coffee table to face Abby. 'What now?'

'We stick to our story,' she says.

'Our story? You mean the one we made up on the spot? It doesn't make sense.'

'It will if I add in what I told Dad about us having an argument. That fills the gap. I don't want to talk about this anymore, Charlie. My head is about to explode.'

'Abby, we should've told the cops before now that we stayed at the pub. We don't want them to think we're keeping secrets.'

'Is that a joke?'

I look away to think, out through the open sliding doors towards Mt Coot-Tha. When I turn back to ask her why Doyle would've mentioned Eumundi, she's gone.

Early afternoon, before she collects the kids, while Mark takes their car to the mechanic, and Dad is catching up with a mate who runs a fishing tackle shop, Abby and I commemorate our mother's death. We have about an hour, and that's plenty.

We do this each year on December thirteenth. Mum died on December twentieth, but Abby decided early on that we shouldn't mark her death too close to that festive time of year. The thirteenth is a Friday this year, but Abby reckons it makes no difference. Given the amount of bad stuff that's happened to her she's strangely unsuperstitious, unlike me; I'm all in with that shit – tarot, palms, witchcraft, you name it. Ignoring my reservations, Abby begins setting up the table with our mother's things.

When we were kids, Dad would take us to Toowong Cemetery on the morning of the real date, even if it was a school day, and we would put flowers on Mum's grave. At some point, when Abby and I were both in our late teens, after one too many ferocious family arguments, we stopped going to the cemetery with Dad. He went alone. Abby and I would go together.

And then Abby created the memorial day ritual. As adults, when we were in the same city, we'd go to Mum's grave and then back to wherever Abby lived at the time – the share house in Paddington, the flat in Highgate Hill, the house in Kenmore. We kept up our ritual when we were both at uni, and when she dropped out to have Sarah. Neither Mark nor the kids have ever joined us.

Today, Abby and I sit in front of the shrine she's creating on her dining table: photographs (Mum, Abby and me with Nan and Pop and their mangy dog at the farm, Mum and Dad's wedding photo, a hand-coloured photo of Mum a few years into her marriage, painted so her cheeks are rosy circles and her teeth freakishly white), a vase of flowers, three candles, Mum's copy of Amy Vanderbilt's *Complete Book of Etiquette* and a silk scarf with line drawings of roses, leering Italians and skinny vamps. Abby has, as usual, arranged the objects around Mum's sewing machine, which seems weird to me since I don't remember her using the thing.

At the front of the shrine is the Memory Box, to which, every year, we each add a handwritten memory about our mother. After we've put our memory inside, Abby pulls out a selection of memories from previous years and reads them aloud. Sometimes we have a drink. Not always. Not today.

'Where's her ring?' I ask. 'Should we put that out, too? Since nobody else is around.'

She shakes her head. 'I've hidden it in my jewellery box. Mark never opens that. But I think it should stay put.'

I think about this. 'Abby, it's evidence. I reckon we should bury it or throw it in the river.'

'No. It should've been with me years ago. Don't worry – I'll keep it hidden. The only other person who'd recognise it is Dad.'

'Who's living in your house,' I say.

'Not for long.'

I change tack. 'So what did you write?'

She turns over the piece of paper in front of her. 'I wrote: I remember the bruise spreading on Mum's arm where the drip went in. It got so large the bandage couldn't cover it. I waited for Dad to tell a nurse but he didn't. So when my mother died from cancer she also had a sore arm.'

I glare at her. 'Jesus, Abby. I don't want that in the Memory Box.'

'It's my memory. I'm putting it in.'

'It's always been good things before.'

'You can't vet my memories. What did you write?'

I read my memory. 'When I was sick, Mum sat on my bed and ran her fingers through my hair. Feeling her hand on my sweaty scalp and the cool air on my skin made me relax and feel better.'

'That's nice.'

'Well, I didn't know we were going gothic this year.'

There are noises I find comforting because they were part of the backdrop to my childhood. One of those noises is the opener to the ABC Radio news bulletins. I've been hearing that a lot lately; Abby and Mark keep the radio on all day in the kitchen. I don't know if it's supposed to be a deterrent to thieves or if they think it's disrespectful to shut the machine off when someone's mid-sentence.

A cloud mass is gathering over the Arafura Sea, and the weather bureau says it's becoming a cyclone. They say it's nothing to worry about because it's miles off the coast, and will hit land way up north where nobody lives. It's an enjoyable act of displacement to listen to someone else's drama though.

The whirring sound that comes before every warning bulletin is playing as we sit down to dinner. I'm glad for the noise, since Dad is stubbornly silent over our meal of sausages, green salad and baked potatoes. The kids have eaten early so there are only adults at the table. We take it in turns to cheer Dad by introducing topics he'd usually find interesting. Mark mentions that it's Friday the thirteenth and says we seem to have gotten off scot-free. Abby and I avoid one another's gaze. I'm sure lying to a cop on Friday the thirteenth is asking for trouble.

'Charlie,' Mark says. 'Here's something you probably didn't hear in Bali: colour television's only a few months away. It'll revolutionise the medium.'

Dad doesn't bat an eyelid. It's unlike him to ignore a moment that's begging for historical context or a meaningful quote about change. We discuss colour TV without him.

'*The Two Ronnies* is on in an hour, if anybody's interested,' Abby says.

'It's goodnight from me, and it's goodnight from him,' Mark adds, looking to Dad for a reaction.

When Dad doesn't take whatever that strange bait was, I change the topic. 'Sarah's stoked about Christmas. You know she wants a unicorn?'

Mark and Abby smile. I'm not sure it'll be funny on Christmas morning.

'All right, listen,' Dad says.

Abby's mouth is open, the fork hovering by her chin. Mark ignores the glass he was about to lift. I let my hand drop slowly from my itchy scalp to my lap, as if a sudden movement might spook Dad back into silence.

'You lot are doing my head in. The woman I love has died. I don't give a fig about television or Christmas or anything else. As for bad luck, well I don't know what you think qualifies if not this.' He slides his plate away angrily. 'You don't seem to care.'

'Dad –' Abby starts, as Dad raises his voice and ploughs ahead.

'Skye was pregnant. Pregnant with my child. Do you understand?'

'Dad, you've told us that,' she says. 'And we do care.'

'She has a son.'

'No,' Abby whispers.

'That's the "him" you were talking about? The guy?' I say.

'She has a child?' Mark says. 'You do mean a living boy, not that she was pregnant with –'

Dad nods brusquely. 'Yes, a living boy. Beau, five years old.'

Mark folds his arms on the table. 'Where is he, John?'

CHAPTER FOURTEEN

Saturday 14 December 1974

Abby

I wake early, again. My brain has spent hours with the same wild and raggedy thoughts, like a greyhound chasing a track rabbit. I wake terrified.

As quietly as I can, I leave the bedroom and pad through the house, moving couch cushions back to where they should be, straightening the tea towel that hangs from the oven door, rearranging the photos on the kitchen sideboard.

I check on the twins then go to Sarah's room, lift the mosquito netting that drapes her bed and sit inside her little cocoon, cross-legged near the footboard. I smile at her uninhibited sprawl, her parted lips, her halo of hair, the Holly Hobbie bedspread she so badly wanted.

Skye had a son. I wonder if the boy knows his mother is dead. I wonder, like Mark does, where he is. Dad stormed off to his room after dropping his bombshell, unwilling to offer any more information.

There'd been no sign that any child other than my own had ever been at the farm – no drawings, no toys. Perhaps she'd put him up for adoption as a baby. Or into an institution. Is that what Dad wanted to tell us that weekend – that he was engaged to a pregnant woman with a damaged son? Perhaps the woman drove off the road intentionally, because she couldn't stand the grief of it. Maybe Charlie didn't cause the accident at all. I can almost see my thoughts bouncing off the walls. I really need sleep.

Sarah rolls over, further twisting her nightie around her, as though she's wringing herself out. I tug the fabric, to smooth it, where it stretches across her hip. I catch myself thinking it might not be bad were she to wake up and steal me from my thoughts.

A warm wind pushes between the pink cotton curtains. They lift and drop, as graceful as a dancer taking a bow. Through the gap, softened by a veil of netting, I see a full moon. Frogs croak beneath the window.

I walk back to my own bed then lie on my side, close to Mark, and silently chant, 'I'm sorry, I'm so sorry.'

Before sunrise, I slide out of bed as quietly as I can, find shorts, a t-shirt, sandals. I need to be out of the house, to think and also to not think. I leave Mark a note on the kitchen bench saying that Woof was whining for a walk and I'll be back soon. In the living room, I pat Woof to wake him, try to coax him off the couch using increasingly dramatic expressions and gestures to indicate to him how exciting it will be to leave his comfy spot and come outside. He lifts his eyebrows, then lets his lids drop closed again. 'Come on,' I whisper. I push him close enough to the edge that gravity does the rest of my job. He jumps back up on the couch. I push him down again, more easily this time, and he gives in.

Once we're outside, Woof peps up. We walk down the street in the early light. The air holds a hint of tea-tree and the coming day's warmth. Magpies offer warbles and trills. We walk, Woof in front of me, his rump swaying in a slow wag, down the hill to the side of the playing field where large rocks make a bridge across the creek.

Woof plods through the mud into the creek, snout down. He regards the trickle of water with curiosity then laps at it. I stand and watch him, and the gentle flow, until he jerks his head back. His wag quickens. He's seen something that excites him. He makes a low growl that I know will end in a string of barks. He prances on the spot. A cluster of brown tadpoles wriggles downstream. Woof fixes his eyes on them, makes two, three short barks until I cut him off. 'Woof!' I click my fingers for added effect. He looks at me and appears to instantly forget about the tadpoles. What bliss such a short memory must be.

I make my way across the rocks to the other side of the creek and Woof plods through the water, eyes up now in search of fun, until we're both standing on the edge of the field.

Woof runs off because he can, because the field is large and wide and empty. I wander to the closest tree, a towering ghost gum that appears to glow pink and cream in the dawn light. I touch the trunk. Long strips of grey bark are peeling off, draped and drooping like swathes of fabric. As I stand with the tree, the sun rises and elbows the darkness to the fringes.

How will I be able to stand in a courtroom and fight for justice after what I've done? So many indefensible choices. I've turned my back on everything I value, on life itself.

As Woof and I lope back to the house, I go over the encounter with Sergeant Doyle, trying to figure out what information he could have gleaned from our inconsistent responses. I think about why he'd been interested in how Dad met Skye and in her life before that. Perhaps he's exploring whether someone who knew her forced her off the road, or whether someone from her past had been in the car. Maybe there's something about Skye that the sergeant knows and Dad doesn't. Or something they both know. Who was this woman before she met my father?

I'd forgotten we were going to dinner at Jim and Karen's this evening. Jim is a uni friend of Mark's, a robust, athletic man with a booming voice and strong opinions on politics, movies and architecture, especially the architecture for which he is responsible. His wife, Karen, is thin, stylish and of impeccable pedigree. When she's given the space to speak, Karen is articulate and erudite, but in the presence of her husband she is most often silent.

I have no wish to sit at their table tonight and listen to Jim wax lyrical about Mark's attributes and achievements. I have no wish to hear him tell me, again, what a lucky woman I am to have caught Mark. And the thought of playing audience with Karen, fighting to inject myself into the men's conversation, makes me slump.

'I barely slept – my head's all over the place,' I say to Mark. 'If you hadn't pointed this out –' I gesture towards the label that indicates I've put my t-shirt on inside out.

144

'You would've noticed sooner or later. And that's not a reason to cancel dinner. Why can't you sleep anyway? Kids were good last night.'

I take my shirt off, move it about like seaweed in a wave, and put it back on so the label is where it should be.

'I don't know. Dad, Christmas, Charlie. Is that enough?'

'Glad I didn't hear my name in that list.' He walks to the end of the bed and gives me a kiss. 'I won't be too long.'

It's strange and unexpected that he's become so handy in the past year. I'm not sure what sparked it, but the kids are going to help him build a cubbyhouse and that, evidently, involves many runs to the hardware store.

We walk down the hallway, and at the point where we'd take different directions – left and down to the front door, right to the kitchen – he groans. 'Jojo,' he says, then steps aside so I can see. Joanne is standing next to Woof and holding a bottle of red food colouring in her alarmingly stained fingers. Woof, mercifully lying on the tiles, a foot away from the carpet, is covered with red blotches.

'Leopard,' Joanne says.

'Ah,' I reply, thinking that at least she'd remembered something from the documentary on Africa we watched last night.

'Do you want me to –?' Mark begins.

'No, I'll do it,' I say.

Only last week, a visiting plumber had commented on Woof's thick golden coat. And his gait. 'You could train him up to show standard,' he'd said. 'Still young.' I'd told him I had no time for a hobby, though I was sure Woof appreciated his compliment. The plumber had seemed more offended that

I thought showing dogs was a hobby than I was at his suggestion that a mother of three had time for training a dog.

'Can I have a hand with the sheets?'

'After the news,' Mark calls back.

By the time he shows up, I've stripped the twins' beds and
ours, and am tucking a clean sheet under Joanne's mattress.

'Had to call Geoff,' he says, picking the pile of discarded
sheets off the floor. 'This is the big one, Abby. This cyclone's
stronger than Wanda. Geoff's putting the Bureau's advice out
as often as he can get airtime, but none of the other networks
are picking up on it.'

I walk to our bedroom and he follows me, throwing the twins'
bedding in the laundry basket, obsessing about the weather as
I unfurl a fitted sheet and let it drop onto our mattress like a
massive shower cap. I point to the corner of the bed.

'It's making its way to the coast. Geoff's been telling them
for days, it's building up to hammer them, and we're sitting
here doing nothing.'

'Who's them?'

'Darwin.'

'Darwin? How many people live there? Anyway, the world
can't jump whenever Geoff has a panic attack.'

I shake the top sheet so it billows out. Mark grabs one edge
and pulls it down.

'Abby, he knew how bad the flood would be before anybody
else did, remember?'

'Would you tuck the ends in?' I check his handiwork.
'What's the point of saying you'll help and doing such a bad
job I have to do it over again?'

'No point, Abby. None at all.' He stares at me, hands on his hips. 'You know, if you want to be a good lawyer you need to be ready for what's coming, you need to pre-empt it.'

'I'm ready. I'm the one who makes sure there's food for dinner, clothes to wear, candles for blackouts.'

'I meant you need to think about what's happening outside the walls of this house.'

I wish I could tell him it's not that simple, that the air from outside flows through this house, poisoning it, that I think about what's coming all the time. The wave that's heading our way grows bigger every day – because, despite what I say to Charlie, I know that no secret stays locked away forever, no matter how hard you try.

I wear my most fashionable outfit to dinner: a pantsuit with stripes of ginger, yellow and maroon, and a white shell top. The swoosh of the wide legs as I walk usually makes me feel peppy, but it's not enough to lift my mood tonight. Before Karen has served the prawn cocktails, my jaw is clench-sore.

Mark adores Jim and Karen, and they adore Mark. And there is my problem. Jim is enthusiastically vocal about the things he finds impressive, and I am not one of them. I'm not famous or accomplished, have no unusual skills or knowledge. Mark, however, impresses him. And he's on TV. In the glow of their approval, he shines even brighter, while I shrink back, small as a mouse, furious as a lion.

The first time I met Jim, before he knew Karen, one warm afternoon on the downstairs veranda of the Regatta Hotel, I stood and listened while he and Mark talked about Keynes, whose writing they were both studying at uni. I knew nothing about Keynes. For the first few minutes I smiled, tipped my head this way and that, tried to steer the topic towards something I might join in with, to no avail. I'd watched the boats on the river, the traffic on Coronation Drive, gone to the bathroom, fetched another round of drinks and still – still! – they discussed Keynes. Jim was oblivious to my discomfort, but he didn't matter to me. I'd hoped I'd never see him again. But Mark, who'd been attentive right until Jim had arrived – how was he not noticing how comprehensively they'd excluded me with their arcane topic, their precocious debate? When we'd finally parted company, and I found myself alone with Mark on the footpath, waiting for a taxi, I was livid. Without the right words to explain why.

Some version of that encounter played out every time we met Jim, and none of my efforts at changing the dynamic had made a scrap of difference. In fact, now that there was another woman involved, even the most cursory attempt at inclusion vanished. Both Jim and Mark seemed relieved to be able to sink into the velvety depths of whatever subject they settled on, knowing the women had one another.

Tonight, though, is the first time we've seen Jim and Karen since I decided to go back to uni. Tonight, I have a chance at impressing Jim and letting him see the relaxed, confident me.

But the evening takes its usual path without me finding an opening. Jim talks about himself, his work, Mark, Mark's work, the glory of them separately and the glory of them together.

'And blow me if he didn't say yes,' Jim roars.

'We had him in a corner,' Mark says with a smile. 'He couldn't deny it anymore.'

Jim hits the table in glee, making his plate jump. 'Classic. Incredible piece of reporting. *Four Corners* should be showering you with gratitude – booze and broads. No offence, Abby.'

They relax back, spent, at the end of each anecdote, and guzzle beer while Karen and I bring out food, fill glasses, and talk about the smalls of life.

Mark tells Jim he's investigating where the traffickers are getting their drugs. 'Every illegal club, brothel and gambling joint is selling dope. Every *legal* club is selling it. And the police are turning a blind eye, must be getting kickbacks. But I want to know where it's coming from.'

Jim nods energetically. 'Exactly, mate. Where's it coming from?'

In the kitchen, while Karen is scraping steak bones into the bin, I say, 'It's like being Alice in Wonderland, isn't it? Your Mogs can be the Cheshire Cat.' I point to Karen's tawny cat, who is rubbing himself against her legs. 'All this talk of blood and slaying has put me off my tea.'

Karen straightens up. 'They put you off your food?'

'It's from the story.'

She frowns slightly and counts out four dessert plates and spoons. 'I made a pavlova.'

'Of course you did.'

She winces, confused by my words, by me.

'I'm sure it'll be delicious,' I say. 'I wish I could cook even half as well as you do.'

By way of apology, I compliment her remodelled kitchen with its orange cupboard doors and gumleaf-patterned tiles.

'Finally made use of my engineering degree.' She looks around the room and smiles. 'It felt good.'

'You have an engineering –'

'Melbourne Uni. Can you bring the plates?'

Karen carries the pavlova into the dining room as though it were a crown on a cushion and places it in front of Jim.

'What's this then?' he says, one hand squeezing her bum through her skirt.

He and Mark marvel over Karen's culinary skills then return to their conversation. Jim is prodding Mark to share insider information about how he'd managed to get one of the watch-house staff who'd been in the room with John Stuart to talk about the faked confession, how the TV voice-disguise works so you can't tell who it is, what's likely to happen next, and shushes Karen when she raises the serving spoon and asks if anyone would like more dessert.

'Mate, magnificent job. Bloody brilliant.'

I feel like something vital has torn in my throat, as if all the spiky words I've swallowed back, for years, have ripped into my flesh. But I know if I said that there are so *many* people who are good at what they do, who never hear a word of praise because they aren't on television, who never get slapped on the back at dinner parties or treated like rock stars because they're busy working in emergency wards, or teaching kids how to read, or collecting our garbage – or using their engineering degree to calculate how many tiles are needed per square foot of kitchen wall . . . Pointless. My words stick in my gullet, where they fester and burn. I won't tell Jim I'm going to uni. The approval I wanted seems unsavoury now, as though his sanctioning my choice would grant him some ownership of it. And I don't want that – this is mine.

'Abby?' Mark says.

'What? Sorry.'

'No worries,' Jim says. 'Grab us a couple more, Karen?' He holds up an empty bottle.

'Want to give her a hand, Abby?' Mark asks.

'Carrying beer?' But I look from Jim to Mark and realise I don't want to stay at the table anyway. 'Sure.'

When we return to the table, Jim speaks with fresh vigour. He wants me on script. 'You're a lucky woman, Abigail. To be the first to hear these things he gets up to. Incredible stuff.' He holds my gaze, stern, waiting. 'Quite the husband you've got here.'

I offer him the smallest smile, and Mark notices our stand-off. 'Time to head home, I think. We have a busy Sunday ahead of us.'

'Pig.' I flop into the car seat and slam the door. 'He's a pig. He treats me and Karen like we're his servants – his servants and your fan club. And you go along with it.'

'No, I don't. I tried to keep the night civil. How much have you had to drink?'

'Not nearly enough.'

I'm still scratchy after we've arrived home, after I've stomped to the bedroom and clumsily made my way into my nightie. I'm sure I've woken Dad, don't even know if Charlie is here. But no sound from the kids. All the while, Mark is going about his night's rituals and ablutions more slowly than usual. His composure incenses me. I'm dealing with something more enormous than he or Jim could imagine, and without an audience.

Mark walks into the bedroom, wiping his face dry. 'Jim can be a clod. Don't take it to heart. It was good to see Karen, wasn't it?'

'No, it wasn't good to see her. There's no solidarity in humiliation.'

'Bit dramatic.'

I throw my hairbrush at him, then apologise, then cry. I'm angry at Jim's smugness, Mark's relaxed self-assuredness, at my self-pity, Charlie's dependence, Dad's misery. I'm scared of being discovered. I'm scared of having my future snatched from me, scared I'm losing my mind. And I can't say any of this to my husband.

I try to think of something soothing. When I was pregnant with Sarah, Mark and I went to Sydney for a holiday. There was no Dad, no chores, and nobody knew Mark as the most gifted student in the English department, the boy who would be prime minister or write the Great Australian Novel. We were a young couple expecting their first child. We rode the harbour ferry. We strolled Manly Beach promenade, eating iceblocks. We walked the trail above the Gap, marvelling at the cliffs, the churning sea, and the huge height from which so many tortured souls had flung themselves. At the lookout, Mark kissed my salty lips through strands of windblown hair.

When I wake, Mark is touching my shoulder. We're in the living room, in the black of night, lit by star shine coming in through the veranda's sliding doors. I am doubled over, my hands on my thighs, as if I'm recovering from a running race. I curl myself up slowly.

'Why am I in here?' I ask.

Mark seems as baffled as I am. 'You walked in here asleep, I guess. I woke up when I heard you.'

'Heard me doing what?'

'You were . . .' He shakes his head. 'You were trying to move the couch, I think. Do you remember what you were dreaming about?'

I freeze in horror. Has my brain decided this is how I'll cope? That I should behave like Lady Macbeth of the suburbs?

'What's going on with you?' he asks gently, then puts his arm around my waist and leads me back to bed.

CHAPTER FIFTEEN

Monday 23 December 1974

Charlie

I pretend to be asleep when Dad opens the curtains, even though the metal rings make a racket, even when he threads his jangly belt into his slacks and taps me on the shoulder.

'Charlie.' His knees crack as he bends down to speak directly into my ear. He taps me again. 'Charlie.'

I give up. 'Dad, I get it.'

Dad walks around to the other side of my fold-out bed, a rumpled mess of sheets, thin bedspread kicked to the end.

'Let me sleep.' I pull my pillow from under my head and put it over my face. He yanks it off. 'What, Dad, *what?*'

I reach under the canvas bed and bring up a balled t-shirt, which I pull on without smelling for wearability.

'I had a thought.'

'Nope. Coffee.' I push myself up. 'Whatever you're going to lecture me about, I at least deserve that first.' I stand up, pull on my jeans. 'It's not even daytime.'

Before he can reply, the phone rings. I look at my father, but this doesn't seem to be connected to our ridiculously early rising. From his expression I can see he has no idea who would call this house before dawn. Would the cops call this early? I guess they can call whenever they feel like it. Especially if they have news.

Mark shuffles down the hallway to answer. And then, a minute later, he's standing in our bedroom doorway. 'Charlie, call from Bali. Didn't catch her name.'

I walk quickly to the kitchen, Dad following me.

'What's happening? Are you okay?' I say into the phone.

Dad puts his hand on my shoulder. 'Who is it?'

'Sal.'

He grunts, walks to the sink, and fills the percolator pot with water.

'So, are you okay?' I ask her as Dad ferrets around in the pantry.

'Ryan's having a meltdown. He says we have to leave Bali on the first flight we can. He's spent the last two hours shoving clothes in our backpacks. He's freaking me out. I don't know what to do.'

'Put him on the phone.'

'He's at home.'

'What brought this on?'

'Who knows? Everyone was at Jack's place – and you know Ryan hates it there – but he was in a good mood. And then he lost it. Stands in the middle of the room and rants about how

155

life has no meaning and we came to discover paradise and now we're destroying it and ra ra ra. He grabs my arm and says we're leaving – leaving Bali.'

'You mean for Christmas? I thought you weren't doing that this year.'

'We're not. He means forever.'

'Was he stoned?'

'Yes, but it's not that. He's been in a mood since you left. Can you come back early? He'll listen to you.'

'Sal, I can't. There's some heavy stuff going on here right now.'

'I need you.'

'What if you close up KD and hang here with him for a couple of weeks? Maybe he needs a break. We can fly back to Bali together.'

'Charlie, you haven't seen him. He's deadset serious about this. He wants to give KD to Ketut. If he goes to Australia now, I don't think he'll ever come back.'

Her words hit me. Bali without Ryan is unthinkable, because that's Bali without Ryan and Sal. Thinking about going back is all that's keeping me afloat.

Dad huffs and whacks his hands against his sides. 'I don't know where she keeps anything.'

I point to the fridge. He mutters something about Abby putting things in illogical places (meaning places he wouldn't choose himself), and stands with the door open, as annoyed and befuddled as he'd been at the pantry. The light from the refrigerator beams out like a spotlight.

'Sal, flights are going to be booked out. You guys probably can't leave right now. But can you get him to the phone anyway, soon as you can? Doesn't matter what time.'

Dad slams the fridge door and puts the coffee tin on the counter. He spreads his palms on the brown-tiled bench as though he's about to do push-ups, stares crossly at the tin and then at me. 'Filters?' He doesn't bother lowering his voice.

I gesture at the middle of three drawers.

'Sal, it'll be okay. Go to Ketut and Made and ask them to help talk some sense into him. And get him on the phone to me.'

She hangs up.

Dad stands with his arms folded, adopting a grim expression. 'It sounds like your friend's in some trouble. Are you going to tell me what's going on?'

'Are you going to make a pot of coffee or did you just want to give me the shits?'

'I'll make coffee if you can find the lid for the blasted machine.'

I resist the urge to swear at him. The lid is in clear view on the dish rack.

'What'd you wake me for anyway?' I ask as the first drops of coffee hit the glass-bottomed pot.

'We're going to fetch the boy,' he says, then slaps the laminex by way of full stop. 'Today.'

He walks me out to the veranda so we can talk without fear of Abby or Mark overhearing. They're up now, going about their morning routines. I balance my mug on the wooden railing and watch the street wake. A powder-blue Kingswood reverses down a driveway, a sprinkler flicks sparkling drops of water across a lawn, a bare-chested man framed by an open window calls his labrador – 'Ruuuby' – who bounds towards him.

'He's living with his dirtbag father, in a tent on a hippy commune.'

'Eumundi?'

'No place for a child.'

'I don't know about that. And he's not your kid, right?'

'Drug addicts and dropouts. And they're into some extremely dodgy business, Charlie.' He stops, as if to decide if I'm up for whatever it is he was about to say. Evidently not. 'They don't send the kids to school, let the young girls run around with nothing on, work the women like they're animals. The boy's father is their self-styled leader and –' Again with the half-thought. 'Brute of a man, a criminal. The stories I heard from Skye would curdle your blood.'

'Let me know when you're up for telling me what those meaningful pauses are for. Whatever you've seen or heard, it won't shock me.' I flick the ash from my cigarette over the railing. 'Did she live there for long before she met you?'

'For a time.'

'A time. And she had Beau with her at this commune, right?'

'She did.'

'Well, if she left him there it can't be that bad.' I lift my mug, feel the smooth warmth against my bottom lip.

'It's complicated. You wouldn't understand.'

I laugh.

'I don't see what's so funny.'

'Nothing, Dad. But if you want me to help you kidnap a child I'll need more than "it's complicated". I can't think of anything that's not complicated right now.' I take a drag on my cigarette. 'Seriously, if it was such a bad place why did she let her son stay there? Why did you, for that matter?'

He lifts his head up. A plane makes its way across the sky, leaving a thin white trail in its wake. *I'd give a million dollars to be on that plane, flying away from all this, flying to Bali, to Sal.*

'She went back for Beau three times, only once when I knew her, early on in her pregnancy. But she didn't tell me until she came back. I wanted to call the police but she . . .'

'She what? Why don't you call them now if you think there are kids in danger? Call Doyle.'

He scoffs. 'He's the last person I'd call. Anyway, they'd put Beau into some type of state care. He needs to be here where I can look out for him.'

'I hope you don't mean *here* here, as in Abby and Mark's house.'

He ignores me. 'Listen, I have no legal connection to that child.'

'Glad we agree. So why is kidnapping him okay?'

'*Rescuing* him. The boy needs to be with a proper family. I should've forced the issue with Skye months ago.'

'Is this bunch a cult or something?' I ask.

'Enough questions, Charlie. Do me a favour and believe I know what I'm talking about.'

'I gotta ask, Dad. What kind of woman leaves her kid behind with a man like that?'

'A good one, an angel. A woman you wouldn't understand. You gad about with women who don't know the first thing about selflessness or sacrifice.'

'Sweeping generalisation.' *Also, 'gad': don't think that's a real word.*

He looks down at his polished brown brogues, dappled from the sunlight pushing through the leaves of the eucalyptus tree. 'His name is Finn and she thought he was going to kill her the night she left. He would have. She had to get out to stay alive, and she was in no state to take a child with her. Bastard broke her collarbone, beat her black and blue.'

'Whoa.'

'Then told the other dumb-as-dirt hippies Skye'd turned on them, turned on their ideals, abandoned her son and gone back to the world they rejected. Because –' he gestures to the street in front of us, its green gardens and neatly parked cars – 'it's so horrendous. So when she showed up for Beau they chased her out. They'd been brainwashed, the lot of them. And I couldn't care less about what they think or what they get up to, except that Beau's there with them and he meant the world to Skye.'

'Dad, I still don't get why she didn't call the police and report the assault, get her son brought to her.'

'She abandoned the boy. She left. And there's no one at that place who'd hold up her side of the story about why she left or who'd hurt her.' He hits the railing with his palm. 'You think you're worldly because you're scruffy and unemployed and own a backpack, but –'

'Not unemployed.'

'You don't have a clue about this type of thing. You don't call the police to a drug farm when the police are running it. You don't demand the police arrest someone they're doing illegal business with. They have millions of dollars growing up there and even the fact she knew that was dangerous. Skye is –'

'Collateral damage,' I say.

I stand in silence for a moment, taking this in. 'Okay, I get it. And that's totally something you want to stay out of. But to the boy, this place is home. And you don't know what they've told him about his mother or the outside world or strangers. So we can't show up out of nowhere and tell him to come with us. Even if he knew us, he wouldn't want to leave his dad and friends, would he?'

'They lock them up, you know. Lock the kids in a hot, gutted kombi for the day with no food or water if they misbehave. What do you think about that?'

'That's fucked, obviously. But it doesn't answer my questions. If we did manage to get him out of there, people will ask where he came from, and he'll tell them. And since the cops are in cahoots with these guys – Wait, is Doyle in on this place?'

'Well he mentioned Eumundi, so he knows about it. But it's possible Finn is a suspect somehow. As for the rest, we'll sort it out once the boy's here. The main thing is to get him out. I want him with us for Christmas.'

'Which is the day after tomorrow.'

'Yes.'

'Two days, Dad.'

'That's why we need to go today. And he'll live here, in this house. He'll have a proper family, and he'll eat normal food, wear normal clothes and go to school.'

'Dad, seriously. A boy from your fiancée we'd never heard of, who lives on a drug farm cult commune whatever-the-hell place run by cops? When are you going to tell Abby? Tell me you're planning to talk to her.'

'She'll be fine.'

'Are you kidding me?'

The woman in the house next door is hosing her driveway, chasing leaves and wattle flowers into the gutter. The smell of cold water on hot bricks wafts up to me. From inside the house I hear a squeal of 'Muuum'. It sounds like Joanne.

'Abby's going back to uni in February. Mark works full time. You can't drop a kidnapped child into their life. Who's going to take care of him?'

'Abby will. She already has three, one more won't sink the boat.'

'Right, women's work, kids and kitchens.'

'Well it bloody is. I'm not having this conversation with you, too. Raising kids *is* what women do well. I'll pay for whatever he needs. And between you and Mark and me he'll have men around to teach him things.'

'I'm not going to be here, Dad. And why do you think any kid would come with us and wait until we're back here to ask what's going on? And that nobody will come after him? Like, *his dad*? Or the police?'

'I'm not a fool. I've thought this through. But you don't need to know any more right now.'

I suspect he's trying to be profound or mysterious but I don't want any surprises if I agree to go with him. And despite everything, I'm considering it. 'I reckon I do, Dad. For starters, how would you get him to leave the commune with you?'

'Right.' He moves closer to me. 'We'll need to be quiet and not raise any alarms. I'll take a rag and some chloroform. We'll carry him back to the car. And once we're –'

'You're going to *drug* him?'

'It's the kindest way.'

'You're going to drug a child and kidnap him?'

'That's *enough*,' he bellows. 'Enough. You're twisting my words, making this sound – After what I've told you, you *know* this is the right thing to do. That child needs me, and I'm going to fetch him. And you.' He points a shaking finger at me. 'You are coming with me.'

The sliding door opens, letting through the smell of buttery toast and the faintest hint of a song on the radio. Sarah sticks her head through the gap.

'What are you doing?' she says.

'Morning, Miss Sarah,' I say.

Dad turns his head and offers her a small smile.

The woman next door has left her hose whipping like a cut snake in wide arcs on her driveway.

'Are you fighting?' Sarah asks.

I flick my dead cigarette over the railing. 'Not anymore.'

Abby asks me to keep an ear out for the kids while she's in the shower. I say yes, though I'm not entirely sure what she means. Mark is outside washing the car. Dad walks into the kitchen, sits, and watches as I unwrap a slice of cheese.

'I'm making a grilled sandwich,' I say. 'Want one?'

'Strange breakfast. Is that what you eat in Bali?'

'I have tomato, onion, cheese.'

'I'm not hungry.'

I rest the knife on the chopping board. 'You've got to eat, Dad.'

'We'll aim to get to the commune before sunset. Too early in the day and they'll be working outdoors. And once it's dark we won't have a hope of finding him. Two-and-a-half-hour drive, I'd say. We'll leave here at two o'clock.'

I spread mustard onto a slice of bread.

'Plenty of time to gather yourself.'

'I'm gathered, Dad. Just not sure I want to steal a child.'

He stands up. 'I'll find a reason to borrow Abby's car. Setting off on the dot. I hope you'll be with me. You could be an asset.'

'Asset?'

'Long hair and unwashed t-shirt, you'll fit right in if we're seen.'

'Thanks. Thought I might be an asset because I'll stop you getting killed.'

He raises his eyebrows. 'Your old man's tougher than you think.'

I drop a lump of butter in the frying pan and watch it sizzle. 'You want me to go or not, Dad? It's not much of a pitch so far.'

He walks around the bench to stand by my side. 'I need you, Charlie.' Suddenly everyone needs me.

Outside, a tinny rendition of 'Greensleeves' grows louder as an ice-cream truck drives along the street. Sarah thunders down the hallway, shouting for Abby.

I use the spatula to flatten my sandwich. 'Broad daylight, Dad. That's a dangerous choice.'

'He can't answer to his name if he's asleep.'

'If you call his name, other people will hear you. People you've just told me are brainwashed and growing dope for corrupt cops and most likely protecting that crop with guns. People who'd rightly be suspicious of two strangers rocking up with no good reason to be there.'

He doesn't bother offering any rebuttal, just huffs. There'll be no talking him out of this. It's the shittest plan I've ever heard. But I can't let him attempt this alone. For my grieving father, for the woman I ran off the road, I'm in.

*

'Don't cook anything for us tonight.'

Abby is mopping the bathroom tiles, beige ceramic with spider veins of brown. I don't know who their tiler is but he's laid the tiles too far apart from one another; the grout's thick and it'll crumble. And he should've used caulk in the joins. I learned about tiling from Ketut, when we remade the bathroom at KD. I watch water pool in the grooves in the wake of Abby's mop. Though she's opened both tiny sliding windows, the room is crazy hot. I never know what's going to bring on a wave of protectiveness for my sister, that weird feeling that I'm not looking out for her the way I should be. But tiling, evidently, is one of those things.

'Why don't you do this later?' I ask.

'Because I want to do it now.'

'Less muck in the air at night, isn't there? You'll get all kinds of tree gunk coming onto your floor now.'

She turns and closes the windows. I'd wanted to offer her a reason to leave the job alone until the air cooled but she's misunderstood me. 'Since when do you know anything about cleaning?'

'I clean at KD.'

'Should've gotten you to do this then.'

'Sure, next time.'

She stands with one hand over the top of the mop as if it were an outsized walking stick. 'Where are you going again?'

'Dad wants to help his friend Rick. You remember him? He used to have all those half-made old cars in his backyard.'

She nods.

'So Rick needs help moving a bunch of stuff. He has a van. We're the muscle.' I hold up my arm as a joke but I'm fit from surfing and KD so I do, in fact, have muscle. She shrugs. 'Anyhow, we'll help him out then probably stay for a barbecue or go to the pub.'

I hate how easily this lie tumbles out of me. I could keep going, layer detail on detail. That Rick's wife would most likely want to feed us, that their older son who'd normally help his dad out had a hernia operation last week.

'Okay.' She narrows her eyes. 'You're not going to say anything to Dad, are you? Not now.'

'Nope, that urge has well and truly passed.'

This really is one spotless bathroom. No mean feat with three kids, a dog, and a husband who showers twice a day. And those tiles.

'Dad's driving, right? I guess I can ask Mrs Lewis to pick up Sarah.'

'What about Mark?'

She rolls her eyes. Which is fair. He's never here.

The phone rings. 'Don't answer,' she says. 'It'll be Constable Roberts. He's been calling me with strange questions. It's like he and the sergeant are following different theories. I don't understand, but it's making me nervous.'

'He's going to be more suspicious if you avoid his calls.'

'Don't answer it.'

CHAPTER SIXTEEN

Monday 23 December 1974

Charlie

An empty chip packet falls out into the gutter near my feet when I open the passenger's-side door to Abby's station wagon. What is it with chicks and cars? It's like they don't care. I pick up the ripped plastic bag, throw it back on the car floor and sit on the crumb-dusted seat.

'Why did you tell Abby we were helping Rick? I told you I'd come up with something,' Dad says.

'It's not that bad of an excuse.'

'It'll do, I suppose. Won't matter soon.' He turns on the engine and slowly backs down the driveway. 'Suspect she'll be glad of some time alone.'

'She spends plenty of time alone. Seems like the world might implode if Mark made it home before his kids went to bed.'

'Stay out of it. Their marriage is none of our business.'

I close my eyes. I can't figure how Skye put up with his old-school thinking. A woman who had a kid without being married, lived on a commune, then wound up with my dad. Weird. Though maybe it was his old ways that appealed to her. I could see how, given what I'd heard, she might crave stability, predictability, a man who used the words 'chivalry' and 'gentle-man' without irony. Dad is rigid in his thinking about women's roles, but he treated my mother like royalty. He opened doors, pulled out chairs, poured her drinks, made sure her petrol tank was always full, bought her flowers. I don't recall seeing him do one thing that could be called domestic, but I think my mother felt loved. And safe.

'So you're clear on the plan?'

'Dad, if you tell me again I'll throw myself out of the car.'

'It's important you understand.'

'Okay, for the last time: we head towards Eumundi, into the hills, take one road to another road, find a sign that says Arcadia, laugh at it, and walk for about a half-hour – not making noise. Once the trees start to thin out, we look down the hill and see communeland. At which point we become invisible and steal a kid who won't make a single noise because we will have rendered him unconscious. We'll take turns carrying him and, magically, no one will see us. Tell me a word that rhymes with failure and I'll make a poem out of it.'

He frowns at me. 'Don't you know that calling this a failure before we've even left the city is a cop-out? You're giving in before we've begun. It's the same old –'

'Same old what, Dad?'

'We have a plan. I know what to say to the boy. And this *will* work.'

'Same what? Same way I live my life? I'm helping you carry this out and you want to judge me?'

We ride in silence for a while until he says, 'Your friend sorted, the one in Bali?'

'Not quite. It's *complicated*.'

'Well, I'm sure she can survive without you for a while. How much longer do you plan to live in that place anyway?'

'Forever.'

He's pursing his lips to resist saying the things I know he wants to. I watch him calm himself. 'You have friends in Brisbane. We have beaches here, the best in the world. You wouldn't need to work as a waiter if you moved back.'

'When I wake up in Kuta I feel happy. The morning smells like incense and watered plants and heat, and people smile when I walk down the track to KD. It's awesome.'

'Did you lose your manhood over there?'

'Say what you want, Dad. Doesn't change a thing.'

'We're not lacking sunshine here. Friendly people aren't unheard of either.'

'I like having rice for breakfast and surfing in the morning. I like hearing Made's sister practise the gamelan in the afternoon. It's –'

'Escapism,' he says.

'Home.'

He turns onto the freeway that will take us north. 'Good luck to you then.'

When Dad nudges me awake we're driving in rainforest on a winding road made shady by the tall gums that arch across the bitumen and knit into a blanket of mottled green, brown and grey, letting in needles of light. I open my window to the forest air, better than anywhere aside from the beach. Rainforest air is moist, rich. You can smell the wet leaves giving back over to the soil, the eucalyptus and myrtle oil, the rot and renewal of it all. Strips of peeling bark hang from tree branches. Whipbirds 'whoee' and bellbirds 'ping'.

'Here,' Dad says. 'Open this up.' He takes a piece of folded paper from his shirt pocket and passes it to me. 'Map.'

'Skye drew this?'

'I told you I was going to come here for the boy. Hadn't planned on these circumstances, obviously . . . The first turn-off road should be near here. Once we're on that we'll need to follow her instructions carefully.'

I unfold the hand-drawn map and a sheet of lined paper with tidy writing on it. The two sheets of paper have been folded and refolded so many times they're near transparent on the crease marks. A small tug from each end and they'd fall to pieces.

He brakes. 'There. The purple sticks. Those are what we're after.'

We turn onto a dirt track humped in the middle and marred with holes. Dad drives slowly but the undercarriage of Abby's car occasionally scrapes and bumps the earth. I study Skye's map. 'This road goes for five miles till we turn onto the next one.'

After a while, the road becomes smoother and flatter, the surrounding landscape lush.

'Read the part where she says what we do now.'

'Uh, five miles blah blah, sign blah blah. Okay, she says, "The road will get steeper. On the passenger's side of the car

170

you'll see a cluster of big boulders, three of them, clumped together. There's a sunrise painted on the middle one and the scrubbery has been brushed away to make a clearing."' I look over at my father. 'Scrubbery?'

'Keep reading.'

"'After you pass the sunrise rock, drive up the hill until the road forks and you see a path barely wide enough for a car. Go up here but not too far or you won't be able to get back out. Only go so far that the car is hidden. From here, you need to walk. At the top of the track you'll find a cleared spot – a lookout. You can see the whole commune from here. Hoping there's no one on duty when you show up."' I sigh. 'Well that's encouraging.'

'Sunrise.' Dad points at a cluster of boulders, one of them painted as Skye described.

'What are they, two-year-olds?'

'Would've thought you'd like that kind of thing. Living with hippies.'

'Totally different scene.'

He mumbles something but I don't care that I can't make out the specifics. I don't want to tell him how different our tribes are, that sunrise aside I reckon these guys won't have a childish bone in their bodies. From what he's said, I think my life of surfing and bonfires, fresh fruit and running water would seem like *Play School* to them. Now, seeing how cut-off they are and with a bit of educated guessing, I know these outliers will be hardcore, self-righteous. And they're in bed with the cops. To the untrained eye our clothes and hair might look similar, but we couldn't have less in common. Creedence acoustic vs Zeppelin on acid.

'Sign,' I say. 'Arcadia.' Neither of us laughs as Dad drives deeper into the rainforest.

'You know I'm not one for violence,' I say. 'But these folks might be, especially if they catch us with Beau. I brought a few things.' I reach for the canvas bag I put on the floor behind my seat.

'What's in there?' he asks. 'I have everything.'

'You don't have weapons. Neither do I. But I found these – better than nothing.' I pull out a spanner and wrench. 'From Mark's toolkit. Mint condition.'

'We don't need those.'

'Correct. We need rifles. But this is what we have.'

I watch Dad fold one arm across the other to make the turn into the wannabe driveway. The skin of his forearm, where no hair grows, shows lines like wood grain. My father is getting old. He needs a foot soldier who won't dick around and undermine his plan, however dumb it is. He needs me to help him.

When I step out of the car door I imagine I'm in the wilds of Vietnam, a strange place for my subconscious to bring me since I went to such epic lengths to *not* go there. And nobody went on more anti-war marches than Ryan and me. We were front of the crowd at the moratorium.

I adjust my bag (makeshift weaponry, two apples, matches, fags), check my shoelaces, and once again try to convince myself I'm doing the right thing. We're not about to kill innocent peasants and babies; we're not acting in the name of colonialism or capitalism. We're rescuing a kid from abusive adults.

'Hurry up, Dad.' Now that I've found my focus I want to get on with it, and Dad is taking forever getting his pack from the back of the car.

He stands beside me and keeps his eyes on mine as he untangles the straps on his pack. 'Settle down.'

We walk along the track, not talking, Dad in front. Mostly, I watch my feet. Left, right, left. There's usually a song in my head when I walk, but not today. I hear my footfall, the crunch of leaves, the peep of birds.

Panic hits me, and I make one last-ditch effort to get my father to see reason. 'If Doyle knows about this place, and about Finn and Skye, Abby's house and your farm will be the first places he looks for Beau. This is a suicide mission, Dad.'

'We've been over this. He cares about Beau less than Skye.'

'Well, his dad then. He'll come for him.'

'I've never given the slightest indication to anyone except you lot that I'd want a child in my life. As far as they know, why would I want another man's son? They don't know if she ever told me about him. They won't suspect me. We'll leave no trace. It'll be like he ran off and got lost in the bush.' He doesn't slow his pace. 'Control your jitters.'

He stops and points through the bush to a clearing in the valley below. There is plant life to shield us, but through the gaps I can see about twenty teepees, a couple of humpies and a scattering of kombi vans in a sprawling circle around a large grey fire pit. To the far side of the commune, close to the base of another wall of hills, is a river shaded on both sides by trees. On the side closer to us is a huge tilled field divided into rectangles. Two lie empty but the rest are growing crops, neat rows of thriving, verdant dope plants with a side area for what I guess are the vegetables. There's a discipline in those fields that troubles me. They know what they're doing. I hear a goat bray, answered by a low moo. There are small clusters of people sprayed across the site: kids playing in the river, a dozen men and women squatting in the fields, a girl in a green dress climbing out of a kombi. The scene is peaceful, idyllic, Arcadia. But it's more industrious, quieter than any commune I've heard of, and now I notice there are men pacing the periphery of the clearing.

'Dad, I don't know about this. Seriously.'

'We'll head to the lookout. I need to see the boy before we go down the hill.'

'How will you know which one's him?'

'Leave that to me.'

We walk on until we reach an outcrop of rocks that offers shelter and a panoramic view through the tallest pair of boulders. There's no one else here. Dad takes a thermos of water out of his bag and hands it to me while he peers down at the camp. Then he takes his wallet out of his back pocket.

'You going to bribe him?'

He pulls out a photograph.

'Is that Beau?' I put the thermos down. 'Let me see.'

He holds the small photograph in front of me, won't let me touch it. It's a picture of a smiling baby sitting on the sand. He has a mop of curly blond hair and a toothless grin.

'Why didn't you show me this before?'

'I don't show this to anyone. It's Skye's.'

'Didn't you think it would help if I knew who we were looking for?'

'That's not your job. I'll find him. I'll show this to him. You help with the rest.' He puts the photo back in his wallet with great care, opening it wide and placing his fingers on the bottom edge of the card as it slides in so the picture isn't creased. 'She took it when they lived up north. He's older, but it'll do.'

We head down the hill, down to the commune. The sound of rushing water rises. I hear an axe strike wood.

Dad walks in front of me, making as little noise as possible, ducking under low branches, holding others aside. Soon we are almost at the clearing and there is little bushland left to hide us.

'What now?' I whisper.

He points to the river and walks on. At the river's edge he stops again. I follow his gaze; he's staring at the children who are playing in the water about thirty feet upstream. There are five of them, all long-haired, in various degrees of nudity. They're chattering happily, passing sticks and large leaves from one to the other, scuttling across the rocks and piling up their finds. They are so focused on their task they don't notice us. One of the boys has similar hair to the baby in the photograph. 'Could be,' Dad mutters.

'There are too many kids, Dad. We need to wait for some of them to go away.'

'And why would they do that? Seems like they're having a good time. Smile.'

We make our way up the river, walking on the thin muddy edge or across the rocks that offer a path through the water. A girl in a brown t-shirt sees us first.

'Men,' she shouts. She pushes her long fringe out of her eyes and regards us with suspicion. The children stand tall, alert as a mob of kangaroos.

'Hey there,' I call out. 'What are you building?'

'I'm getting Finn,' the girl in brown says, and breaks from the group.

'Hold on,' Dad says. 'Can I show you something?'

She stops mid-stride. 'What?'

Dad balances on a large mossy rock. He takes out his wallet. 'It's a picture,' he says. He speaks directly to the boy we think might be Beau. 'Is your name Beau?'

The children are surprised.

'How do you know that?' the girl in brown asks. She reminds me of Abby.

Dad keeps his eyes on Beau. 'I have a picture of you when you were little. Your mother gave it to me. I'm her best friend and she's sent me here because she'd like to see you.'

'Is she coming here?' the boy asks. 'Maria said she was coming when I was sick but she didn't.'

'What's going on?' A short-haired woman in denim dunga-rees marches through the grassy field above us and stops at the top of the riverbank. She flicks her chin towards the children. 'Up here. Now.'

They bound over the rocks then skit up the slippery slope to her.

She gathers them around her like chicks, folding an arm across the shoulders of those closest to her.

'What do you want?' she asks us.

'He has a photo of Beau,' the girl in brown says.

The woman stares at Dad. 'How did you come by that?'

'Skye gave it to me.'

She softens her face for an instant before it hardens again like fast-drying concrete. She turns her head and shouts, 'Jackson.'

'I'll get him,' the girl says, and starts to run off.

'Wait,' I say. 'It's all good. No need for alarm.'

'Jackson!' The woman looks behind her to see if the men are coming. And regrettably, they are. Two muscled, stern-faced men walk to her side. They could be brothers: both black-haired and bearded, wearing worn jeans, except one has a tattoo across his chest, a green-and-blue dragon in flight.

The other, in a white singlet darkened with sweat, holds a rifle. 'Gentlemen,' he says.

'I'm John. This is Charlie.'

'Reporters?' the tattooed man asks.

'Nope.' The man with the rifle takes a few steps towards us, staring down from the bank. 'I'm Finn, and if you're who I think you are, you'd better leave.'

'Skye sent me,' Dad says. 'She wants to see Beau. That's why we're here. How about you let him come with us, for a visit?'

'Skye's dead,' the tattooed man says, frowning.

My eyes shoot to Beau. He's shocked.

The woman thumps the tattooed man in the arm. 'You fuckwit,' she shouts. She turns to Beau, kneels down and hugs him. 'Oh sweetheart.'

Finn addresses Beau without turning around. 'Go with Maria.'

Beau stares at us, mouth open, forehead corrugated in pained confusion. 'Is Mum dead?' Maria strokes his hair. 'Is she?'

Several of the children start to sob.

'Shit,' I say.

'Beau,' Dad says, his voice breaking.

Finn speaks to Maria without taking his eyes off me. 'Get them out of here.'

She gathers the children together. As she leaves, she says to Dad, 'She was my friend.'

'Then why the hell are you here? Why didn't you –' I start.

'Go!' Finn bellows. He makes a move towards Maria and she flinches.

'Beau, get up, sweetie. Come with me.'

But Beau sits on the ground, staring at Dad, tears welling in his eyes. Maria lifts him up with a grunt.

'Beau,' Dad calls out. 'We'll come back. We're coming back.'

'No you're not.' Finn steps closer to us, and the tattooed man follows. 'You're going to piss off out of here and never show your face again.'

I glare at the tattooed man, a person I'd normally spend my energy trying to placate, a giant of a man who could knock me over with a single blow. 'What is wrong with you? Why would you tell him like that?'

'I didn't know –'

'Shut up.' Finn glowers at me. 'This is none of your business.' He uses his rifle to point. 'You better start moving up that hill.'

'He's a little kid! Who does that?'

'She left him. Who does *that*?' Finn says.

'Someone who's scared for her life. Someone who's too beaten up to carry a child with her.' Adrenaline is coursing through my veins. I reach into my bag and grab the cold metal handle of the wrench.

'Get off my land,' Finn snarls.

I walk forward into the river. The water surges up and over my shoes.

'Charlie, no.' Dad grabs my arm. He raises his other hand to Finn. 'We're leaving.'

Finn steps closer, rifle held like a hammer. 'Give me a reason, Water Rat.'

'Charlie, don't.' As Dad pulls me back, his foot slips and he stumbles.

Finn laughs. I steel my arm so Dad can use me to right himself.

We walk up the river towards the bush track we came from. When it feels safe to do so, I turn around. The two men are watching us. Finn lifts his rifle as though he's aiming at me, and the tattooed man laughs.

When we reach the top of the hill Dad drops onto the ground. I walk away from him and throw up at the base of a tree.

CHAPTER SEVENTEEN

Tuesday 24 December 1974

Charlie

I make my way to the kitchen, where Abby hands me the phone then goes back to washing dishes. At least Ryan doesn't call as early in the morning as Sal does. I say 'hello Kuta' to a rumble then boom of thunder, along with Sarah's chant of 'one more sleep' as she stomps up and down the hallway. I hope Abby's found a unicorn toy or there'll be an ocean of tears tomorrow.

Ryan's calmed down since Sal's call, but is still resolved to move back to Brisbane.

'Man, I wish I could send photos through the phone to remind you why you left,' I say. 'There's nothing you want here. The city's crowded with people in a shopping frenzy, there are cranes everywhere throwing up dodgy skyscrapers, you can't breathe through the car fumes. And in the burbs it's the other extreme: dead. I take Abby's dog for a walk and I'm lucky if I see one old lady pruning her roses.'

'You're describing a city with suburbs. I know what Brisbane's like. But man, you should see how many people have shown up here even in the last week. It's like they're falling from the sky.'

'Good for KD, right?'

'But shit for Bali. I'm worried about this, Charlie. Things are changing fast here. Beach is littered with crap every morning now, and I have to fight for space in the waves. I heard a guy yesterday talking about how they should put roads down so he can get up north more easily. It's out of control.'

'They'll leave. They don't get it. Bali won't change.'

He sighs. 'It's already changed. It's time for us to move back, try being adults at home.'

'You're not thinking straight. Do you remember why we left? Brisbane's all capitalism, no culture – a police state. The rest of the country still laughs at us, but it's not funny. It's never been funny.'

'Again, this is not news to me.'

Abby and I lock eyes for a moment as lightning quickfires across the sky.

'Nah, you don't understand. Petersen's getting worse. He's going to run this place until he dies. And we're too old to endlessly protest about his latest shrugged-off act of tyranny.'

'People are never too old to care. And you're getting me fired up about why I should be there, doing something useful.'

'But you won't. You'll take a job in some law firm, get a mortgage and go to the Gold Coast for your holidays. We'll moan about things and nothing will change. Don't give up what we have in Kuta, man. It's still paradise. Get fired up about keeping it that way.'

'We got seats on a flight tonight,' he says.

'How?' I'm gobsmacked. 'Christmas Eve?'

'Sal's dad pulled some strings.'

'Right, okay. Well, make nice with your family for Christmas, and then let's get on the plane to Kuta. I'm counting the days until I'm back there.'

He's noncommittal, but I'm not giving up. I know tourists are invading Bali. We all know that. But they won't stay: there'll be some other place to go. Bali is for surfers and people genuinely searching for a better way to live. We have a restaurant, a whole bunch of friends, and the perfect losmen a minute's walk from the ocean. Giving that up would be insanity. But it'll be okay. Ryan'll enjoy concrete footpaths, modern cars and eating different food for a few days then he'll hear something racist or read a newspaper and he'll remember why he left. And I'll join the chorus whenever anything here bugs him.

I want to tell Ryan what's going on with me, about the car crash and Beau, the commune and the cops, but I don't want to muddy the waters. I keep to my lines of Brisbane bad, Bali good. When the dust settles here I want to be sure I have a place to go.

Abby is back home from taking the kids to wherever she took them. She lugs a brown paper bag of groceries onto the counter then goes back to the car for the rest. They go through a lot of food.

It's oppressively hot; a downpour of rain causes the temperature to drop for about as long as it takes to drink a glass of juice, then the sky clears and the sun ratchets up the heat. Then there's the never-ending pre-Christmas organising to do and drive and buy, which makes it feel stressful in this house. The rush is not mine to deal with so I watch and listen, but I know for sure this is not how my family home will be, if that ever happens.

The days here have felt long, and aside from my excursion with Dad I'm not sure what to do with myself. When Ryan and Sal get here they'll need to spend most of their time with family, in the beginning at least. I decide to read through the newspaper and see if any bands are playing tonight. Might catch up with some friends I haven't seen since I was here last.

I try to chat to Abby while she puts her groceries into the pantry and fridge, fills Woof's water bowl, wipes muddy paw prints off the floor. 'Where's today's paper?'

She makes a grumbling sound to indicate she's annoyed, though I don't see how answering a question is such a big deal. 'No idea, Charlie.'

'You keep them in the living room, yeah?'

'Why don't you get up and go look?'

She's cranky about something so I drop it. The phone rings before I can search for the paper.

'I'll get it,' I say. I'm worried the call could be something to do with our visit to the commune.

'Well it probably won't be Roberts,' she says as I pick up the phone.

'Hello? Hang on a sec.' I cover the receiver with one hand. 'Why not? Anything I should know?'

She frowns and points at my hand. 'Don't do that.' But I indicate I'm ignoring the call until she answers my question. 'God, Charlie. So rude. He rang yesterday. I'll tell you after.'

'What time yesterday? What did he say?'

'Charlie, talk to the person who's on the phone right now!'

It's Abby's friend Lou. I pass it to Abby then pace around while she's talking. I didn't think Roberts knew about the commune, but maybe he does. It could be that the 'good cop, bad cop' thing is a ruse. Maybe someone left the commune right after we did, told Roberts what happened and – no, Abby would've said something. But if she inadvertently made it clear she knew nothing about what Dad and I were doing, that's bad, too. These guys would love to divide us, play us against one another.

'What's your problem?' Abby asks when she's off the phone. 'I thought you wanted me to take his calls.'

'What did he want to know?'

'Times. He's as obsessed as Doyle about getting the timeline straight. I was convincing on the phone. I told him about us arguing. As far as I can tell they have no evidence, and I've answered for the missing hours. Charlie, this might be okay.' She flushes.

'It's all right. I want it to be over, too.'

At dusk, I'm back in the kitchen again. I went for a walk, read a little, slept a little and now I'm sitting next to Dad at the bench, drinking a cold beer. No bands on tonight and no friends at a loose end. The radio is on but the sound is low. Woof is lying on the floor near my feet, snoring. And Abby is working the stove like a pro, turning the kids' lamb chops and quickly moving her arm away from the leaping hot fat, checking on their corn cobs and peas boiling in separate saucepans. We could use her at KD.

When the phone rings, I mentally put money on it being Mark calling to say he'll be home late even though he'd seemed relieved this was his last workday for the year.

Dad is aggravated by the constant ringing. He pushes his chair back, picks up his glass and stands. 'You get half a dozen phone calls a day! It's noisier than being in an office.'

'This is more than normal,' Abby says, draining the peas into a colander. 'We don't usually get calls from Bali or the police. I'd go out of my head if it rang this much every day.'

Dad makes a face that suggests it's still somehow Abby's fault, and heads out into the backyard with his book.

I'm not going to indulge his tantrum about modern life but he's right that it's noisy in here. Between the cooking sounds, the radio, the TV on full volume in the living room, Woof barking at who-knows-what and the occasional kid shout, I struggle to hear who's on the phone. I turn off the radio, wave at Abby to keep it down as she calls the kids to dinner. But it turns out to be a call I should've let ring out.

'I hear you and your father took a drive yesterday,' Doyle says.

While Sarah clambers into her designated seat, Abby lifts the twins onto chairs made high with stacked cushions. She places a small plate of food in front of each of them.

I wish I could take the call in another room. I don't want Abby or the kids to hear this. In a house this size, you'd think they'd have a second phone.

'Who'd you hear that from?' I want Doyle to admit he knows Finn and his henchmen, or Maria.

'The man in the fucking moon. What does your father want with that boy?'

'Not sure who you mean.'

Abby looks at me. I cover the phone and whisper, 'My mate Jason. All good.'

'Don't get smart with me,' Doyle says. 'What does he have that you want? Did she give him something? A letter, photographs? Maybe I'll ask him myself.'

Abby cuts the kids' meat into small chunks and butters the corn, then leaves the room, thinking, I suppose, that I'll supervise. I ignore Petey's instantly spilled water and speak quickly.

'Beau doesn't have anything. Dad wanted to make sure he was okay. He promised Skye he'd do that.'

'And all of a sudden he knew she'd lived on a commune and how to get there. Should've told me the truth when I asked the first time.'

'Sure, yes. She recently told him she had a son and wanted Dad to check in on him. Which we did. End of story.'

He's eating something – is everyone eating right now? – and makes me wait while he chews into the phone. 'Not quite. It's been brought to my attention that your brother-in-law is that *Four Corners* reporter.' I'm amazed he didn't already know that. Not much of a cop. 'Did he send you out there? Because if he did, we have a problem, you and me.'

'No, we didn't tell him we were going there. It was only a quick drive to see that Beau was all right. Nothing else there is of any interest.'

'You lot need to compare notes.' He goes back to eating and I'm glad I can't see him. Sounds like his snout is deep in the trough. 'You see, your brother-in-law is unhealthily curious about what goes on there. Seems to have a keen enough interest in farming that he's been asking people about it for *months*.

186

He hasn't gone as far as trespassing like you did, but he is behaving in a very bloody intrusive manner. And I'm going to have to insist he stick his nose somewhere else.'

I have no idea how to respond to this. If Mark *is* investigating that commune, it's news to me.

'So what's going to happen,' Doyle swallows, 'is that I'm going to offer you a deal. And it's a good one, so you'll say yes. See, I'm not exactly sure how you and your sister – maybe your father – are involved in this woman's death. But you are. I don't have evidence but I've been doing this long enough to trust my gut. I'm prepared to drop the whole thing, and say she had car trouble, blew a tyre, skidded off the road, alone and unaided, if you get your brother-in-law to stay away from Eumundi and anyone involved with that place. Got that?'

'Won't that make him suspicious?' Petey looks up and I turn my back on him, twisting the phone cord across my chest.

'Not my problem. You'll find a solution.'

I'm whispering now, but Doyle doesn't seem to notice. 'I hear you, I do. And I'm not saying we had anything to do with anything, because we didn't. But hypothetically, if Mark thinks there's something going on at that commune he won't stop poking around because I ask him to. Why would he?'

The kids are digging into an intense argument about who-cares-about-what, which suits me perfectly.

'To protect his wife. I presume he'd like to keep her out of jail.'

'And my dad won't believe it was an accident, though it obviously was. You told us the body had been laid out and the door was closed.'

'Don't recall saying that.'

187

'Roberts –'

'Makes mistakes.'

'Your men took photographs. The medical examiner.'

He exhales loudly. 'Are you telling me how to do my job, boy?'

I call up flashes of the stories Mark told me about his investigations into the Whiskey Au Go Go, the two men rotting in jail, swallowing metal and clawing the walls, locked up for life with no evidence, the crooked cops and judge in collusion. Doyle holds the power here. The only value I have is in my relationship to a journalist who's educated me about how scared I should be right now. 'No, not at all. But seriously, how do you suggest I keep him away from Eumundi?'

That's a word I've said only a couple of times in my life, and my timing in saying it again could not have been worse. Mark has walked into the kitchen, kissed each of the kids on the top of the head, nodded to me, and is on his way to the fridge. After I mumble a 'Good to talk to you, have to go now' into the receiver and then hang up, Mark asks me – placing a longneck on the kitchen bench, not making eye contact – 'Eumundi?'

I stand still as a lizard as Mark pulls out a drawer, removes a bottle opener and looks up at me.

I feel my face reddening but make an effort to keep my voice steady. 'Yeah, the ginger factory. Friend asking whether it's worth a visit.'

'That's in Buderim.' He flicks the lid off the bottle, takes a tumbler from the dish rack.

'That's what I said.'

'You said Eumundi.'

'Pretty sure I didn't.' He'll put two and two together, but I'm not going to help speed up the process.

Mark pours the beer and drinks a slow mouthful, letting the silence hang. 'My mistake.'

CHAPTER EIGHTEEN

Wednesday 25 December 1974

Charlie

'Pop. Pop. Pop.' I lie on my side, watching as Sarah taps on Dad's forehead with admirable persistence. 'Wake up, Pop. Santa's been. *Pop.*'

He wipes the crust from his eyes and reaches for his watch.

'Are you getting up?' Sarah asks him. Standing next to my father's bed, bouncing on the spot, saucer-eyed with anticipation, a fairy in front of an ogre.

'It's five in the morning, miss. But I suppose that's as good a time as any.'

Dad heaves himself up into a sitting position. 'Mum and Dad awake?'

She shakes her head. 'They'll make me stay in bed. Come to the tree, Pop.' She makes a show of pulling him upright.

Once he's standing, Dad gives me a whack on the foot. 'Merry Christmas.'

Dad holds Sarah's hand as she tugs him down the dark hallway to the living room. I follow. She stops when she sees the tree, now circled by a dizzying number of brightly wrapped presents. Abby has left the lights on overnight so the tree flashes gaudy colours, and the tinsel and metal decorations glow and dim with each throb of light. Sarah runs to the tree and kneels, overwhelmed by the number of gifts, the excess of it all, as the twins run down the hallway, screeching in excitement.

I feel a light touch on my arm. 'Merry Christmas,' Abby says.

'If you guys haven't got a unicorn chewing grass outside, I'm leaving.'

She smiles back at me. Mark stands next to her, his arm draped across her shoulders. 'I'm sure Santa came up with an alternative.'

'What's an alternative to a unicorn?' I ask.

'You want to do the honours, Sarah?' Mark says, and she leaps into action, picking up one parcel after another, reading the name on the tag and handing it to the right person. She quickly becomes annoyed at Joanne's slowness in unwrapping, and Petey's insistence on grabbing his own gifts, and gives up the job, turning her attention to tearing into a gift labelled for her. Abby takes over.

I've brought gifts from Bali: a sarong and wooden salad servers for Abby, wood carvings for Mark and Dad, miniature gamelans and twangy instruments made out of coconuts and metal spikes for the kids. Abby shakes her head at the sight of the musical toys, but Petey seems happy. Kids love noise.

It's a spectacular morning, the sky a bright blue, air warm but not hot. After we've admired one another's gifts of books, bubble bath, jewellery, aftershave, tools and appliances, after Petey has shown me his G.I. Joe and Joanne has held her Viewmaster to Dad's face so he can enjoy it, too, Abby makes us breakfast: scrambled eggs on toast, coffee and Tang for the adults; Froot Loops for the kids. While she's cooking, Mark balls up the torn wrapping paper and puts it in a box to take outside. I sit with the kids and check out their presents with them. Sarah clutches her toy unicorn, which is the size of a large cat, with enormous plastic eyes, a horn decorated in pastel-coloured glitter and a pink ribbon collar studded with diamantes. I thought she'd be disappointed when I watched her unwrap what clearly was not the living unicorn she'd asked for, but she adjusted in a heartbeat, and now declares her love for the toy in her arms. Dad stands watching, hands in pockets, unsure what to do with himself since there's no newspaper on Christmas Day.

By the time we've finished eating, it's 7.15 am. I stand outside, mug in one hand, cigarette in the other, and try to imagine what Beau might be doing now. I'm not sure if he'll know it's Christmas, if that's even something they acknowledge on the commune. Maybe Maria has made him a gift?

I wish I could tell him that the first Christmas without your mother is the hardest, and it'll get easier – not better – that the pain will dull each year until it feels sad but normal she's not there. I wish I could do the things for him that I'd wanted someone to do for me. I'd fill his day with activity and distraction, keep him moving, make him laugh. The worst thing is to be alone, sitting in the quietness with no escape from the ache of loss in your gut.

At four in the afternoon, when by rights we should be sleeping off lunch, Abby wedges the front door open to a pulsating flow of people who, one gush at a time, fill the house. Abby introduces them as 'from the street', 'from Sarah's school', 'from Mark's work'. There are women who ask after the twins before anyone else, women who carry gifts of potted poinsettias, bowls of trifle, plastic trays of sandwiches, and know where they need to go, and men who seem befuddled about why they've brought their family to this house for more Christmas carry-on. Before even an hour has passed, the house resembles a zoo at feeding time. The air is filled with talk and laughter, with kids running and spilling.

I want to go back to bed, but Abby tells Dad and me to talk to the guests. I stand next to Dad as a man with a thick black moustache and puffy hair says he's sorry to hear about his loss. He asks Dad how he's coping. Dad still has no coherent answer to this question. The man drifts away, then one woman after another comes over to offer Dad more chicken, more coleslaw, more watermelon. He wants none of it. He's hardly eaten in weeks. The rest of us ate our own body weight at lunchtime, and in this hot, crowded room the food smells swill in the air, mixing with sweat and cigarette smoke. Dad is jollied and talked at. I'm finding even a sideline dose of this exhausting, but I'm better than Dad at coming up with shut-it-down answers: 'Yep, Bali', 'Soon as I can', 'No one special right now', 'Well, hey, it's summer, it gets steamy, right?' I don't know how he's coping with the ramped-up version. I head outside for a break, watching people socialise while I smoke.

As I squash my cigarette stub under my thong, Mark calls out to me through the back door. 'Charlie, phone.'

I have no idea how he heard it ring but I go into the crowded kitchen, cover one ear with my hand and press the phone against the other.

It's Constable Roberts. 'Sorry to disturb you, Mr Scott. But I need to ask you about a few things your daughter said when we spoke yesterday.'

'You've got Charlie, Scott Junior. My brother-in-law must've misunderstood. And, uh, I know you take your job seriously. Respect for that. But it's Christmas Day. Can this wait until tomorrow?' Why would Roberts be calling when Doyle has already laid down the law? They don't seem to be sharing notes.

The kitchen is not as packed as the living room but still, these people are making a hell of a noise, flicking their ring pulls at invented targets, pouring dregs of warm wine down the sink, laughing and back-slapping, crunching on chips and peanuts. A line of kids, led by Sarah, elbows their way through the room to run into the backyard. I concentrate to hear what Roberts is saying.

'Skye's body,' he says. 'I can't imagine anyone without some degree of compassion taking her out of the car, folding her arms –'

'I reckon we've covered this.'

'If someone ran her off the road then tried to make her comfortable but left her there, maybe that person wasn't able to get her to their car – because it would take two people – or else there were two people who disagreed about what to do. Do you see where I'm going?'

'Can't say I do, no.'

We're both less guarded, bolder, with Christmas drinks under our belts.

'I think she was alone,' he says, 'and that there were at least two people in another car that forced her off the road, probably forced her off unintentionally. And I think one of those people was a woman, to lay her like that. And the driver might've been a man who didn't want to get involved with local trouble since he wasn't planning on staying. Does that strike you as a possible scenario?'

I fumble in my pocket for a cigarette but the pack is empty. 'As possible as any other I suppose, but wouldn't you want some evidence to back up a wild idea like that?'

I watch as Petey pours a can of lemonade into a hole he's dug in the lawn then stirs it with a stick. He has two mates with him, who are adding fistfuls of grass and dirt.

'Are you with your family today?'

'I'm at my mother's house,' Roberts replies.

'You're from a big family?'

'Eight kids.'

Catholic. 'Well, I don't want to keep you from them. And your girlfriend I suppose? She won't be too happy about you working today.'

'Hardly any cars drive along that road, and since you and your sister were travelling, and stayed in Chinchilla . . . I'm still unclear about why you did that. When you were so close to your father's farm.'

'You've met Abby. Once she's got an idea in her head, that's what she does. It was a night in a hotel, no biggie. We'd been fighting, not thinking straight. She told you that.'

'What were you fighting about?'

'Nothing much. You have sisters, yeah, in that eight? You must fight with them sometimes.'

He pauses. 'I do need to speak with your father.'

'Yeah, there's a lot of people here right now. I don't see him anywhere. Might have ducked out for some air.'

'I'll give you the number I can be reached on today.'

'Sure.' He tells me a phone number. I offer a few uh-huhs, pretend I'm writing it down.

'I'm not giving up on this,' he says. His tone has changed, suddenly sober and professional. 'I know I'm right.'

I hang up, push through the kitchen crowd to get to the bathroom to think, tamping down my urge to find Abby and recite the conversation to her. Last I saw her she was actually having fun, drink in hand, laughing with a group of her friends. I close the bathroom door and sit on the edge of the bath, staring at the cross-pattern of wire reinforcing the mustard-coloured glass shower screen. The shower door is askew. It would take a minute to fix, but getting Mark's toolbox from the shed would entail navigating a maze of small talk.

I'm terrified at how close Roberts is getting, and nervous he'll find out his boss has offered us a highly suspect deal. I wonder how many cops know about the commune, how many cops aren't corrupt.

There's a knock on the bathroom door, then a woman's voice. 'Hello in there? I'm busting.'

I rise unsteadily, flush the toilet and turn on the tap. 'One minute.'

I open the bathroom door to Lou. She's wearing a long red-and-white-striped dress and reeks of sweet perfume and cigarette smoke. She's holding a champagne flute on an angle so precarious the liquid touches the lip of the plastic on one side.

'Charlie!' Her smile is large and generous, lopsided. 'How have I not seen you today?' She gives me a hug, spilling champagne on the back of my shirt. 'Are you having a good Christmas, babe? Better now you're in Brisbane, after all that car crash, fiancée stuff.'

Before I can reply, she puts her hand, sticky and warm, on my arm. 'Sorry, not "stuff". Tragic, obviously.' She holds up her glass. 'Idiot juice. I've had a few.'

I smile at her. She's got a louche, unbuttoned sexiness about her, wet lips. 'Not a problem,' I say.

She looks at me with great concentration. 'Are you okay? Coming home to drama must be the last thing you wanted.' She gestures at the crowded living room with her glass, sloshing champagne onto shag carpet. 'I mean – y'know.'

There's so much of this woman, so much hair and breast and hip, so much energy and volume. And she's crazy drunk.

'You were wanting –' I tilt my head towards the bathroom door.

She blinks vaguely for a beat, then speaks in a rush. 'Yes. Desperate.' She lets go of my arm.

I stand aside but rather than going into the bathroom she slouches against the doorframe and continues talking.

'Knows how to throw a party, doesn't she? It's all going to plan. Tick, tick, tick.' She gulps down another mouthful of champagne. She looks over her shoulder into the living room, where a group of revellers is dancing near the stereo. 'See that?

197

She made that happen. Doesn't happen by itself, you know.' Her smile is gone. 'Has it all, doesn't she? Twist in the road won't kill her.'

Her gaze is set on Abby, who is shouldering her way through the crowd holding aloft a round white tray. I'm suddenly terrified that Abby might have confided in her boozy friend, and that by road she means our road, *the* road. But she doesn't elaborate, just gives me her glass. 'I shouldn't be allowed to drink.'

'People's lives are never as simple as you think,' I say. 'Everybody has troubles, even Abby.'

She laughs. 'You're a funny one.'

When Lou goes to the bathroom I return to the gathering for lack of anything else to do, dumping her glass on the first empty surface. I'm about to make my way over to Abby, who's standing near the veranda door, topping up people's drinks, when Mark holds his arm up to get my attention, then comes towards me, slapping backs and clinking cans on the way.

'Get you a drink, Charlie?' he asks. 'Beer, Bundy?'

'I'm taking a breather. Party's going well.'

He takes a slug of his beer, crushes the can and locks eyes with me. I see the face of the journalist, the interrogator, considering the best approach. 'Abby tells me you and John went to help his mate Rick out on Monday. How'd that go?'

'Yeah, fine. Moved some things.'

'Did you? I could've helped if it'd been on a weekend. Kind of strange he asked you to help on a weekday. You know he still works – teaches at TAFE. I guess he took the day off.'

'Pretty sure everyone but you ended their work year weeks ago.'

'Got it done then?'

'Yep.'

His eyes haven't left my face, not when he's been jostled, not when a drink is spilled on his hand. I feel sweaty and try to think of a way to disengage. I've told him I don't want a drink, and he knows I've come from the bathroom . . .

'Charlie, I don't think you went to Rick's house. I think you went to Eumundi. And you're only now realising how out of your depth you are.' I look for someone to make eye contact with. 'I've been searching for that place for months. So the fact Skye's boy is there is more than a little interesting to me.'

'Bit of a leap.'

'I know more about that commune than you can imagine. I know what goes on there and who's running it. And I'm not on board with you taking one of their kids and bringing him into my home.' No more pussyfooting around.

'Mark, I get it. But Dad's decided.'

'To take another man's son?'

'The kid's in a dangerous situation.'

'Do you have any proof he's in trouble?'

'I met his father. And the place is – like you said, it's no apple farm.'

He leans closer. 'Describe it.'

Given that Doyle wants Mark to become less interested in the commune, this is dangerous turf. I want Mark to believe Beau shouldn't be there but I don't want to whet his appetite about the place or give him any information he doesn't already have.

Mark looks around to see if anyone is listening in on our conversation. But the people near us are gleefully unaware. 'How far out of Eumundi is it?'

Children run past us and between us. Abby's dancing with a man who's wearing a metal bowl on his head and mouthing lyrics into a wooden-spoon microphone.

'*Mate.*'

I make a move to walk away but Mark puts his arm across my shoulders.

'Jim. How you doing? Meet my brother-in-law, Charlie.'

'Charlie, *mate*, merry bloody Christmas. You're related to this bloke? You lucky bastard.'

When Jim is distracted by a woman carrying a platter of cheese and pineapple chunks on toothpicks, Mark speaks directly into my ear. 'I'm going to need you to take me there, soon as we can.' He pats me jovially then walks away.

Someone has turned up the music. The half-dozen people nearest the stereo holler the words to 'Kung Fu Fighting' and jump about. Lou is in the centre of the group, arms above her head, eyes closed, singing. A man wearing gold chains, shirt unbuttoned to show his hairy chest, stands behind her with one hand on her waist. They chop at the air in clumsy rhythm: 'Ha!'

I turn back to Jim, who is regaling the three men now circled around us with a tale of his past prowess on the rugby field. Then I head to the kitchen.

Dad is getting himself a fresh beer while a woman wearing a purple headband talks at him. I should have fought him harder. I should've stopped him from going to the commune, shouldn't have helped out.

Once the record ends, the dancers gather around the stereo, choosing what they want to hear next. Abby holds up one album cover after another to shouts of 'naaah' or whoops of approval.

For a moment there's no music, and the radio that no one bothered to turn off bays for attention. Mark is standing in front of it, turns it up, and people begin to fall silent and funnel into the kitchen, aware that something has changed, something important is being said.

Mark leans on the benchtop, his brow furrowed in concentration. His mate Geoff stands beside him, hands on hips.

Abby cuts through the crowd to get to the radio. 'On Christmas Day? Turn it off. We're playing records.' She reaches for the radio, but Mark grabs her wrist. 'Ow, that hurts.'

'Sorry.' He releases her, but his eyes don't leave the radio.

'What's so important?' She rubs her wrist.

The radio newsreader is grave: '. . . city of Darwin destroyed by Tropical Cyclone Tracy. Reports of the devastation are only now making their way to the rest of the country. Eyewitnesses say the city has been levelled, with the remains of thousands of homes scattered across the town. Winds of 135 miles per hour were recorded by the gauge at Darwin Airport before it was blown away. Never has Australia seen a disaster of this magnitude.'

Lou joins the back of the crowd. 'What's going on?' Low murmurs of explanation ripple across the room.

Jim is standing beside me. A lit cigarette dangles from his parted lips, ash dropping onto the floor. 'Holy Christ.'

'Prime Minister Whitlam has ordered a mass airlift of citizens from what remains of the city, and has sent Navy boats, armed services and police from southern states to assist with the disaster.'

I hate to admit it, but my first thought is that a disaster of this scale is good for Abby and me, that it will draw focus away from us, make Mark forget about the commune and Beau, make Roberts think about bigger things than a country-road car crash. Maybe some of his sprawling family or workmates come from Darwin.

'. . . number of fatalities is not yet known, and with people already evacuating the town by car, authorities are struggling to determine the full scope of this disaster . . . We'll bring further information to air as it comes to hand.'

When the news story finishes, the kitchen comes back to life with a rustle of talk like leaves caught in a wind. I don't want to process this with a bunch of strangers so I go to my bedroom. As I walk past Sarah's room I see Joanne sitting cross-legged and alone on the bed, stroking Sarah's toy unicorn like it's a beloved pet.

Dad joins me in our room. 'Skye's there, in Darwin,' he says.

'Right, I forgot that. Her family too, yeah?'

'Her brother. Parents are dead. I don't know if she had cousins, or if her grandparents are alive. I should know that.' He takes a jerky breath. 'I hope they put her deep in the ground, Charlie. I hope she was safe.'

CHAPTER NINETEEN

Thursday 26 December 1974

Abby

Geoff's wife, Margot, calls while I'm making lunch. I wipe tomato juice off my fingers with a paper towel, holding the phone between my shoulder and ear.

'They'll be on the news tonight,' she says. 'Geoff got an emergency line out of Darwin and called the station. They're both okay and Mark says to tell you he'll be in touch as soon as he can.'

I phone Lou. 'I'll be on your couch at five-thirty,' she says.

Radio reports have drip-fed us information about the cyclone. It turns out the rest of Australia hadn't known about the cyclone until Christmas afternoon because there'd been no way of getting word out. In the end, a ship not too far off the coast, taking its own beating in the storm, got news to Perth.

It'd taken them four hours to make radio contact. The ship's captain said that when the cyclone changed course and headed for Darwin he'd feared the worst: 'It wasn't like any wind I'd seen before. It was colossal.' He'd told his men to keep calling until they made contact. And, he said, he prayed.

Wind had battered Darwin for seven hours. It cut a line across the city, missing nothing, destroying everything. And, as is the way with these things, those awful hours were followed by a series of insults. With an earthquake, it's aftershocks; with a tropical cyclone, it's fear of typhoid and an infestation of mosquitoes and flies. All of this I learned from the ABC.

Mark, Geoff, a cameraman and a sound guy flew up in a Hercules late yesterday, hours after the reports started coming through. Tonight, we'll see the first images of Darwin on the news.

At a quarter to six, Lou and I usher our kids into the living room. The cyclone will be the first story and I want everyone to be settled when the news comes on. I've made Dad a pot of tea, put it on the table near the armchair. Charlie has kicked off his stinky sandals, plopped down onto the floor, and is nursing a can of beer. The kids bump one another like dodgems before finally agreeing on a seating arrangement where no one is touching anyone and no heads are in the way. Lou and I take the couch, each holding a glass of moselle.

'This year,' she says. 'What a debacle. Starts with a flood, ends with a cyclone.' She doesn't mention Skye but yes, this year . . .

We hear Mark before we see him. 'We arrived in Darwin last night and what we've seen since then defies belief.' My heart lifts at the sound of his voice, so measured and authoritative.

'What's the population up there, do you think? Before this,' Charlie asks.

'I heard 47,000, and they're expecting to evacuate almost all of them,' Dad replies.

'To where?' Charlie asks.

Dad rattles off the list of potential towns people could be taken to.

'Look,' I say and nod at the TV.

We watch as the camera pans across the devastated streets of Darwin. Mark's team has filmed from a helicopter, and what's left of the town beneath them looks like a sprawling rubbish dump. Over the sound of chopper blades, we see collapsed, dishevelled skeletons of homes. They sit along the edge of streets strewn with wooden boards, metal sheeting, upturned cars, and telephone poles pointing every which way, wires draping despondently between them. We see footage of life on the ground, too. Men, some slim, some with pregnancy-sized bellies, wearing shorts and work boots, haul great hunks of whatever they can carry into garbage trucks. An elderly Aboriginal woman in a faded sundress watches.

The footage cuts to Mark, handsome and composed as always, standing alone on ground covered with detritus. He's wearing tan slacks and a short-sleeved white shirt, and has one hand on his hip. He points to a snaking line behind him.

'There's Daddy!' Sarah points at the screen.

'Daddy!' Petey stands up.

'These men and women, mums and dads and grandparents, teachers and bus drivers, are queuing for ice,' Mark says. 'It's about thirty-nine degrees in Darwin today, and the water is running out.'

Joanne begins to cry. I lift her onto my lap and smooth her hair off her forehead. Dad touches Petey on the back. 'Sit.'

'The people here have an unbreakable spirit, despite all they've been through,' Mark says. He talks of the neighbourliness – encouraged by the presence of law-enforcement officials – of the food and medical supplies making their way to the schools, which are now shelters. It's horribly familiar, words we heard following the flood. But this is worse, as much as disasters can be compared. It's much worse.

'All public services have been severed,' Mark says. 'There is no electricity, no sewage, no clean water flowing from the taps, and aside from emergency services and the media, there is no way of contacting the outside world.' He pauses for effect. 'This is a tragedy of unprecedented scale.'

I don't think Mark should have let the cameraman shoot footage of the children's toys and Christmas decorations that litter the ground, soiled and wet, but Mark has told me many times his job is not to show what's palatable but what's true.

He interviews a woman called Nan who says she and her children have only the clothes they are wearing.

'Barney got thrown against the shed wall.'

'Barney is your dog,' Mark says.

'My dog, yeah. Went up like a piece of paper and off down the street. Down there.' The camera follows her sightline to the end of a ravaged street.

'And what did you do, Nan? How did you survive?'

'We went under the caravan, didn't we? Stayed there in the mud for hours till the wind stopped enough to crawl out. Kids were screaming and we were all a foot in the muck and

I thought the caravan was going to come down on top of us. Not much of a Christmas for the kids.'

'But you made it through,' Mark says.

The camera moves closer, ready for tears. Nan remains stoic. 'Can't find the dog, but.'

Mark speaks with local mechanic Sam who describes his night, saying the rain had been heavy, and the wind immense.

'Sheets of corrugated iron scraping across the road and smashing into cars. There was an almighty wind, like standing near a plane. Deafening. I watched my kids screaming at me, right in front of me. Couldn't make out a word.'

'Well, at least people are getting out,' I say to Lou. The television shows a crawling line of cars leaving the city on a cleared road.

'People are fleeing this shattered city by air, land and sea,' Mark says, 'leaving those whose job it is to clean and care. People who go by plane are being sent to Alice, Sydney and Adelaide. Those who drive are heading to Katherine and Tennant Creek. Some are heading by sea to parts of north Queensland or down to Brisbane. And no one knows when, or if, they will be coming home.'

He ends his story with a shot of a sign outside the local cinema. It's fashioned from a piece of old board, with the hand-written words, 'Gone with the Wind, starring Cyclone Tracy'.

'If I didn't know better, I'd think Mark wrote that himself,' Dad says.

They cut back to the studio, where the program's host stares gravely into the camera. 'That was Mark Campbell reporting from Darwin. And the prayers of the nation are with the people of that city tonight.'

'Prayers?' I stand up. 'If there's anybody up there who let this happen, why would you pray to him?'

Lou whistles. 'You'll be in for it if the nuns hear that.'

But I don't think I believe what the nuns forced on us as teenagers. I'm not sure I believed it even then, since I'd wondered from a young age why any god worth worshipping would allow children to starve or loving mothers to die.

'I just think it's strange to hear people thank God for their survival,' I say. 'He could've stopped this happening in the first place. If it was the work of the Devil, why didn't God blow the wind back out to sea? What kind of god lets wind destroy a city?'

These are the sorts of comments that Dad would have leapt on in years gone by, since he remained resolutely Catholic even after Mum's death. He'd have offered a 'God works in mysterious ways' or 'There's a larger plan at work than we understand.' But he says nothing.

'You think God lets people die because he doesn't care about them?' Charlie asks.

'No,' I say. 'I don't think that.'

When Lou has gone home and the kids and Dad are in bed, I sit outside with Charlie. We slouch in the butterfly chairs and look up at the night sky. The air is hot and humid, and carries the anxious scratch of cicadas, *ratatatatat*, insistent agreement of frogs, *uh-huh-uh-huh-uh-huh*, and the acrid smell of our insect repellent.

He reaches into his shirt pocket and pulls out a joint and a box of matches. 'It's a shame for us you're married to a reporter.' He puts the joint in his mouth, lights it and takes a series of short, sharp drags. He tips up his head and blows out a stream of smoke, grey-white against the black sky. 'Here.' He passes the joint to me.

'It's never been a problem until now.' I sink into my chair, almost relaxed for the first time in months. I take another long toke before I pass it back to him.

'Cyclone won't hold his interest for much longer. How are you going to keep him away from the commune?'

I groan. 'You tell me. I wish either you or Dad had told me about that place before it got to this point. You know Mark's like a bloodhound once he gets a whiff of something. I would've told you not to go there.'

'That's exactly why Dad didn't want you to know.'

'Well, yes, that's fantastic. My father not telling me so he could bring back a stolen child. My husband not telling me because –' But that one is on me. Mark doesn't tell me the details of his stories because I've made it clear I'm not interested or am annoyed or want to get him to do something useful around the house. And bloodhound is the wrong dog: when it comes to investigating a story Mark is a pitbull, a pitbull attacking a poodle. 'Charlie, he's been investigating illegal brothels, gambling places, drug trafficking, the criminals coming up from Sydney – everything that goes on in Fortitude Valley – for two years. He's obsessed. If he's found out there's a police-run dope farm that's funnelling drugs into the Valley, no one will be able to keep him away. Not me, not his boss.'

'He'd drop it if he knew it'd keep you safe.'

I hold my hand out for the joint. 'I'm not telling him.'

'I don't see any other way.'

I don't either. But I have a few more days to think of one, and Charlie's making me anxious. I change the topic. 'Remember the summer Dad decided we had to learn about physics?'

'Bread always lands butter side down?'

Which makes me laugh. 'That is not a law of physics.'

'Pretty sure it is.'

'You don't remember him explaining the laws of motion?'

'I really don't.' He smiles at me. 'And if this is your best stoned riffing, I'm cutting you off.'

'So funny. Dad was teaching a grade ten physics class, which meant our ignorance was suddenly outrageous. Nothing?' He shakes his head. 'It's amazing how much you've blocked.'

'My superpower,' he says.

'First law of motion: Everything stays in its state of rest or moving straight ahead, except when it's compelled to change its state by another force. Third: For every action there's an equal and opposite reaction. Second one's not relevant right now.'

'I don't see how any of them are relevant right now.'

I sigh. 'Charlie, you interfered with the motion of things, the way things were supposed to go, when you ran Skye off the road. She was moving somewhere, going to her child. She was thrown off course and now Beau's stuck somewhere he shouldn't be, and a woman and a baby are dead.'

'You know what? The car accident is good for Doyle. If it wasn't for that, Mark would storm into the commune with his crew and Doyle wouldn't have any leverage to stop him. But now he can use you.' He sits forward. 'And we can use Mark's work.'

But I'm not done explaining the laws to him. 'We changed Skye's course, *the* course, some action of the universe. There has

210

to be a reaction to that, equal in force. Do you know what I mean?'

He pulls on the joint, considers the stars.

'Charlie?'

'Because it's not like Doyle cares that some chick had a car crash. But now she's tied to you, and you're tied to Mark. So when you think about it, this all circles around you.'

'No, listen. We – you, mostly – caused something to veer from its natural trajectory. And now we need to do something to put everything back on its right track.' I stop, struck by an idea. 'It's like the cyclone. Some force flicked it in a different direction and now a whole city has been destroyed. Because –' But I don't know who to blame for that, or exactly how it relates to our driving – though I'm sure there's a connection.

This seems to strike a chord with him. 'Karma. There needs to be a right to balance a wrong.'

'Karma? What?' I can't follow our conversation anymore. I don't smoke often and I've never found myself in such a convoluted mental mess. But somewhere in my brain I'm clear on two things: I have to talk my husband out of doing his job, and Dad was right when he said the third law was the one you had to look out for. For every action there's a reaction. Nothing and no one escapes that fact.

CHAPTER TWENTY

Saturday 28 December 1974

Charlie

I sit on a park bench in the treeless playground near Indooroo-pilly Shoppingtown while Abby pushes the twins on swings, first one then the other. She's like a hydraulic machine. One arm in, one arm out. Yelling at them to hold on to the thick chains. Grim.

There's a long gulley in the ground where kids have dragged their feet to slow down. Petey draws a line through it with the front of his thongs, lifting the dust. I can call up the feeling of my own shoes stuttering against the ground, the vibrations going up through my ankles. But the dust – the dust brings other things to mind that I don't want to think about.

To my left, two boys are kicking a football across the dry grass. They're both wearing short shorts and jerseys. One of

212

them, with flame-red hair, leaves his arms hanging in the air after he kicks, and watches the curve of the ball against the sky until it thuds into his friend's arms.

I'm the sole man in the play area. Four or five bored women watch their children, sometimes chatting to one another. A kelpie zips around the climbing frame, which is shaped like the skeleton of a rocket, and has a steep slide coming down from the top. The dog barks anxiously, ears pricked forward, shifting his weight from one front paw to another like a tennis player not sure which way he might need to run after the serve. His small human must be inside the rocket.

A girl in green shorts comes zooming down the slide, her legs held up so her skin doesn't burn on the metal.

A toddler with a mask of freckles lets go of the large spinning disc that serves as a self-propelled merry-go-round. He falls down, face-first.

I watch and smoke and think. We're a hundred feet away from the beast of a shopping centre Abby dragged us through before directing us to the park. Thick white plastic letters shout the name *Westfield* above the glass doors near us.

'This is child abuse, Abby,' I'd said as we walked through the fluoro-lit, noisy passageways past pinball machines, record shops, shoe shops and a giant ball of a fountain with coins littering the tiled bottom. What were people wishing for here? To find a way out of the labyrinthine building without buying some hideous dress or sickly guinea pig?

Abby's desensitised to the horror of the place. Mind you, it was a whole lot cooler in the air-conditioning than out here.

'Can we go now?' I call out, but she shakes her head, still pushing the swings as though it was a full-time job.

Abby had some kind of mental flip-out before we left the house. I thought I'd calmed her down, but evidently not.

'I don't see how I can be a lawyer now.' She'd looked from the sink to me. 'I shouldn't even bother going to uni. I'm compromised.'

I shouldn't have laughed but I did. 'Compromised? Like a spy you mean?'

'No, like a person who's committed a crime that the police know about. Compromised. They could use it against me, against my clients, at any time.'

'But they won't, because we're doing a quid-pro-quo thing.' I'd thought she'd be impressed with me throwing some Latin in, or at least smile at it, but she was genuinely spooked. 'You should do your course like you planned. You'll be a great lawyer, probably help a bunch of people the police don't care about. Anyway, it's Queensland. Everyone's compromised.'

It's three nights till New Year's Eve. Abby says I should go with her and Dad to the street party being organised by Lou, and that Ryan and Sal can come, too. But New Year's in the suburbs doesn't appeal.

Ryan and Sal have been pinging between his family in Hamilton and hers in Noosa since they flew in on Christmas morning. Which could mean he's ready to leave by now. But just in case, I'm stockpiling stories of tedium and small-mindedness for when Ryan starts to romanticise life in Brisbane, as I promised Sal I would.

I'm glad they've arrived in time for New Year's. That means we get to spend two of them together in one year. Back in March, we celebrated Balinese new year, Nyepi, the way the locals do. Apparently it's not universally agreed that ringing in

214

the year involves vats of alcohol and bags of dope to help you forget all the bad decisions, wrong words, wasted days of the past twelve months.

Ketut had invited us to spend Nyepi with his family at Wayan's house. He told us to be there in the morning with plans to spend the night. That seemed like a long New Year's event to me, but they like to celebrate. The previous three days had included statue scrubbing, exorcisms and public displays of handmade effigies – fangs and bug eyes and crazy hair – which were later destroyed in a bonfire.

Ryan, Sal and I showed up at Wayan's in the morning to a full house. Made was there, as well as a bunch of aunts, uncles and children, and Ketut's sister, who always regards me with the disdain owed a foreign moocher. I began the day in good form, asking Wayan how old she was, before taking Ketut aside to find out when we'd start sharing spliffs and drinking beer.

'Not today, friend. Juice and water. We stay indoors, thinking and resting.'

So Ryan, Sal and I sat on chairs, lay on day beds and slept, which would've been fine except we'd only woken up a short while before. We talked about leaving. But Ketut explained the whole island was closed down – no shops or bars open, nobody wandering about – and roving police would be enforcing that, so we agreed to stay.

Since Wayan was there I figured at least we wouldn't go hungry. That is, until I noticed she wasn't occupying her usual position in the kitchen but instead lying on a mat, with two small sleeping children wrapped around her.

'Should we help Wayan with lunch?' I asked Ketut. 'Or has she made it already?'

'Oh man, I'm sorry. No food till tomorrow either.'

On the upside, Sal was there, too. And sex, like food, alcohol and drugs, was verboten, so Ryan wouldn't be hiding her away in one of the bedrooms for the day.

Since Ryan and I are both prone to cabin fever, we sampled different locations around Wayan's house, peeking out windows when we could get away with it. The day was sunny with a good breeze, and it seemed a waste not to be surfing.

'What are we doing here?' Ryan asked, as we lay on our backs in the bathroom. This room was part of the house so we were playing by the rules, but the lack of a roof allowed us to gaze up at the sky.

'You heard what Ketut said. We'd have to stay indoors even if we were at our own place.'

'I mean Bali. What are we doing in Bali?'

Ryan's black periods never last long, and his moodiness doesn't normally bother me too much. But since I had an empty stomach and nowhere to run, I had limited patience. 'Try to enjoy life, Ryan. Give it a shot.'

He turned his head towards me. 'That's all we do, enjoy ourselves. Get stoned and surf, junk up paradise. It's not ours, man, none of this.'

Again with the misery, the guilt. 'We're running a restaurant, and people love it. And we're not junking up anything. We're living, Ryan, and you're turning what could be the most incredible life into a goddamn endless whinge.'

His discontent troubled me, not because I was concerned for his peace of mind – like I said, he can be a bit Eeyore – but because having Ryan here was part of my Bali experience.

Without Ryan, there was no Sal. And while I wouldn't say it out loud, I didn't want to be here without her.

Wayan walked into the bathroom through the batik curtains that served as a door, regarding us with her usual irritation. She began tearing leaves from a large plant growing in a pot in the corner, to weave into one of her daily offerings boxes.

'Too much talking,' she said. 'Time for thinking.'

'Too much thinking in our quarter, Wayan. Anything different today?' I sat up and pointed at the leaves.

'Same but more.'

Wayan's offerings consistently included cut fruit, uncooked rice, betel nuts, flowers and incense, all of which struck me as reasonable gifts, but on occasion she also included Camel cigarettes.

'More cigarettes?' I asked. Once she left the room I'd nick one.

'Good for demons,' she said. 'Keeps them happy.'

'Hear that, Ryan? Need to keep your demons happy. Fed and fagged.'

I shouldn't have joked around with his dissatisfaction. He was more serious than I'd known. And I actually believe you need to pay attention to demons.

'No, no.' Petey is shouting at Abby as she holds him around the belly and pulls him off another child. The other boy has thrown himself on top of a yellow metal tip truck and is hugging it. Abby hauls Petey over to me and drops him on the bench by my side.

'Take him please. He's being a monster.'

He sits next to me, arms crossed, humphing.

'Are you really a monster?' I ask. 'Did you eat one of the other kids?'

He fights a smile.

'Did you breathe fire? That'd show him.'

'Yeah.'

'Is it about that truck? You feel like it should be yours?' Petey looks at me wide-eyed. 'I know things, buddy. I have powers.' He laughs at me. Not even a little kid believes that. He slides off the bench and runs to the climbing frame.

I watch him play, spread my arms wide across the top of the bench to let some air into my sweaty pits. I think I should tell Ryan and Sal about the accident. Because they're my friends, and it *was* an accident. They'll have some ideas about what to do next, especially how to handle the cops. And I want to start out both my new years with some kind of plan about how to move past this.

When we're back at the house, Abby puts the twins down for a nap. Sarah sits cross-legged on the living-room floor to watch TV.

'I'm catching up with Ryan and Sal today,' I tell Abby. She's changed into old shorts and a ratty t-shirt in preparation for washing something in this forever-spotless house. 'They're going to swing by in about an hour.'

She's pulling her hair into a ponytail but stops mid-job. 'You should've told me before. I need to –'

'Need to what?' I watch her. She's been awkward around Ryan and Sal since uni. A crush on Ryan – that'd been obvious, as had his disinterest in her. But her attitude to Sal? Some soup of jealousy about Sal's looks and ease, and a need for her approval. Which almost nobody gets, especially not women. Sal doesn't have many female friends, in Brisbane or Bali, but there are a hundred men who'd stand in front of a moving train for her. There's no way Sal will ever see my sister as her equal. And the fact Abby kept up the cloying routine with both of them after Sal and Ryan were a couple and she became a mother is . . . it lacks a little dignity. I'd told Ryan to beep his horn, not to come up.

'Abby, they're dropping by to give me a lift to the pub. It's no big deal.'

She ignores me, and heads down the hallway.

I remember I haven't had lunch. I open the fridge door and peruse my options. A head of lettuce, a carton of eggs, some jam, half a grapefruit, a jar of pickles, leftover sausages and chicken, and a box of Mateus. Slim pickings. Abby comes into the kitchen wearing a lime-green halter-neck dress and yellow shoes.

'Are you going out, too?'

'No,' she snaps. 'Why? Do you want me to be gone when they get here?'

I'm about to tell her they're not coming inside when I hear the car horn. It sounds like some old-guy jazz instrument; Ryan will be driving his dad's Mercedes. I glance at my watch: they're early. Ryan's parents must really be shitting Sal. Late is her usual M.O.

'That's them. I'll see you later.'

'They don't want to have a quick drink here, a bite to eat?'

'I told you, we're going to the pub. Is this –' I point at her latest outfit – 'is this for their benefit?'

'Shut up.' She blushes and leaves the kitchen.

CHAPTER TWENTY-ONE

Sunday 29 December 1974

Charlie

Ryan, Sal and I walk into the beer garden entrance of the Royal Exchange. It's five-thirty on a hot afternoon so the pub is crowded for the Sunday session, filled with happy drinkers done with weekend chores, students, packs of kids running around and dogs. The music is pumping – Sherbet's 'Slipstream' when we walk in – and people are smiling, holding glasses, stubbies, cans, cigarettes. I hear snatches of upbeat conversation: 'Come here you big poofter!', 'Bloody oath I am', 'Fourteen, mate. That's close enough to legal.' I'm glad we three are back together again, and in a place we've spent so many days and nights, but I'm worried about taking Ryan somewhere fun. I reckon I can enjoy myself without losing perspective, but a good afternoon at the RE might fuel his romantic notions about moving back.

Ryan goes inside to the bar to get us a jug of beer while Sal and I scout for a table under the fig tree, our preferred spot. I'm about to ask her what kind of mood Ryan's been in since they arrived when I instead freeze on the spot. People are moving about on the dirt floor, obscuring my line of sight, so it's only a glimpse at first. I tell myself I'm being paranoid, that it can't be, wouldn't be. Sal wanders away, and I wait until I get a good look. Then I'm certain. It's Finn.

He's leaning against a brick wall, talking to a hefty, heavily bearded man wearing an unzipped leather vest and patched jeans. My first thought is that Finn is following me. He must have arrived here minutes before us and ducked into the pub while we parked. Question is whether he's here to punish me for trying to take Beau, or if Doyle sent him to keep an eye on who I talk to. I try to think of an excuse to get Ryan and Sal out of here, then think about whether, instead, I can get into the bar unseen and tell Ryan I have to leave on my own. Family emergency or something. Finn isn't looking my way so maybe I should just go, and explain myself to my friends later.

Sal calls out to me that she's found an empty table, then raises one arm to signal to Ryan also, who's walking our way, holding a full jug and glasses. Three or four men, Finn included, flick their eyes to watch her with undisguised appreciation. And in a snap I realise that this place is so public, so crowded, that it's my safest option. Finn won't do anything to me with this many witnesses around. My best bet is to sit down and wait him out.

But before I can join Sal at the table, she walks away from it, squealing. 'Oh my God!' And then she is throwing her arms around Finn.

221

I stand back from them, as though I'm watching a scene in a film. The sleeves of Sal's blouse slide back to her shoulders, exposing her tanned arms and jangle of silver bracelets. She lifts her head to Finn and he kisses her full on the lips, pulls her close and puts his hand on her ass. Her headscarf drops to the ground. Sal puts her arm around Finn's waist.

'Ryan, look who's here!' She's flushed with joy, her voice high.

Finn makes a mock salute at Ryan.

'Finn, my man!'

It's when Ryan deposits the glasses and jug on our table that Finn notices me, standing behind a chair.

'You've got to be kidding,' he says.

I raise my eyebrows. 'Thought I wouldn't notice you?'

He seems even more of a mountain man here in a city beer garden, his beard wild, skin brown, short-sleeved shirt open. He locks eyes with me. 'Are you following me, Water Rat?'

'You know each other?' Ryan asks as Finn lets go of Sal to greet him, grabbing his arm and thumping him on the back.

'Could say that. I think your man here is stalking me.'

'Believe me, the last thing I want to do is follow you around. I came here for a drink with my friends. It's you who –' But I'm not sure what's going on.

Sal and Ryan seem confused. Neither Finn nor I makes a move to explain our animosity. I'm worried he'll tell them Dad and I came to the commune to take his son. And maybe Finn's reluctant to explain why the mother of his child ran off and hooked up with my dad. We stand in uncomfortable silence until Ryan speaks. 'So, you're in Brisbane? Thought you'd moved to the coast.' He pours beers for us three, tops up Finn's.

222

'I'm down here for the day. What about you two? Where're you living?' He's speaking to Ryan, but still glaring at me. I want to ask how he knows Ryan and Sal. He wasn't at uni with us; I never saw him at any parties or marches.

'We moved to Bali,' Sal says.

'Oh yeah? I hear it's incredible there,' he says. 'You always did like sunset on the beach, huh?' How is Ryan putting up with these two flirting so hard right in front of him?

'Sunsets there are amazing,' she smiles. 'Everything they say about Bali is true.'

'Great surf and even better weed?'

'And the people, my god.' She puts one hand to her chest. 'They're beautiful.'

'Paradise lost, that's what it is,' Ryan says. 'It was perfect until we showed up. Place is infested with tourists now.'

'Don't start,' I say.

'Which is why we're back,' Sal says. 'We've been looking around Brisbane for a house, somewhere near the river.'

I frown at her. This is news to me, big news. And she's said it in such a cavalier way. But Sal's attention is entirely on Finn, as though she's in the presence of a rock star.

'So how are you doing, man?' Ryan says. 'It's been years. What do you do for a crust nowadays?' He moves himself around to break Finn's gaze on me.

'Bit of this, bit of that.' Finn grins at them. I gulp down my beer. *Bit of beating up women*, I think. *Bit of growing dope for the cops, lording it over little kids. Bit of being a cult leader. Bit of threatening Charlie and his dad. The usual.* My snort of contempt goes ignored.

223

'Take a load off,' Ryan says, pointing at a chair. 'We've got a lot to catch up on.'

Sal is rubbing Finn's back. 'So good to see you, babe,' she says.

'How *do* you three know each other?' I ask. I can't hold it in any longer. They look at me as if I'd spoken German, or Dog.

But before anyone answers, Finn's leather-vest-wearing friend pushes his way through and whispers in his ear.

While they're talking, Ryan says to me: 'I was going to ask you the same thing. How do you know Finn?'

'And why are you being such a dick to him?' Sal adds.

Finn turns away from his friend to address Ryan and Sal. 'Got to finish something. Good to see you.'

'Sure, yeah,' Ryan says.

He kisses Sal. 'Where can I find you guys?'

Ryan reaches into his jeans pocket and pulls out a receipt. 'Pen?' he asks me.

I dig into my canvas rucksack and hand him a biro.

He rests the paper on the table between wet coasters. 'This is our number. We're mostly staying with my folks. And when we leave, they'll know where we are.'

Finn takes the paper. 'Cool. I'll be back this way in a few months, probably.' He slaps Ryan on the back. 'Good to see you.' Kisses Sal. 'Spunk.' He looks at me and shakes his head.

I watch Finn go inside the bar. I can still see the top of his head but he's well out of earshot. Sal stands behind Ryan's chair and hugs him from behind, resting her head atop his. They lift their eyes in sync, a two-headed creature regarding me thoughtfully.

'Atherton,' Ryan says. 'Remember how Sal and I took a semester off in third year and lived up north? We stayed in this wild house at the top of a hill, with a river running next to it and this incredible view across a valley. A mattress floor in the living room, bunch of musicians, chickens and goats free-ranging.' He waits for me to indicate I remember hearing about any of this.

'Yeah, vaguely,' I say.

'That was Finn's place.'

'Heaven,' Sal says. 'We should've stayed longer. That seed bread Lucy used to make?'

Ryan smiles widely.

'So you'd have met his girlfriend, Skye?' I ask.

'Sure,' Ryan says as Sal sits beside him. 'We know Skye, and her baby, Beau. You loved that kid, didn't you?'

Sal coos. 'My little lamb.'

'Haven't heard from Skye in years,' Ryan says. 'Are they still together? I should've asked about her.' He twists around in his seat to see if Finn is still here.

I take a mouthful of beer. 'Don't ask him about Skye.'

'They broke up?' he asks.

Of all the sick twists of fate. 'Skye was living with my dad.'

'What? Living with, as in –?' Sal wrinkles her nose. 'Ew.'

'My dad treated her way better than that scumbag.'

'Honestly, Charlie, what's with the aggression?' Sal says.

'Skye and my dad were engaged. She was pregnant.' I look from Ryan to Sal. They aren't making the connection. '*Was*. I told you about the woman who had the car accident, the one who was living with my dad.'

'That was Skye?' Sal asks. 'Skye's dead?'

Ryan moans. 'No.'

Maybe it was a good thing Finn showed up before I had a chance to tell them the whole truth. But if they see Finn again, he might tell them Dad and I tried to kidnap Beau, and I'm not certain now how they'll take that. I want to keep them firmly in my corner.

'Finn used to beat her up,' I say.

Ryan scowls at me. 'Why would you think that? Did Skye say that?'

'That's why Skye left him and ended up with my dad. Finn was hitting her.'

'He'd never,' Sal says. 'I can't believe she'd even say that.'

'You don't know the whole story,' Ryan says. 'They had an intense thing going on – mutually intense.'

'She got pregnant really young. She more or less trapped him,' Sal says. 'We loved her, but –' She lifts one shoulder in a shrug.

'She was kind of hysterical, Charlie,' Ryan says. 'Sort of crazy.'

Sal agrees. 'Didn't you get that vibe?'

I'm dumbfounded by what I'm hearing. 'Whoa, she's dead, guys. This is not cool. And from everything I know, Skye was the victim of the story. There's no version of crazy that makes it okay –'

'Everything you know?' Ryan says. 'You never met her?'

Sal interrupts us. 'Wait, does Finn know?'

'That she's dead? Yeah, he knows. You didn't see how devastated he was? How he was mourning? Or were you distracted by his grope?'

Sal flicks me on the shoulder. She turns to Ryan. 'I'm going to see if I can talk him into staying in town a while longer. We can all go back to Addison Street, crash there.'

Ryan nods. 'I've got nothing against your dad, Charlie, but him and Skye? I don't know, man.'

I don't want to have this discussion. I watch Sal walk through the crowd and inside the pub. I look at the head-high wall of cream and steel-blue tiles, the rust-coloured wall above them. I see a long-haired blond surfie with his back against the tiles, blowing smoke over the head of a girl dressed like Hiawatha before moving in to kiss her. A swarthy guy standing next to the jukebox watches them like he's at the drive-in. Finn smiles as Sal walks towards him.

'Ryan, how can you think it was okay for Finn to hit Skye?'

'I don't think that's okay. I don't think it ever happened. They argued a lot. But I never saw him do anything remotely physical. You might want to think about why your dad's telling you that. Sounds like a classic power move.'

This, like 'Bali is ruined', is one of Ryan's current obsessions. He's become a broken record about it. His theory, sparked by something he read, is that every interaction between people is a power play, sometimes subtle, sometimes unrecognised – but everything is about power. It's a depressing way of seeing the world.

Sal calls out from the doorway. 'Ryan, our little lamb is here.' She stands on the top step next to Finn and has her hand on Beau's shoulder. He's wearing denim shorts, a Milo t-shirt and thongs that are at least a size too big for him, and his hair sticks out awkwardly over his ears. It's all I can do to stop myself from jumping up and throwing Beau out of their reach, away from all of us.

As Sal, Finn and Beau walk towards our table, I notice that the boy is staring at me with a look of worry: I'm the dangerous one, I realise, the one who came to kidnap him.

'Let's go back to the house,' Sal says once they reach us and Ryan has greeted Beau. 'Finn says he can hang out a while.' She puts her hand on Finn's arm. 'We had no idea you'd been through such a terrible time, babe.'

Beau stands next to Sal, holding her hand.

'Wait, where was Beau while you were talking with us?' I ask Finn.

Finn cocks his head in the direction of the street. 'Outside, playing. Not that it's any of your business.'

Beau lifts up a calico bag, unsure whether he's supposed to offer evidence. He looks to his father for guidance but Finn has fixed his eyes on me again so Beau slowly drops his arm back to his side.

Ryan, Sal, Finn and I sit on the veranda of a run-down Queenslander on Addison Street. The house belongs to Sal's cousin Colleen, a nurse, who has gone to work a night shift.

We occupy a lumpy armchair apiece, with a potted umbrella tree standing by the front door, parched. The neighbour's tabby cat slinks along the top of the crusty wooden railing and settles in the shadows offered by an overgrown jasmine vine. I feel the warm boards under my feet, the layer of grit sticking to my soles. I'm here because I'm anxious about the conversations that might happen in my absence. Otherwise there is no way I'd want to spend another second in Finn's company.

There's still enough light in the sky to watch fruit bats flap towards the banana groves. Nearby streetlights jerk awake. Sal has put a radio on the floor beside me, the volume on low because Beau is sleeping on Colleen's bed. I smoke a spliff and munch on salt-and-vinegar chips, listen to 4BC.

Finn agrees with Sal that it's a good thing her cousin moved to Red Hill and found this house on stilts with its sloping backyard, its mango and avocado trees and out-of-the-country landlord. They talk about the house they lived in with Skye, when Beau was a baby. The three of them share memories of Skye. Ryan cries. Sal doesn't. I watch Finn's face for any sign he knows the police suspect Abby and me, but I see nothing to suggest he does, and neither of us mentions Roberts or Doyle. No one mentions my dad.

Cars roll along the road below us, gathering speed as they travel down the hill, spraying water when they hit the puddle of sludge that's formed in a dip. A dog howls. I exhale and watch the smoke curl and rise against the darkening sky, up and then gone, motion without consequence. I make a note to tell Abby. Then think about how many cigarettes it would take to cause air pollution.

There's a knot in my gut from listening to their affectionate stories about Skye (crazy, evidently, but loved), from waiting to hear my dad's name, from knowing that Beau is only a few walls away, from being unsure if Finn knows anything or every-thing or nothing. Separate from the accident, Finn has to be angry that I tried to take his son but he says nothing, doesn't mention it aside from calling me Water Rat. His calmness is freaking me out.

We need food. Around nine o'clock, Ryan drives with Sal to Milton Road to get hamburgers. Ryan's the only one of us remotely straight enough to drive, doesn't see why that means he should have to go on his own, and the decision about who stays, who goes is arrived at silently, poker faces all round. Sal's already made it clear that I'm bugging her, and while Ryan would never admit it, leaving Sal alone with Finn is asking for trouble. And Finn's not going anywhere.

So here I am with Finn. It's not exactly comfortable but what's he going to do? I've been hit before and survived, and he doesn't have his rifle. I've seen curlier situations. My fear lifts a little more with each mouthful of beer, each breath of dope, and I find myself – ludicrously – wanting to win him over. I'm not sure if everything I've heard about him is true. It's not like Ryan to misjudge someone that badly, whereas my dad and I haven't always agreed about people.

I hold the longneck out and tilt it towards Finn. 'Top up?' He nods, lifts his empty glass.

Is it possible my father lied to me, or that Skye lied to him? Finn's a dope grower, but I have no problem with that. In bed with the cops, but sometimes bad things happen to good dope suppliers, so I can excuse that, too. And his aggression towards me was to protect Beau from would-be kidnappers. That's more than reasonable behaviour – it's what a responsible father would do. And it wasn't him who blurted out news of Skye's death. Maybe Finn had been shielding Beau from that until he could break it to him gently. Also, I can't think of a single time either Ryan or Sal has expressed any tolerance for violence, so . . . My head is spinning.

Finn stretches his legs out, sinks further in the chair, then says: 'I'm a little curious how you came to be at my farm.'

A fair question. 'My dad promised Skye he'd make sure Beau was okay. And he did, so we won't be back. Seems like he has friends, lots of space to run around.'

'You came to take him. But I asked how, not why. Arcadia's way off the beaten track. And we value our privacy, which you and your father violated. So I'm wondering how that happened, how you found us. Did Skye tell your old man where we were?'

'Guess so.'

He turns his head my way and raises his eyebrows. 'And have you shared that information with anybody else? At a guess?'

'Absolutely not.' I shake my head vigorously. 'I wouldn't do that.' Ah, perhaps Doyle has sent him after all, to find out what I've told Mark, if I'm going to lead him to the commune.

Finn speaks slowly. 'So what exactly is your story? Can't figure you out. A third wheel. Do anything for Daddy's approval. Living with your sister. You don't strike me as a halfwit but that's some stunted life you've got going.'

I frown. 'Not stunted. What you're seeing now is an aberration, temporary. In a few weeks I'm heading back to Bali.'

'On your own, by the sounds of it.'

I'd forgotten for a moment what Sal had said at the RE. Surely she's only looking at houses to keep Ryan happy.

'Sal and I are walking Ryan through a bit of a meltdown. We'll be back in Bali before the end of January. You'll see.'

He smirks. '"We". She's out of your reach, Water Rat. I know that woman, and you are not enough man for her.'

'She's not in or out of my reach. We're friends, the three of us,' I say. 'You don't get it.'

'Think I do.'

How many beers have I had? How many spliffs have we shared? My words are chewy in my mouth. My head moves about like a ball on a spring. 'So the rifle,' I say. 'That was unexpected.'

'Feral pigs.'

'Right. Right.' I stare out at the night sky. 'Ryan said you and Skye had something intense going on. But you know, that doesn't explain her running away without Beau. I mean, she kept trying to get him back, so it's not like she didn't want him. She told my dad you had a bit of a temper, said a bunch of stuff about her that wasn't true.'

He squints as if he hadn't seen me until now, or isn't quite sure what to make of me. 'What happened between me and Skye is none of your goddamn business.'

'Well it sort of is, since she was about to marry my dad. And the baby would've been my half-brother or sister, technically. So Beau would be something to me, too, I guess. No. Hang on.'

'She was pregnant?' he says.

Why wouldn't the police have told him that?

'Pregnant with your dad?' he asks. 'Your twice-her-age dad?'

'He loved her. She left you, chose him. So that's . . .'

'Pregnant.' He pauses. 'Let me ask you something: were you with your dad when she had the crash? The police told me she was alone. But where were you, Water Rat?' The air takes on a chill. His voice has a snarl in it now.

'First I heard about it was the morning we got to the farm and some cop was telling Dad.'

'Who's we?'

'Abby, my sister. We drove there together.'

'Morning after the crash. Didn't you say he's near Chinchilla? You must've left Brisbane at the crack of dawn.'

I reach for my glass but it's empty. I can't believe I told him earlier where Dad's farm is, but I did. Stupid. Tried to make him laugh at my description of the turkeys. 'I don't know exactly what time we got there. Doesn't matter anyhow. I didn't know about Skye until then, is what I'm saying.'

He twists in his seat to face me. 'She was a good driver, cautious. Like, boringly cautious.'

'Maybe there was something wrong with the engine. Or there was a kangaroo. Or she'd gone into labour.' I think I'm talking faster than normal, but I can't be sure. 'Maybe she fell asleep.'

He waits a moment before replying. 'Maybe.'

A car pulls up outside the house and parks on the gravel driveway. I hear the slam of doors, then Ryan talking to Sal.

Finn speaks in a low voice. 'It's been a real treat having this chat. But if you or your father come near my farm again I will break you.'

CHAPTER TWENTY-TWO

Monday 30 December 1974

Charlie

I stand next to Dad on the veranda, in the morning shade, drinking black coffee, giving him an edited version of what I told Abby in full about my evening. I want him only to know I saw Beau and that he's okay. And that 'rescuing' him is entirely off the table.

Ten feet away from us, perched on a thick branch, a kookaburra tilts its head from one side to the other as it considers whether to leave the safety of the gum tree to eat the shreds of ham Dad put on the wooden balustrade, shreds that are darkening and warping in the heat. It isn't far for him to come: the tree almost touches the railing, so he could inch his way along and get to the meat in a small jump. But he keeps his distance.

'Did you wear that?' Dad points to my t-shirt. It's pale blue, with a drawing of two of those big-headed, tiny-body nude

234

kids, smiling and hugging, the words *Save Water. Shower with a Friend.*

'No, why?'

'Bloody ridiculous,' he says. 'You know, if you'd called me from the pub I could've come down.'

'To get Beau?'

'That didn't occur to you?'

'It's still kidnapping. And Finn will know it's you or me if Beau goes missing, and he'll come take him back – legally. How would that drama be good for Beau?'

Dad stares at me, a hard, unwavering stare that makes my gut clench. He really hates being told he's wrong.

I hear a screech of tyres. A green ute flings around the corner into Abby's street and the driver stops suddenly, right in the middle of Abby's driveway. A woman gets out of the ute.

'It's the chick from the commune.'

'Maria,' Dad says.

She's more tanned than I'd noticed in the half-light of our failed rescue, lean and muscled. Not as ironman as Finn but jeez, they must log a lot of hours in those fields. She walks to the passenger's side and opens the door. Beau clambers out.

'What?' I spook the kookaburra: it hits a brace of leaves and flaps madly to keep its balance. I look at Dad, who's smiling as if he's somehow manufactured this situation, as if Beau's presence here is proving him right.

We head downstairs and open the front door. Maria nods a hello, keeps one hand protectively on Beau's shoulder. I peer inside the ute but Finn isn't there.

'How'd you know where I was?' Dad asks.

'Ryan and Sal, Dad,' I say.

'Hello, young man,' Dad speaks to Beau. 'I'm sorry we scared you when we first met. And I am very sorry about your mother. She was a special lady and I know she loved you.'

Beau says nothing. His attention is not on my father or me. He's peering inside the house, letting his eyes roam from one object to the next. He looks at the landscape painting – parched bushland at dusk, a solitary Aboriginal man wearing a loincloth standing stork-like on one leg, holding a spear – that hangs over a brown pot holding dried pussy willows, smiles when he sees Woof padding down the stairs. I remember Beau lives in a teepee, and wonder how many houses he's been in, and if they're usually as run-down as Sal's cousin's place.

'Car's roasting,' Maria says. 'Beau and I could use a drink.'

We stand aside to let them come in as Woof licks Beau's hand, sniffs Maria's leg and wags his tail, greeting them altogether more affably than we have.

Once we're in the kitchen, Beau wriggles himself onto one of the stools and sits on the edge of the brown vinyl cushion. Woof stands on his hind legs, his front paws on Beau's bare thighs. Maria stands next to the counter, scanning the room, smiling at something she doesn't share with us. 'Nice place.'

'Yes,' Dad says.

'Beau, do you want some cordial?' I ask. 'Lemonade, chocolate milk?'

'He doesn't drink that sugary stuff,' Maria says. 'Juice or water. Doubt you have soy milk.'

'You doubt correct. What would you like, buddy?'

'Juice please,' Beau says. He sounds relaxed, his voice peppy and light. It doesn't seem interesting to him that he saw me last night, or even at the commune. I'm just another grown-up now, hanging around with the other boring grown-ups.

'Make it two,' Maria says. 'Since you're offering. Is your sister home?'

Beau scratches behind Woof's ear and looks out the back door at the trampoline.

'Just us here,' Dad says.

'Shame. It's her I'm after. Wanted to meet the adult of the house.'

Dad bristles. 'Now listen –'

'Spare me. You clowns aren't running any of this.' She looks around the kitchen, which is well equipped, spotless, and at the neat line of sandshoes and thongs on the swept back porch.

Beau drinks most of his apple juice in one go, then wipes his arm across his mouth.

'Go play,' Maria says to him. Beau shakes his head. 'Go on,' she says, gentle but firm.

'Why don't you take him out to the trampoline, Charlie?' Dad says. 'Seems like that might be of some interest.'

'Yes please.' Beau slides off the stool.

'Hold it till I come back. I need to hear this, too,' I say to Maria. Why would she be here after Finn told me, just last night, to stay away from his commune – and, by obvious extension, Beau? Maybe she's been sent to hit us up for money.

I come around the bench and touch Beau lightly on the head. 'You have your mother's hair. Bet you hear that a lot.'

The instant the words leave my mouth I stop – stop moving, stop breathing. Then I suddenly suck in air, as though my body wants to vacuum the words right back inside me. Beau has gone outside, is on the trampoline. I flick my eyes to my father.

'How do you know what Skye's hair looked like?' Dad says.

'A photo,' I say. My heart beats double time.

'You've got a photo of Skye?' Maria takes an apple from the fruit bowl.

'There are no photos,' my father says. His voice is a low rumble. 'How do you know what her hair looked like?'

I stand in the doorway, frozen.

'Can we talk about her *son* please? I don't have all day,' Maria says, polishing the apple on her shirt. 'She did have good hair, though.'

Surely Dad won't press the issue in front of Maria.

'Things are going down at the commune,' she says. 'Finn wants Beau to be somewhere else for a while. Not today, but soon. We figured since you were so desperate to have him he could stay here, have your daughter take care of him. He said the way Charlie described her last night made her sound super straight. And that's what Beau needs, until we get ourselves sorted again. He wanted me to check the house though, make sure it was a legit family place.' She points her apple at me. 'But your stuck-up friends Ryan and . . . whoever his bitch girl-friend is . . . you can't say anything to them. I don't trust them to stay quiet. That's not from Finn, that's from me, okay?'

Dad hasn't taken his eyes off me. Maria seems blind to what's happening in front of her. She eats her apple, watches Beau through the glass. I hear the squeak of trampoline springs, and Woof barking encouragement.

'So,' she says, 'the house looks like a house should. I'll tell Finn it'll do.'

Dad turns his glare on Maria. 'Is this some game, some trap you and Finn have cooked up? Drop the boy here then call the police and say we took him?'

'No. We want to find Beau a safe place *away* from the –' She frowns. 'Look, shit's about to get too heavy to have the kids around. Finn's not the world's best father but he doesn't want Beau getting hurt.' She stands up. 'Maybe this was a mistake. He thought you'd be pleased about it.'

'We'll take care of the boy,' Dad says. 'Keep him away from your train wreck. You can go now. I'll explain to him.'

'I'm not leaving him here today. I said *soon*.' Maria rolls her eyes. 'I can see your daughter is the details person.'

'Do what you need to. We'll be here,' Dad says.

Maria picks her backpack up off the floor. 'Beau,' she calls out. 'Time to go, buddy.'

Beau runs into the room, Woof at his heels. 'Thanks for the juice.' He offers us a small, odd wave.

And then Dad and I are alone.

'How do you know what her hair looked like?' He narrows his eyes at me. 'There's no photograph.'

'Well, it's nothing like Finn's hair so it must be like hers.' I want to run.

'Don't screw with me.'

'People talk about things when you're not around, Dad. I asked about her at the funeral. Donna told me –'

'Bullshit. You've seen her.'

I don't reply but I know he catches the anxious dart of my eyes, the flash of panic. 'You were at the car, weren't you? You took her out.'

He reaches across, grabs a fistful of my t-shirt and yanks me closer. I stumble, caught off-guard. 'Didn't you?' He spits the words out. 'Answer me!'

He's not as strong as when he was young, but my father can still punch. And though I push him away, and duck to avoid his swings, I'm not quick enough. He slams his fist into my jaw with the force of a twenty-year-old. The blow sends vibrations up through my head. He shoves me against the closest wall.

I shove him hard and he falls back against the pantry door. I run out of the room, down the stairs and onto the street. I keep running.

CHAPTER TWENTY-THREE

Monday 30 December 1974

Abby

I pull into the carport and beep the horn. Mark won't be home yet – he's helping Geoff build a pergola – but Dad or Charlie might be here to help me get Sarah, the twins and the groceries into the house. Nobody responds to my beeping.

'Bugger.'

'Bugger,' Sarah echoes.

'Don't say that.' I wind my window up, sling my handbag over my shoulder. 'Out you pop.'

By the time I get to Sarah's door it's still closed, though I can see her trying to push it open. I lift her out and heave the twins one by one onto the cool shaded concrete, touching my palm to it for quick relief from the relentless heat of the day.

'Go see if anyone's inside, Sar. Tell them Mum needs a hand.'

Putting three-year-olds down in an open space is asking for trouble. Joanne walks down the steep driveway; Petey heads to the hot front grill of the car.

'For the love of –' I scoop up Joanne while yelling to Petey, 'Don't touch the car. It's hot. Hot.' I hear a small howl that builds to a scream before I can get to him. I pick him up so I have a twin dangled under each arm, my handbag pushing into my hip. They're both whining, and squirming like puppies. 'Stop, please, both of you.'

Sarah appears at the boot of the car with Dad.

'Great. I have a car full of food. Can you get the bags on the front seat?'

'Sarah, take the little ones inside. I need to talk to Mum.'

'Dad, can it wait? I've got ice cream –' But I stop speaking when I see the fierce expression on Dad's face.

Sarah, Petey and Joanne make a game of walking up the stairs to the front door, the girls holding hands and all three jumping when they reach each tread.

Dad takes a step closer to me. 'Did you meet her some-where, you and your brother?'

'Who?' Though I know who he means, the instant he says it.

'How would Charlie know what Skye's hair looked like?'

I am flustered, flummoxed. What has Charlie said? I glance behind Dad to see if Charlie is nearby. 'Well, I don't think he does. Why would you ask that?' I pull my bag higher onto my shoulder. 'Can I bring in the food?'

'Forget the bloody food. Charlie said Beau had Skye's hair. You were there that night, weren't you? Pulled her body out of the car and left her.' He points at me with a shaking finger. 'That's what happened, isn't it?'

'No, Dad, we – no.' Where is Charlie?

'Beau was here. Charlie said to him, you have your mother's hair. Your *mother's hair*.' Dad stands an inch away from me, fire in his eyes.

'Beau was here?'

'How could you?' he bellows. He is breathing heavily, hands on his hips, glowering at me. 'You get her out and then, what, you drive off? What possessed you?'

My lips tremble but no words come.

'Is that what happened? Say something.'

'I tried to move her up to the road. But she was so heavy, and –'

'Pregnant, she was pregnant! *Christ*, Abigail. I –' He makes a gesture as if to erase me, then turns away. He takes the sleeper stairs two at a time and I scurry to catch up with him as he storms inside, down the hall and to his room. As I pass the kitchen I see the children are outside. Sarah is standing on a wobbly chair so she can swing on the Hills hoist. The twins are watching, will want to try, she'll egg them on, and while none of this should be ignored, I have to ignore it. I hurry to the doorway of the spare room and watch my father hurl his suitcase onto the bed and fling the top back. He grabs his shoes, pyjamas and the stack of books beside his bed and throws them in.

'Dad, we didn't mean to. It was an accident. Where is Charlie?' Where *for the love of God* is Charlie?

He turns. 'You didn't *mean* to?'

The air rushes out of my chest so I cave in on myself. 'Dad, I'm sorry. So, so sorry.'

'You caused this?' He yells with such ferocity I shrink backwards out of the doorway. 'You did this to her?' He walks towards me.

'I wasn't – I'm not saying I was blameless. It was an accident, a terrible accident. And the instant her car hit the tree, she was dead. There was nothing we could do.' Before I can decide whether to tell him that Charlie was driving, drunk on beer I'd bought, that we were both asleep, before I can decide whether throwing my brother between my father and me is shameful and selfish, before I can think through whether that would make the slightest difference to my father's rage and pain, before any of this mad mental dust can settle or form coherent thoughts, my father lurches forward and slaps me across the face. I had no idea a hit could hurt so much.

I run to the backyard. Where else can I go? I sit on the edge of the sandpit with my arms folded tight across the top of my knees, shaking, staring at the door and praying that Dad won't yell at me or hit me again with the children nearby. I watch as Petey throws a bucketful of sand out of the sandpit and onto the grass, and waits for my usual admonishments. I hold out my arms. 'Give me a hug.' He shakes his head.

I try not to panic. I drop my head onto my folded arms, ignore my stinging cheek, stare at the ground through my legs and try to breathe. Just breathe. He's not coming outside. If he was going to follow me he would have by now. I concentrate on the ants crawling across the sand in the triangle of space beneath me. I smell my coffee-scented breath and feel the sun burn through my shirt. Anything not to think.

I hear footsteps on the porch. I'm not sure how long I've been sitting here. I may have even slept or passed out. It feels as though time has somehow moved on without me. I want to look up and see if the children are still in the sandpit – there's no sign of them in my small range of vision – but if it's Dad on the porch I don't dare move.

'Hey, hi everyone.'

'Mark,' I say in a sob and lift my head up.

'Mummy's sad,' Sarah says. 'Is dinner soon?'

'Whoa,' Mark says. 'What's going on?' He pulls me up and shepherds me to the wooden bench near the barbecue, which is still close enough for the children to hear, so I point to the house. 'Inside.'

'Is this something you want John to hear?'

'Is he still here?'

'Where else would he be? Abby?'

We sit. He rubs my back the same way I rub Sarah's back when she can't sleep. I need his comfort, and I know once I tell him the truth he'll take it away from me.

'I don't want to talk right now. And the kids are hungry, so –'

'Why did you ask me if John was here? Did you have an argument?' I should've known my deflection wouldn't work. Mark won't be denied information.

'It's nothing.'

He wraps his arms around me. I let myself soften into him.

'Abby?' He lifts my head off his chest. 'Tell me.'

Before I can speak, Dad is at the back door, calling to the children.

'John,' Mark says. 'What –?'

My father cuts off the question. 'Only the kids. I don't want a bar of you two.'

Mark screws his face into a frown. 'Maybe open a bag of chips for them.'

I am mortified. How can it be that this is how I have to tell Mark?

'I've called a taxi to take me to the bus station. Kids, come inside. Pop has to leave. I want to say goodbye.'

'Why?' Sarah says.

'Do it, Sarah,' I say.

'John, it's the night before New Year's Eve,' Mark says. 'Loads of people go out tonight. Getting a cab will be impossible. Why don't you come out here and tell me what –'

'Then I'll bloody well walk.'

'I'm hungry,' Petey whines.

'Woof weed on me,' Joanne says, holding her hand up as evidence.

'Why are you going?' Mark asks. 'And why now?'

'Come inside, kids,' Dad repeats. 'I'll give you chips.'

Dad pats each of the children on the head as they file past him to go inside. 'Wash your hands.' He stays on the porch, closes the sliding door behind him. 'You should be ashamed.'

'Of what?' Mark says. And then he slaps his thighs. 'Okay, one of you needs to tell me what you're fighting about. Why are *you* leaving? And why are *you* crying?'

'You weren't there!' I shout, though I'm not sure who I'm speaking to. Both of them, everyone. 'You weren't there so you don't know. I'm sick of having to cover for something I didn't do. Well, I didn't – Not all of it. I *tried*. I tried to get her to the car and I tried to get Charlie to the farm and I tried to pretend I wanted to go to the farm and I tried to act like juggling three kids and Christmas and Charlie and Dad and getting ready for dinner and cleaning the house and – bloody hell, do either of you know how exhausted I am?'

'Wait a minute.' Mark holds his hand up to stop me. 'What do you mean you tried to get her to the car?'

'You are *never* home,' I say.

'How is this about me? Are you saying you were involved in Skye's accident?'

'Yes, Mark,' Dad says. 'But somehow she's feeling sorry for herself.'

I slump back onto the bench. 'No, Dad, I'm not. I don't know how to explain. I didn't see the car. I was asleep. We both were.'

'Skye was asleep?' Mark asks.

'No. She pressed her horn. She was awake. Charlie and I were asleep.'

My father is standing with his arms taut by his sides, his mouth a straight line. 'Who was driving?'

'Does it matter? We were both in the car.'

'Who?' Mark echoes.

I turn away from Mark and look up at the darkening treetops. I draw a slow breath. 'Charlie. But I let him.'

Dad yanks open the sliding door and goes inside.

Mark stares at me but I can't meet his eye. The hairs on my arms rise. I hear the frogs begin their evening chant, growing louder as though they're an advancing army.

'She swerved to avoid us, but there was nowhere for her to go, nowhere safe. Such a narrow road and we were right in the middle of it. If I'd woken a minute earlier . . . I think about it nonstop, Mark. I wanted to tell you but . . . It was never the right time.'

I wait for him to speak. I know he'll be angry but I feel some relief. He'll know what to do. But when he does finally look at me, his eyes are ice-cold.

247

'There's so much wrong with this I don't know where to start, Abby. A hit and run. A pregnant woman. And you've been lying to my face for weeks. Lying,' his voice rises, 'to me, your father, the police.'

I should speak. He's right about all of it. But I'm in shock, and my words have fled to someplace less painful.

'You handed your keys over to someone just off an eight-hour flight then went to sleep? Knowing he's never been to the farm and is mentally a child.'

'I know, I know,' I say quietly. 'He wanted to drive.'

'Oh, and God forbid Charlie doesn't get to do whatever he feels like. How could you be so stupid? And, what, you tried to get her into the car by yourself? He didn't want to help you? Abby, you wouldn't leave a dog to die like that.'

'She was already dead.'

He swears, then goes inside.

Left alone in the sandpit, I watch as the lights come on in the kitchen, the bathroom and Sarah's bedroom. Mark moves between the fridge and stovetop, making dinner for our children. What feelings will rear up now I've purged myself by speaking the truth? Everybody knows nature abhors a vacuum.

CHAPTER TWENTY-FOUR

Tuesday 31 December 1974

Charlie

I take the window table at Melina's coffee shop in West End, a small, laidback place in a weatherboard worker's cottage. It sits between the Anarchist Centre, a grey besser-brick building with a locked glass-covered noticeboard out front – the irony of which seems to have escaped them – and the Greek grocery store. Across the road is a row of peeling, raggedy-garden share houses. I'm waiting for Ryan and Sal before I order food. They've ducked up the road to get coffee, bread, olives and other supplies for us to take back to Sal's cousin's place. We've crashed there for days and while she's a very relaxed chick, we get the feeling she's had enough of us. We'll be party-hopping tonight but hope to end up back at hers, so food will go some way to securing us one more night in her house. While

I wait, I'm considering how to broach the topic of Bali with them. I know in their hearts they must want to go back. And life will be cool again once we're there.

I look out at the street. It's late morning, so the local Greek residents have done their watering and weeding and are walking up and down the treeless footpath, catching up. The elderly women are clad in black, stockings and all, the men with their hands clasped behind their backs, stopping to talk to people they know and taking the pulse of the neighbourhood before heading back to continue work on their gardens. A man in a navy-blue fisherman's cap and a waistcoat buttoned over a white collarless shirt yawns as he passes by the window.

'Hey.' Ryan and Sal sit down opposite me.

Sal wrinkles her nose at the plastic blue-and-white-checked tablecloth, then runs her eyes around the restaurant while Ryan peruses the blackboard menu. The man at the table closest to ours is reading a small hardback and making notes with a stubby pencil in the margins. I watch his long hair sweep across what's left of his scrambled eggs as he reaches for his glass. Cat Stevens' 'Wild World' plays in the background.

'Any reason?' I ask, pointing at Ryan's clean-shaven face as he rubs his fingers across his chin.

'I couldn't stand one more comment from my mother.'

I laugh. 'Betty can be quite persuasive.'

'You remember?' He smiles.

Sal strokes his cheek. 'You're gorgeous no matter what.' Then sighs. 'I'd forgotten how boring Brisbane is.'

Since I'm keen for them to feel this way I don't defend the place. But in truth, her comment doesn't make sense in this part of town, a suburb I frequent because it's never dull: there's a mix of factories, a cinema, market gardens. I don't point out the man and woman who've wandered out from the Anarchist Centre and are heading towards the bus stop, both visions of West meets East or, rather, West steals clothing from India, hairdos from Jamaica and jewellery from Africa. Sal has more or less given me an opener to the conversation I want to have.

'Probably time to think about heading back to KD,' I say.

The waitress puts our coffees on the table and Sal gives hers right back, ignoring my words. 'Too milky.' Working in a restaurant hasn't changed the way Sal deals with people whose job it is to serve her. 'I'll need another one.'

'Sal, honey,' Ryan says as the waitress takes her cup.

'Why should I drink bad coffee?'

He gazes at her as though she's said something delightful. I don't know why we both find her arrogance endearing, forgivable, almost elegant, but we do.

'Anything to eat?' The waitress regards us with contempt. 'I'll be sure to hold the milk.'

As so often happens, I try to compensate for Sal's rudeness. 'A toasted ham-and-cheese sandwich, please. Thank you.'

'Is that all?'

'Same,' Ryan says. 'Sal?'

'A decent coffee.'

The waitress walks away, shaking her head.

'So, hey,' I try again. 'What's our go-home date? I'm thinking I can leave by February.'

'February?' Ryan says. 'Why are you hanging around that long?'

'There are a few things I need to sort out.'

'Are they to do with Skye and your dad? Because I reckon it's better if we don't talk about *that*, man.'

251

'More than happy to leave that subject alone.'

'Good. You need to get back before February if you want to run KD. Otherwise we should give it to Ketut and Made.'

'Why would we –?'

'We're staying in Brisbane, Charlie,' Sal says flatly, and though the music has cranked up and a car with a hole in its muffler roars down the street, I hear her as clear as a bell. 'It's over in Bali.' She ignores the waitress when she places the fresh coffee on the table.

'You don't mean that. You just said Brisbane was boring. Why would you want to live here?'

'I told you at the pub. I said we were checking out houses,' Sal says.

'That's Alan Nolan from the co-op.' Ryan knocks on the window. The man on the footpath, twenty-something, tall, lanky and thin, is wearing loose patched jeans and a dark green t-shirt. He smiles at Ryan, waves to Sal.

'Back in a sec,' Ryan says.

Sal makes no move but smiles at Alan.

'What are you doing?' I say. 'I thought we were going to convince him not to stay here.'

'He wants to come home.' She makes a what-are-you-going-to-do shrug.

'You can't stay in Brisbane. You'll be miserable.'

She sips her coffee, pushes the half-full cup away from her.

'Do you want to go back to the place you first met Finn and –? Is that what you want? Or Byron? We could go to Byron.'

'There's no "we". Ryan and I need to do our own thing. You can't follow us around all the time, Charlie.'

I pull my head back in surprise.

'First of all, I didn't follow you to Bali, you invited me. And second, you're saying now we're back in Brisbane we're not friends?'

She watches Ryan talk to Alan Nolan. 'I'll treasure our time in Bali forever. But we're done there. Ryan and I need to make a new life and it won't work if you're hanging around telling us to go back to Kuta.' I open my mouth to speak but she cuts me off, turns steely eyes towards me. 'You're going to have a lot more trouble letting go of Bali than we are. We need to get some space from you. *I* need some space from you.'

'What's that supposed to mean?'

She rubs a smudge of something off her thumb. 'You think Ryan doesn't notice the way you look at me?'

'Get over yourself.'

'I love Ryan and I would never –'

'Never run your fingers up my arm, never kiss me?'

She laughs and tips her head back. 'Oh, cute. You thought I'd leave Ryan for you?'

'You're such a bitch.'

'Hey, cut it out.' Ryan walks towards the table. 'I could hear you from the doorway.'

'Then you know what he said.'

He remains standing. 'I could hear what you were saying, too.'

Sal is unrepentant. The waitress appears next to Ryan and puts our toasted sandwiches on the table. She's smirking.

Ryan clenches and unclenches his fists. 'What's going on?'

'Nothing, sweetheart,' Sal murmurs. 'Charlie's got a little crush on me. I'm letting him down easy.'

'Don't bullshit me,' Ryan says. 'Are you having sex with him?'

'No, baby, *no*. He doesn't mean anything to me.'

'Charming,' I say.

'You don't.' And I see in her eyes that it's true.

'You know she felt us both up in the truck that day we went for the fridge? She could've gone with you or me, wouldn't have made any difference to her,' I say.

'Charlie,' she says. 'You are delusional.'

'You want me gone? Consider it done.' I turn to Ryan. 'You can't trust her.'

'Don't think I can trust you either.'

I stomp out of the coffee shop then stand on the footpath, queasy, not sure what to do, feeling the heat come up through my thongs. Across the road, a group of Aboriginal men walk towards Musgrave Park. I look back through the window at Ryan and Sal. Ryan is hunched over his plate, eating his sandwich. Sal, chin up, flicks her hair off her shoulder, her hand moving like the tail of an irate cat.

CHAPTER TWENTY-FIVE

Tuesday 31 December 1974

Abby

It's late morning, and the air is gummy, cloying, with dark clouds blocking out the sun.

I'm leaning against the pushed-open sliding door, holding a mug of coffee that I have no interest in drinking. A task that had filled empty minutes. The kids are burying Matchbox cars in the sandpit. For the moment, they don't need or even want me. And I have no idea of what to do with myself. Most days I move around this house like a pinball: from veranda to backyard to kitchen to bathroom to laundry to bedroom, quick detour to letterbox, then back to kitchen. Picking up and watering and chopping and folding along the way. Right now I can barely summon the energy to stay upright.

I don't know where Mark went, but I'm guessing he's at Geoff's house. Dad will be at the farm. I won't try phoning either of them because even the thought of how those calls would go makes me want to fall into bed and sleep for a hundred years. What could I possibly say other than repeat that I'm sorry? I know that's not enough. I have no idea where Charlie is, though he'll be with Ryan and Sal. Tonight, I'll see out this sorry year with my children, who'll probably be asleep before the first fireworks light up the sky.

I look to the sandpit as Sarah and Joanne giggle. Petey is putting a fistful of sand into his mouth.

'Petey, don't do that.' I hear the exhaustion in my voice.

He spits out the doughy muck, leaving a ring of it around his lips. 'Sarah told me to.'

I hold a hand out to Sarah in a 'why?' gesture.

'I want to know what it tastes like.'

'Then eat it yourself.' She's rightly surprised by this suggestion. 'Forget I said that. Get your sandals. Let's go visit Auntie Lou.'

We need to do something to fill our day, and I need the company of an adult who won't look at me with disgust. I'll tell Lou I won't be coming to the street party tonight, and that Mark has gone and I'm scared because I don't know when he's coming back. I'm not sure what reason I'll give for our fight, but I know I can think of one.

The two-minute walk to Lou and Andrew's house is made longer as the children stop to pick up sticks and rocks and flowers, peek inside people's letterboxes, and squat to peer at a white cat hiding in the shade under a car. Which is fine. I'm in no rush.

When we're close to Lou's house, the kids break into a run and scurry up the driveway, arguing about who gets to knock on the door. They all bang on it at once.

When Lou opens the door, smiling and making faces at their noise, I can see she's three sheets to the wind.

'Shhh, Uncle Andy's snoozing,' she says to the children. 'Kids are out back. Tiptoes.' She turns to me. 'Went to a champagne breakfast. Head Something Someone from Andrew's work. Boring as batshit. What could I do but drink?' She points at Sarah's all-white outfit and the headband to which I've taped an empty toilet roll.

'She's a unicorn.'

'Ah, be the change . . .' Lou makes a shushing noise as we pass through the living room to the sun-drenched deck. Andrew is lying on the couch, snoring so loudly I can't imagine what noise the kids or I could make that would be heard. My kids and Lou's fall into a happy tumble on the lawn, shaded by the tall leafy line of bamboo that grows alongside the fence. I sit on a bench beside the slat table, under a canvas umbrella patterned with pink and orange flowers.

'Wine?' Lou asks, and before I can answer she's heading back into the kitchen, muttering, 'Yes. A little. Nearly lunchtime.'

She returns with a bowl of peanuts, a cask of moselle and two plastic cups. 'Hair of the dog.'

'I don't think you can call it that when you haven't stopped drinking,' I say with a smile. 'But sure, fill her up.'

Since she's my friend, Lou agrees with every word I say, every edited half-truth and deluded justification, every lie about Mark and I arguing about the unfairness of our domestic arrangement. Since she's spent the morning drinking, she agrees voluminously.

'Bastard,' she says when I tell her that Mark stormed out last night, insisting he did more than most men would. 'Bastard,' when I tell her he hasn't been back since. Her elbow slips sideways, so she's propped up on an angle. Her makeup isn't quite where it should be: lipstick smudges the lip of her cup, mascara flecks above and below her lashes, and there is a rub of blue eye shadow on the side of her face. She stares intently at me, pausing before she speaks again. 'But he's not actually a bastard. You know that, don't you? You'll sort this out. He loves you, love.'

'I know he does.'

She reaches across the table and grabs my wrist. 'Loves you like crazy, one hundred per cent. We both do.'

'I love you, too. Might be enough wine for now. How about I put this back in the fridge?'

She keeps hold of my wrist. 'I'm sorry.'

'Don't worry about it. I've seen you sloshed before.'

'Really, *really* sorry.'

I smile at her. 'Is it my straw hat? I never thought I'd get it back anyway.'

'You're my best friend.'

I sit up straight, my hand still on the wine box.

'It didn't mean anything. Nothing. Which is not to say – you know, it does mean *something* or we wouldn't be having this conversation, would we? The important thing is you're my best friend and that's more important than any bloke. It's urges, biology, but we should be, I mean, there's no excuse. I'm not excusing anything.' She seems to lose her train of thought. I've never seen her quite this drunk before. 'Because that's what they want, isn't it? Women against women. But we're sisters aren't we, so that won't happen.' She pauses. 'It's over. You can be sure about that. Hundred per cent.'

'Okay.' I nod, trying to figure out what she's telling me. Has she had a fling with Charlie? My God, with Finn? No, she hasn't met him.

She makes a childish pout. 'Because at the time you might not recognise a mistake, body chemicals take over, but then . . . And then you do it again. That part is harder to explain away. But I know it was a mistake – *huge* mistake.'

'Charlie?' I ask.

She frowns at me. 'What?'

'Did you and Charlie –?'

'God no.' She stares up at the sky. 'Though not out of the ballpark.' She squeezes my hand. 'You and me would make more sense, you know. Though I've never been physically attracted to a woman. But mentally, I'm much more into you. Boobs though, boobs are good.' She looks off into the backyard, where the children are playing with the totem tennis pole, using their hands to fling the ball around. 'It was the flood, you know, seeing him so ape-man rescuing me and the kids. Andrew should've been here but –' She waves vaguely at the house. 'Doesn't excuse the times that came after that, I know. And like I said, hundred per cent finished.' She takes a deep breath, nods vigorously. 'Finished.'

It's as though I'm watching a hideous beast rise up from the deep sea, seeing its black shadow first, then the glint of its wet back until it rears up to its full height, enormous and terrifying, all claws and fangs. My voice is thin, unfamiliar. 'Mark? You and Mark? No.' I yank my hand away from her. 'No. You're my friend.'

'It's over. Finished, I swear.'

'*No*. Stop talking.' The only words I wanted to hear were that I'd misunderstood, that she'd meant something entirely different and I'd jumped to a crazy conclusion. Charlie, Finn, even Dad! Because she would *never* have sex with my husband. I must have got it wrong. She'd laugh, put her hand on her chest in horror that I could even *think* that. I'd sigh with relief, and we'd share another drink. But she won't stop saying what I cannot hear.

'It was a physical thing. I'd never try to steal him away from you. It was – biology.'

'Stop. Shut up.' I feel dizzy, panic-stricken. 'Kids, we're going.' I stand too quickly and one knee buckles beneath me. I grab the edge of the table.

Lou reaches for me again but I escape her and walk shakily down the few stairs that lead from the deck to the grass. I stand next to Sarah. 'Darling, we need to go now.'

'But we're not finished yet.' Sarah holds up the fuzzy tennis ball attached by a string to the pole. 'It's a tournament.'

'You can finish it next time. We need to go.'

'Abby –' Lou stands behind me and touches my back.

I jerk forward. If my children weren't right here I would hit her with all my strength. 'No!' I shout.

The kids freeze mid-motions and stare at me.

'You're my best friend, in the *world*,' she says.

I shove her away. This much I allow myself. 'We are not friends. And I won't have this conversation in front of my children.'

She strokes the top of Sarah's head. 'Sweet girl.'

'Stay away from her.' I grab Sarah's arm. 'Petey, Joanne, come here now.'

'I want to stay. Why can't we stay?' Sarah whines. She pulls away from me and plops down on the grass.

'Get up.' I yank Sarah to standing. She howls in outrage. The twins sense something is wrong and start to snivel. 'Oh for God's sake, stay here then.' I let go of Sarah's arm and turn to walk back through the house. I hiss at Lou, 'Why not have my kids, too? Take everything. Don't follow me. Do *not*.' I poke her chest with one finger as she leans towards me. 'We are *done*.'

She ignores me, follows me, back onto the deck, through her house where Andrew is still snoring on the couch, to the front door, talking in a loud and relentless whisper all the while.

'He was missing you. You're all about the kids and the house and, you know, it happens. And Andrew's never here. I was lonely, Abby.'

I turn to face her once I'm outside. 'You want me to feel sorry for him? For you? Go to hell.'

The rain splats down onto her drive as I walk away, my legs shaky, my eyes flooded with tears.

I nurse a gin and tonic, picturing the drink as clear glue sliding down my throat, working to hold me together internally, while the children splash about in the plastic pool. Once the rain eased, they'd wandered back home, hungry, Lou having gone to her room to 'nap' according to Sarah. I'm thankful that they seem oblivious to my pain, interested only in lunch and then fun. I watch as Woof cocks his leg and wees on a pile of abandoned goggles and masks.

Mark calls while I cook lamb chops, carrots and peas for the kids' dinner. Sarah picks up the phone – her latest joy – and tells me, once the conversation is done, that Dad has a lot of work to do and will be home late, after sleep-time. He doesn't ask to speak with me.

When Mark walks into the living room after eleven o'clock that night, I am curled up in an armchair, in the dark, a half-empty glass on the side table.

He stands in front of me. 'Listen, I'm sorry I got so mad. It's bloody horrendous, and you should've told me. I'm not excusing you, I can't. I know you've spent your life covering for Charlie, but –'

'You *bastard*.' I spit the word at him.

He jerks his head back in surprise.

While he's been wherever he's been, I've been trapped with my rage in this house, going through each domestic task as if I were a robot, thinking about Mark and Lou, growing angrier, more hurt, more brittle. I've crafted a speech about betrayal and hypocrisy and the wounds he's inflicted. I'd forgotten that he would be thinking about the car crash. That conversation feels a lifetime ago.

'Uh.' He takes a step backwards. 'Don't know what that's for but I can see you're in no state to have a rational discussion so I'm going to bed.'

'You think you're going to sleep here? Lie in our bed like nothing happened?' I stand up and grab his arm, as much for balance as to stop him leaving the room. 'How could you?'

'How could *I*? You're the one who killed a woman then lied to me.'

We face one another in the dark. I let go of his arm. I am barefoot and small, and feel like a child in the presence of a powerful adult. 'Lou,' I say quietly. Even in this dim light

I see the change in his expression as he becomes aware of what I'm saying.

'Abby,' he whispers.

'You had an affair.' I feel myself sway.

'It wasn't like that.'

'You're married, she's married. That's an affair.'

He considers for a moment, then regains his confidence. 'Well, what did you expect? You turn into a plank of wood whenever I touch you. Don't seem interested in me at all.' He waits. 'Is that because of the car crash, the stress?' he says. 'Or – I don't know. How much rejection did you think I could take, Abby?'

I stand still, separate from the world and all that's in it. I want to ask when and where and for exactly how long. And does he love her. And was she the first.

'Okay, well, I'll go then.' His face makes it clear he believes himself to be the victim in this scenario, cast out of his home, misunderstood by his mad harpy of a wife.

There is no law of motion that allows for things to stay the same, silent and motion*less*, at peace. I would like that, for a while at least. To wake to stasis, a permanent sunrise, have the raindrops hugged in white clouds – for life to stay utterly immobile until I can make sense of it.

As if on cue, the still night is shattered by what I first think is a volley of gunshots and backfiring cars. I look over Mark's shoulder and see the black sky spot with puffs of sparkling light, then quick rockets shooting up, zigzagging, bursting open, white at first and then pink, green. The explosions grow in number and speed until the sky is hysterical with them and it suddenly seems so funny that someone is flinging all this nonsense up into the air, faster and faster, until it just stops.

And when the noise abates and the sky is decorated only with pale grey squiggles of smoke, I realise I'm laughing. And that Mark has left.

The next morning, I hear a knock at the front door.

Woof runs down the stairs, barking excitedly. I open the door even though I recognise the knock.

Lou and I are wearing the same dress. I hate her afresh for the fact I'll now think of her whenever I pull this dress off its hanger. I will never again pull this dress off the hanger. Woof leaps forward in enthusiastic greeting.

'We match.' She smiles awkwardly, bends down to stroke Woof's head. I stand on the threshold with my hand on the door. 'Except one of us is a dumb bitch.'

The sun shines onto one side of her face. Worry wrinkles cut into her forehead. I reach forward and grab Woof by the flea collar, pull him back to me.

'Me. I'm the bitch. Abby, I'm sorry. I swear, I'll make this up to you. I'll –'

'Is that it? I have things to do.'

I drag Woof closer, point him towards the stairs and pat him on the rear. He ignores me, stands by my side. I step back so I can close the door.

'Wait, I have something for you. A first peace offering.' She picks up a thick wooden mask she's placed against the doorframe. It's the length of her torso, stained a dark brown, and topped with a shock of coarse black hair. The gawping oval mouth is circled with red, and the cowrie-shell eyes are ringed by thick stripes of yellow and blue. It's the face of a morning-after drag queen as drawn by a child, or Munch's scream made solid.

'That's hideous. Why would you bring me that?'

She's surprised. 'I thought you loved the masks. You always say such nice things about them.'

'I don't want a mask.'

'Andrew says this is a good one.'

'So he doesn't know you've been sleeping with my husband?'

'He does. We're not speaking. He's letting his knuckles do the talking.' She has a large bruise on her upper arm.

'Don't ask me to feel sorry for you.'

She holds the mask out to me. 'Please take it. You might like nailing my head to your wall.'

I put the mask on the floor behind me. I'd drop it but it would crack the tiles. 'I'll enjoy setting it on fire at some point.'

Woof circles the mask, sniffing and growling.

Lou cries in large, loud sobs. 'I'm sorry, so sorry. I was wrong, such a bad friend.'

'Is that what you're going to call it? *Bad friendship?*'

She turns her palms up, lifts her shoulders, wordlessly pleading. Her nose runs, leaking clear thick fluid that touches her lip. I have a tissue in my pocket.

'How long were you a bad friend for? Were you a bad friend in my house? I mean, aside from the day of the flood when I risked my life to carry your garbage here to safety, fed and clothed your children? Were you being a bad friend and fucking my husband while I cooked your children's dinner? Or after we spent a day together at the pool? Were you one of his million trips to the hardware store or work?'

She uses her forefinger to wipe her lip. 'Abby, can you forgive me? I'll do whatever it takes.'

265

'Go away.' I close the door on her. Barely contained behind my rage are the feelings I don't want to make public – hurt and humiliation and crushing fear. There was no one in the world watching my back except for Mark and Lou, and now . . . Now, neither. And in my heart, I think I knew. I both knew and didn't know.

Woof is pawing the mouth of the mask, sniffing at it, pulling back to bark at it. He looks up at me to see if this is what's required. I kick the mask over to the wall, scratching the floor tiles. 'All yours.'

PART TWO

PART TWO

CHAPTER TWENTY-SIX

Friday 21 February 1975

Abby

I spread my towel on the wooden floor of the church hall. The yoga instructor, wearing a long-sleeved leotard, pale orange, offers me a smile of acknowledgement as she pads barefoot around the room. A fifty-something woman with a grey ponytail moves to the right to make more space for me. Sun beams in a bright slant through the stained-glass windows but the open front doors invite in a breeze so the morning's heat is lifted to the rafters, to rest with a pair of swallows sitting in silence above us. The room is painted white except for the bare floorboards. It smells of incense, with notes of shampoo, warm skin and dust.

I've dropped the kids off: two at kindy, one at school. I lie on my back as I see the dozen others are doing and feel my shoulders relax towards the floor. Sarah, Petey and Joanne are safe and cared for, and I am free. My own schooling starts Monday and I'll use this moment of unowned time to consider how to make this year better than the last, to force positive change. I will exercise, clean and organise.

I tell myself that for this one hour I won't weep when I picture my husband and best friend naked together. I'll block that image. I will not obsess about whether I can forgive my husband, or whether my husband and father will ever forgive me. I won't try to think of fresh ways to further explain myself or how I can make amends. Or who exactly is owed amends. I won't think about Skye's little boy. I'll push down my anger that Charlie still doesn't seem as guilty as he should be, as contrite, or committed to healing his rift with Dad. None of this. I will banish this writhing, poisonous viper pit from my mind.

Of course, my brain fights relaxation, accustomed to encouraging anxiety to flare up as soon as I'm horizontal. I tell myself I'll allow five minutes of my punishing self-talk and *then* I will relax into the class. So: I need to talk to Mark, and soon, to have one conversation that doesn't immediately disintegrate into yelling and insults, our ping-pong of blame, so I can beg him to drop his investigations into the commune. Sergeant Doyle thinks this conversation has already happened, even praised my good sense, and I didn't correct him. The truth is that the universe offered me a reprieve when Mark flew to Alice Springs one day after he moved out of our house. He'll be there for another week, investigating something about the American military base at Pine Gap. The previous *Four Corners* reporter who was covering the story is under arrest for trying to get inside the facility. Mark is enraged there's a part of Australia no Australian is allowed into: 'Satellites, radars. Do you know that more than six hundred people work at that base and our government has no idea – none – about what's going on out there.' He said that much when he told me he'd be gone a while, so consumed with the story it wouldn't have mattered who was on the other end of the phone. This assignment should fill me with dread but I'm confident in Mark's ability to keep himself safe, and glad he's immersed in a meaty story. Also, bastard. I'm snapped away from my thoughts by the yoga teacher, who welcomes us to her class.

We stand at the back of our towels with our hands in prayer position then swoop our arms up. The woman on the phone said this was a beginners' yoga class and perfect for my tightly wound body, but the other students seem to know what to do and are able to move from one pose to the next with ease. I am, admittedly, making it harder on myself by second-guessing the instructor. 'Salute' sounds aggressive to my ear. And shouldn't we be doing this outside where we can see the sun? My body resists the chest-expansion exercises, finding comfort in curling my shoulders in. Bending down to touch my toes feels claustro-phobic and brings on a rush of panic. I roll up faster than anyone else. I count the seconds when we hold a position, antsy to move.

The instructor must see the tension radiating off me and strokes my back as I try a downward dog pose. Dog, cat, frog, camel, cow. Foreign words spoken as though I should under-stand them. More pain than I'd anticipated. I'm not unfit but evidently I'm inflexible, in every way. The instructor's hand is warm through my t-shirt. I try to relax, not for myself but because I know this is what she wants me to do.

By the end of the class I've worked myself into a tangle of annoyance and self-loathing, and want nothing more than to be home. I shouldn't have come. But when I think we're about to be released, the instructor walks around the room passing out thick cushions to make us comfortable for our seated meditation.

Once we've arranged ourselves onto the cushions, the room becomes silent. The instructor, cross-legged in front of her altar – a low square table covered in Indian cloth, topped with a Buddha statue, incense, a small vase of frangipanis, a scattering of shells, a lit candle – asks us to gaze with soft eyes on the flame and become aware of our breath. 'Don't try to control it, simply observe. Feel the rise and fall of your stomach, the release that comes with each exhale.' My ankles push into my towel. I hear my heartbeat over my breath. I watch the flame and think of the altar we make to my mother each year, and realise I don't want to do that anymore. I've turned what started as a moment of reflection into a furtive chore to rush through before getting on with Christmas. I'll tell Charlie I want to try a new way to remember our mother, as she was before she got sick. And I'd like to include the children. The decision to drop our shrine-building makes me feel more relaxed than I have since I walked into this hall. My shoulders ease down.

Out of nowhere, I remember Charlie saying 'karma' when I was trying to explain the laws of motion. Perhaps action and reaction and cause and effect are not that different.

'Breathe in, breathe out.' The instructor advises us to find peace in the truth of this moment. I don't know what that means. But the promise of peace, that word used on her poster, is what drew me to this class so I should at least try to experience it. 'Try not to think about the past or the future, or the stories you tell yourself about your life, but instead think about what is happening in this moment. Be here, now. Be willing to truly feel, in all its glorious expansiveness, everything that exists in this breath, and in the next breath.' The idea of not allowing my mind to think about the past or future is intriguing but bewildering. I'm committed to keeping the bad thoughts at bay, and dropping my mind into a lower gear, but to corral my mind into one moment seems incredibly limiting, the opposite of expansive.

'Let go,' the instructor whispers, as if reading my thoughts.

We sit in silence until she says: 'A poem.' Which we all take as an invitation to resettle our bodies.

'Let us consider the words of Zen poet Ryōkan as we begin our brief look into the three paths to peace.'

How strange that the Western scientist and Eastern seer divide their truths into threes: did they artificially construct three laws and three paths, or is that a division preferred by nature that they merely put into words? Surely life is scrappier, messier than their three-part theories would have it.

'*To find truth, drift east and west, come and go, entrusting yourself to the waves.*' The instructor looks directly at me and suggests we close our eyes. 'To find happiness and peace in our lives, to feel genuine contentment, first we must know the truth of ourselves and the moment, and pay close attention to what is inside us; second, we must encourage kind and loving relation-ships with those around us; and third, we must relax with true awareness in the waves.' She pauses. 'This last one can meet resistance from those of us more comfortable trying to control than to observe. But a wise mind entrusts itself to the waves, and is able to remain calm even in chaos, knowing that life is never still, and that we are a part of that perpetual movement and change. Even as you sit here your heart pumps, your blood flows, your lungs empty and fill. And outside, flowers bloom, a bird breaks out of its shell, another may lie down to die. The earth moves around the sun. We don't control any of this. We need only to be aware of it, fully awake to everything around us, both outside and inside our bodies. Live and love, entrusting ourselves to the waves.

'Take a moment now to visualise yourself floating in an endless sea. Be at ease in the calm water, then observe the waves as they rise to swell and crash around you, feel the push and pull of the water and know that life is not meant to be still, that you are part of a vast and ever-changing ocean. Entrust yourselves to the waves.' She pauses again. 'For our last few moments, come into your body and simply breathe.'

And though I am sitting still and my eyes are closed, inside I am like a cartoon character who has thrust a finger into a live power point and become electrified. I've never thought about life in this way. My father taught me the value of pragmatism, practicality, the rigid inevitability of forward motion, the pointlessness of introspection or resisting what is established. Move on, move forward, fix and maintain. Control.

But what I hear now is that life's movement is something more organic than that, messier, more beautiful. The world and everything in it rises and falls and changes and grows, even as I sit and breathe. And I can't control that. And I am only responsible for some of what I can control. And it is possible to feel at peace knowing that.

This, at least, is how I understand her words: I can control what I eat for breakfast, how many hours I study, how I vote, what I say. I can exercise. I can show up again for this class. But I cannot make my brother grow up, my father answer the phone or my husband come home and love me. I can keep my hands on the wheel today, but I cannot undo Skye's death. I cannot rewrite the past or be certain about the future. But I can choose to fully be in this moment of this life. A thought that fills me with fear and delight.

CHAPTER TWENTY-SEVEN

Monday 24 February 1975

Abby

With only one year of uni under my belt – six years ago – I feel like a foreigner setting foot on campus. The students I pass on the footpath that leads to the Great Court are younger than me, and cooler. For all my attention to books and stationery, the logistics of leaving and returning to my home, I hadn't thought enough about how I should dress. In my defence, I suspect neither the girl with the perfect flicks, zigzag-striped skirt, Levi's t-shirt and clogs nor the boy with the blond surf hair, maroon flares and thongs had to wrangle three kids out of the house before coming here, or is thinking about whether their husband is about to file for a divorce. And I'm certain they aren't starting their year with an undeclared crime in their past. As I think this, I catch a waft of dope, watch the guy walking in front of me slip one hand into the back jeans pocket of the man he's with. So, maybe other people aren't living by the letter of the law, but I'd bet none of them wakes in the night remembering the time they left a dead woman in the dirt.

Skye's death hangs over me like a black cloud. I try to take solace in this moment, my new beginning. Neither Dad nor Mark will tell the police what they know. And we've had no more calls from Roberts or Doyle. I'll talk to Mark the first day he's back in Brisbane, to make sure he leaves the commune story alone. While he's still in Alice, and I have no immediate fires to put out, I can focus on being a single-mother student. I can study law.

I hitch my denim book bag high on my shoulder and cross a road lined with parked Minis, Beetles, Holdens. Holden Premiers. An AC/DC song blares out an open car window. I walk through an archway into the court, still a work in progress it seems from the construction equipment and scaffolding, where imposing sandstone buildings – pink and cream and biscuit coloured – circle a large swathe of grass spotted with saplings.

I pass a group of students sitting on the grass and slow down to eavesdrop.

'– handmaids of a fascist government.'

'Told Charles Perkins he should call himself Mr Witchetty Grub.'

'Dan and Carol are organising a rally for Friday. You're going, yeah?'

'Have you seen her new magazine? Interdisciplinary feminism.'

The students want change; they're hungry for it. In other parts of Australia, people are struggling to keep up with change, feel like they're hurtling into the future without helmets. But our premier has dug his heels in, and is resisting every attempt by the federal government to civilise Queensland. Petersen makes it clear he loathes students, feminists, 'darkies', 'homos' and 'communists'. He laughs at the media, while he sells our state to overseas developers – every bit of beachfront and any land that can be mined – and looks away as heritage-listed buildings are bulldozed in the dead of night. It doesn't seem to matter that he's barely able to string a sentence together; he rules with iron-fisted resolve.

I head inside, where the air is instantly cooler, almost crisp. My plaited leather sandals squeak as I walk down a high-ceilinged hallway to the lecture room where I have my first class. The room is vast, with hundreds of chairs arranged amphitheatre-style around a small stage. I take an aisle seat about a third of the way from the front, not so close it seems cocky, not so far back it might seem I don't care. Students file in, talking, dropping bags, clicking pens. There's an air of anti- cipation and tempered eagerness. A man stands at the lectern and adjusts the microphone, which makes squeals of protest each time he touches it.

'Good morning,' he says. 'You are here for the first lecture of Contracts 101. Should that not be the case, you're in the wrong room and will want to make a discreet exit. I can assure you, no one stays unless they have to.'

Perhaps he's jaded from years of teaching this class, but his mood is out of sync with the people in the room. He might have expected laughter, maybe even received it in years gone by, but it seems that I'm not alone in being keen to get on with this, bright-eyed and optimistic. I feel a rush of adrenaline, thrilled to be a part of something, in this room full of like-minded strangers. The lecturer clears his throat, recalibrates now that his joke has fallen flat. 'Let's begin,' he says.

The hour passes in an instant. I file out of the room with the other students, no longer an outsider. I know where the cafeteria is and walk there in a haze of energised happiness, past posters advertising upcoming band performances, a city record store, the new women's journal, notices about student union services.

And then I see Skye. She walks towards me, a friend either side of her, wearing jean shorts and the same cheesecloth smock she had on when we left her, but washed now, no longer muddy, bloodied, a second skin over her swollen belly. She smiles at me. My knees buckle and I collapse onto the concrete.

When I come to, I am sitting on the footpath with my back against a wall. Looking up, I see the three girls crouched in front of me, with the sun above them, sharing a halo. They are asking if I'm okay in overlapping sentences, a harmony of concern. I nod slowly and, remembering why I fell, look at Skye. But it isn't Skye. The smock is the same, her hair is blonde, but that's where the similarity ends. How did I transform this younger girl, her star-sign pendant dangling from a silver chain in front of me, her hair like silk curtains, into Skye?

The three girls help me to stand up and guide me to the closest wooden bench. They offer water and to make a phone call for me, to walk with me to the health centre. One digs in her bag and finds mints. I tell them I'm fine, have low blood pressure, that I'd neglected to eat breakfast, that it's nothing. And while they clearly want to help me, I resist every suggestion until they give up and leave.

I brush my hair with my fingers, straighten my shirt then sit still, staring numbly at the passers-by and cars. Why had I seen Skye here, now, eleven weeks and three days after the crash?

If she'd survived, her baby would be about seven weeks old now, able to lie on its stomach and lift its head, to smile, to reach and clutch. Skye would be tired, up throughout the night to comfort and feed. Would Dad have helped? I have no idea if he helped my mother when I was a newborn.

I sit on the bench and think. Were Skye and her baby alive, they would be changing daily. Their forward movement would affect everyone around them, in ways large and small. But we stopped her in her tracks. Skye will never lower her new baby into her cot, or watch her first wobbly steps, or teach her to read. Beau will never know this brother or sister. A girl, I somehow think. My father may never know love again. There must be a consequence for that. That is surely the essence of law, as well as physics: action then reaction. What should be my penance: should I stop being, too? But what good would another death do? A pigeon perched on the lip of a rubbish bin stares at me, waiting.

How can I have a legal career when I've broken and am now evading the law? I realise, with a sense of deep weariness, sadness, that this can no longer be my path. The students are right: things must change, and it's up to us to make change happen. But what arrogance to think I could continue on as planned, feed my hunger to learn, study how to cast judgement on others, read about contracts while locked in a contract with the Devil. There will be a way I can be my full self, my best self, but first I need to do what I'd mocked Charlie for suggesting: I must, somehow, make amends.

The towering jacaranda tree across the road offers me a floaty nod for finally coming to my senses. I frown at the tree, as if we were in silent conversation. 'Yes,' I say quietly. 'I know. Nothing is the same anymore.'

CHAPTER TWENTY-EIGHT

Sunday 2 March 1975

Charlie

Abby and I sit in her kitchen enjoying the quiet. The kids are at a birthday party and Abby is reading a Stephen King novel, occasionally scooping cottage cheese out of a half-rockmelon in a bowl. I thought she'd have loads of study to do for her law subjects but I don't think I've seen her crack open a textbook since uni started. I'm shuffling a pack of cards, over and over, refining my technique. 'Midnight at the Oasis' plays on the radio, then the news – Whitlam says Darwin will be rebuilt in five years, there's fighting in Cambodia and Papua, the French have declared a year-long news blackout around Moruroa Atoll so they can test their nukes in the Pacific. 'A news blackout announced on the news. Weird,' I say. The biscuits Abby made this morning are still on a cooling rack so the room smells of coconut and golden syrup. It's all good, but I'm bored. I'm glad for Abby that she has a plan for the year but I'm not sure about my own. Ryan and Sal have been clear: Bali is over. I've signed on for the dole, but what next? I put the cards down.

'Hey, did I tell you I read that the lady who wrote Mum's etiquette book died?'

Abby looks up in surprise. 'Amy Vanderbilt?'

'Committed suicide. Seems like one of the ruder ways to die.'

She raises her eyebrows at me. 'How sensitive you are. That woman is responsible for the few table manners you have.'

'I've always said hands are nature's cutlery.'

'Sure, and knuckles can help you walk.'

Before I can reply, there's a knock at the door.

'I'll get it,' I say. Something to do.

Through the amber-coloured glass panel next to the door I see the outline of a woman, and a boy too tall to be Petey. Though he wouldn't be coming home without the others anyway . . . It only takes a moment for me to realise it's Maria and Beau.

I open the door to them standing side by side on the coir mat, close but not touching. 'Hey guys. Long time no see.' I peer behind them, out to the street. Abby's neighbour is hosing her driveway again. The milkman is pulling up a few doors down the road on his usual run. A mickey bird swoops low to peck a labrador waddling across the road. But what I'm looking for is Finn, and there's no sign of him. I ask Maria for good measure, 'Are you alone?'

'Yeah. Are you going to let us in?'

I stand aside. 'Wasn't sure you were ever going to come back.'

'I told you I'd come when the time was right.'

Abby stands at the kitchen sink washing our cups and dishes. She turns at the sound of Beau and Maria entering the room and I realise she's never seen Beau before. She's never met Maria either, for that matter. I introduce everyone. Abby stares at Beau, soap suds dripping down her wrist and onto the floor. Beau is taller than Sarah now, still skinny, could do with a wash, but his expression is relaxed and open.

'You're the daughter, yeah?' Maria says.

At the sound of Maria's voice, Abby snaps back, wipes her hands hurriedly, nods.

'I need more coffee,' I say. 'Anyone else?'

Maria pulls out a chair and settles herself. 'Black.'

'You too, buddy?' I say to Beau. 'Cup of joe?'

He giggles and sits down as Maria has indicated he should.

'Abby, coffee? Join in anytime.'

'Sorry. I'm sorry. You've taken me by surprise. Beau, it's so nice to meet you,' Abby says. 'Cordial or –?'

'Juice or water,' Maria says.

'Still fresh out of soy milk,' I say, to which Maria smiles and Abby looks confused.

Abby pours Beau a glass of apple juice and places a plate of biscuits and cut apple in front of him in no time flat. She is an Olympic-quality mother. Then she addresses Maria. 'My father's not here anymore. He's gone back to the farm.'

'Beau, the grown-ups need to talk,' Maria says. 'Hoof it, darling.'

He slumps in his seat. I have the feeling he hears this a lot. 'It's hot outside.'

'The twins have set up a Hot Wheels track in their room,'

I say. He stares blankly at me, takes a bite of his biscuit. 'Toy cars. Their room's down the hallway there.'

He brightens. 'Okay.' He gulps a mouthful of juice, slips off the seat and scampers out of the kitchen.

Maria crosses her arms, ready to talk business. 'Things are happening at the commune. There's been another change of plans. And this one is kind of on you, or your husband anyway. So Beau needs to be here, out of the way, while we manage our . . . issues.'

'He can't stay here. That was my father's idea. I can tell you where his farm is if Beau needs a temporary home,' Abby says.

Maria snorts. 'We know where you all live. And it might've been your Dad's idea to begin with but now it's Finn's. He wants Beau here, like I said, with a mothering type and other kids, normal meals and all that.'

'Finn knows you're here today?' I ask.

She rolls her eyes. 'What did I just say?' And then she speaks to Abby. 'Also, the men in your family are a bit thick. Finn has a lot on right now so I'm doing the drop-off.'

'Drop-off?' Abby says. 'You plan to leave him here now? For how long?'

Maria sighs. 'My God, the questions. He's a sweet kid and won't be any trouble. He'll muck in with your lot. And Finn will show up when he shows up.'

'No, he can't stay here,' Abby says. 'I was never on board with my father trying to take Beau in the first place, obviously. But if the police show up they'll think we've kidnapped him. And Finn saw Dad – and Charlie – at your commune, so . . .'

'Why would the police come here?'

Abby fumbles to answer.

'Is Finn setting us up?' I ask.

'Yes, that,' Abby says, pointing at me.

Maria shrugs. 'I don't think so.'

'You don't think so?' I say. 'Far out, that is not a good answer.'

'And,' Abby continues, 'not that it's any of your business, but I'm the only adult in the house right now –'

'Excuse me?' I say. Rude.

Maria smirks at Abby. 'You really are.'

Abby keeps going. 'The only adult in the house, with three kids and a dog.'

'Hang on, Abby. Maybe we should let Beau stay,' I say. 'He'll be safe here, and Dad will be pleased, and if it's Finn's idea –'

'Can you *not*?'

'Maybe go play with the toy cars,' Maria says.

I ignore their barbs.

'We're not related to him,' Abby says. 'He doesn't know us. You agree that my hands are full. And – wait: Skye has a brother in Darwin, doesn't she?'

'Had,' Maria says. 'He got crushed by a house during Tracy. Listen, this is where Finn wants Beau. There isn't anywhere else he can go. So,' she stands up, 'end of discussion.'

'Not end of discussion,' Abby says, frowning.

Maria stands firm. 'Listen, Skye was on her way to Beau when she died. She wanted him off the commune. And I understand why, I do. So if Finn is letting that happen for even a short while, you should step up and help the kid. I do what I can to keep the little ones safe, but they're not. Okay? They're not safe there.'

286

Abby visibly pales and rubs her eyes with the pads of her hands.

'I'm going to say goodbye to him now. There's a bag of clothes by your door.'

Abby steps towards her. 'I said no.'

'Abby,' I say. 'You heard her. There isn't anywhere else.'

Maria turns when she reaches the doorway. 'Lady, I get it. But this isn't up to me – I'm doing what Finn told me to. You can take it up with him when he shows. Just make sure you're not alone when you do that, okay?'

That night, after Sarah, Beau and the twins have been fed, bathed and put to bed, Abby and I watch the news, taking turns to get up and change the channel. We're working our way through a box of moselle and a bag of Cheezels. Abby talks endlessly about the difficulties of having Beau stay with her – the legal, the logistic, the financial and emotional.

'Who knows what that poor child has been through? Did you see him in the living room? That was the first time he'd ever seen a television. And she's got a nerve calling that bag of scraps she left clothing. I'm going to have to buy him everything.'

'Sounds like he needs you.'

'And how will I explain this to Mark? You know he didn't want Beau here. But I was railroaded, wasn't I?'

'So now you want to tell Mark things?'

'No more secrets. That's what got us into this mess.'

From what I understand, a loose zipper and a boozy neighbour got them into this particular mess, but I don't want to pour salt on her wound. And after one too many nights of her crying about his affair, I've learned that I'm not good at consoling a woman in distress. Nothing I say ever makes her feel any better.

'Well, I guess you tell Mark you're looking after him because literally no one else is. He'll see Beau with his own eyes anyway. You better make sure to tell Mark and Dad at the same time so there's not any more –' She waits for me to finish 'controversy'.

Abby's in the bathroom when the phone rings, so I answer it.

'Has the boy settled in?' Sergeant Doyle asks.

'How'd you know he was here? You know Maria?'

'I know everyone and everything, son.' He sniffs. 'Except one thing: why hasn't your sister pulled her husband into line? I thought I'd made myself clear.'

'You did, absolutely,' I say. My breath quickens. I'd figured we were in a safety zone until Mark got back to Brisbane. Maybe Abby underestimated Mark's ability to juggle multiple stories.

'Because a boy like that, who's lost his mother and been left to run wild by a pack of hippies, needs a stable home life. I can't imagine how he'd fare in a foster home if you and your sister wound up in jail.'

'Whoa, slow down. Mark's working in Alice Springs, and Abby is going to talk to him as soon –'

'She'd led me to believe that conversation had already happened. But it hasn't, has it? Which means she lied to me. And now –'

'Not lied, a misunderstanding I'm sure.'

He pauses for a moment. 'We had an arrangement. You and your sister haven't kept your part of it. Your brother-in-law hasn't stopped poking around. He's sent other people up here to snoop, and they're getting very close to finding the commune, which is *un-bloody-acceptable.*' He shouts this last mash of words. 'You need to take me seriously because I am not fucking around. I've been doing this job for long enough that I don't need fingerprints or tyre tracks. Your guilty faces and a well-typed confession will be enough. Roberts has done your drive, more than once – with pit stops for arguments and spewing – and it'll never add up. You and your sister ran that car off the road. And unless you –'

'No, we –'

'Don't.' He takes a slow inhale. 'Do not waste my time with more bullshit. I can either let young Roberts run with what is clearly the truth or I can shut this down once and for all. It's your choice. You tell your sister to get her husband to back off and this goes away. Otherwise, I'll have you both arrested by the end of the week. And the kid can fuck off into foster care forever.'

Abby doesn't need to call Mark at his hotel in Alice Springs, though she was pacing the living room gearing herself up to do so. At six-thirty, after the kids have eaten dinner and been bathed, Mark shows up unannounced. Sarah, Petey and Joanne run down the hallway to his call, tumbling into their father as he squats down with his arms out wide.

'I thought you were back tomorrow,' Abby says. I see her anxiously scan the hallway, but Beau stays in the bedroom.

'Yeah, well, I'm back early. Nice to see you, too.'

They're spiky when they speak to one another. I don't know how long that will last or how they'll move on to whatever the next phase is. But because they have kids, there has to be a next phase.

'Not a great time to get them riled up,' Abby says. 'It's bedtime. They have school tomorrow.'

He rolls his eyes. 'Don't make a fuss, okay? I haven't come back early to cause drama. I actually need to talk to Charlie.' He turns his attention to me. 'Got a minute?'

Mark starts talking as we walk into the living room, Abby following after she sends the kids back to their rooms. 'Something huge is about to go down on the commune. We're not entirely clear about it but we have enough intel that we know we need to be there –'

Intel. I'm about to laugh but he's not joking. He keeps talking, on a roll.

'– cameraman and sound guy. Like, tomorrow, Charlie. I'm going to need you to be awake at the crack of dawn, and help us get there. No.' He holds his hand up when he sees I'm about to speak. 'Mate, you owe me.'

'You can't go to the commune,' Abby says.

'I bloody can.'

'Mark –' She pauses.

He shakes his head. 'Abby, this is separate from our stuff. It's work, okay? I'll make sure he doesn't get hurt.'

'It's not that.'

Mark must hear the change in her voice because he turns to face her without any sign of the coldness or steel that's become their norm. He scans Abby's face for information. I watch her eyes soften. She tilts her head and takes a deep breath.

'I know this is important to you but you can't go to the commune. The police have said if you don't back off, stay away from Eumundi, they'll charge Charlie and me with Skye's death.'

Mark's shoulders drop as he makes a quiet groan. 'How much do they know?'

'Enough to follow through on their threats,' she says. 'And there's more. We have an extra child in the house tonight, a boy.'

Mark is smart so his neurons fire fast. 'He didn't,' he says, incredulous rather than angry.

'He? No no, this is not Dad's doing. Or Charlie's. You're right that something is about to happen – they want the kids off the commune. A woman called Maria brought him here. I said no, but she left him anyway.'

Mark tips his head back, stares upwards. 'Okay, right. Well, they might have made a responsible choice. He'll be safe here with you, and that's a good thing.' He's silent for a moment. 'I think we can go to the commune anyway. I'm sure we can get what I need without them –'

'But then what?' Abby says, stepping closer to him. 'Even if you can get in and out of the commune without being caught, what happens when your story goes to air? You can't, Mark. Please.'

'Think of the kids, man,' I say. And they roll their eyes at me in perfect unison.

CHAPTER TWENTY-NINE

Sunday 2 March 1975

Abby

At nine-thirty, once the kids are asleep, after I've cleared the bottles and glasses from the coffee table, emptied the ashtray, washed the dinner dishes and wiped someone's spilled juice from the kitchen floor, I come back into the living room. Mark is lying on the couch and Charlie is on the floor, with his feet up on the coffee table and his head on a cushion he's pulled off the armchair. Mark has one forearm draped across his face, covering his eyes, the wind knocked from his sails.

Neither of them acknowledges me as I scan the room for anything else that needs my attention before the morning. I pick up one of Charlie's thongs, abandoned next to the TV.

I sit on the edge of the couch near Mark's hip. 'I'm sorry,' I say quietly. 'I know how much this story means to you.'

He lifts his arm and drops it on his chest, turns his head. 'I'm sorry, too.' He props himself up on one side. 'I don't mean about the story. I'm sorry I hurt you.'

'Visuals would've been amazing,' Charlie says as he heaves himself up to sitting, his back against the couch. 'There's a view from the top of the hill where you can see the whole place. Almost aerial. Your cameraman would dig it.'

Mark and I lock eyes and smile. 'World of his own,' I whisper.

'I'm sure he would,' Mark says, without looking away from me.

'And there's this painted rock. Yeah . . . Oh well.'

'Oh well,' I echo. 'Guess we'll have to keep living outside of jail and hope viewers can survive without seeing the painted rock.'

Mark reaches for my hand. 'It would've been a shame to deprive the world of a great lawyer.'

'I'm not going to be a lawyer.' It's the first time I've said this aloud. My voice is calm and steady.

'Yeah?' Charlie says, twisting around.

'Why?' Mark says.

'It doesn't seem like the right course for me,' I say. 'I'm going to study, but not law.'

'Semester has already started,' Mark says. 'Though I guess you could –'

'I'll work it out. I'll decide what's right and then start next semester.' I look down at Charlie. 'In the meantime, though, I'm not going to be everyone's personal slave. We need to share the load better. And the thongs, Charlie – I mean, come on. They smell like dead possum. Leave them outside. In fact, take the bloody things now. I'm not picking up after you anymore.'

After Charlie has left the room, mumbling half-hearted objections, Mark and I sit side by side on the couch.

'So,' Mark says. 'That's big news. You've been talking about studying law for so long I'm kind of shocked.'

'Well, after the accident . . .'

'I get that. I guess I'm not sure what happens next, with us, with you.' He pauses a moment, then asks: 'What is it that you want?'

I wake in the dark. Mark is sitting on the bed, saying my name.

'What time is it?' I ask. I glance at the clock. Eleven-thirty. 'Is something –'

'I got to Geoff's and didn't want to get out of the car.' He takes hold of my hand and nestles it in his lap. 'I miss you. I know I've been an idiot, and I mean it when I say I'm sorry. Will you have me back, Abby? I won't hurt you again.'

I sit up against the headboard. I've missed sharing this bed with him. I don't even mind that he reeks of beer. But the moment I allow myself to feel softness towards him, the hurt rises up. 'Do you love her?' I whisper.

He frowns, shakes his head. 'Never. No. You're the only woman I love, I swear. The only woman I've ever loved.'

'Do you still want her?'

'Absolutely not.' He moves closer to me. 'And I won't jeopardise what I have again. I want to be with you.'

Charlie opens our bedroom door and stands in the dark. 'Hey, so, since we're all awake, I want to let you know I'll pick my stuff up. I hear where you're coming from. I can be a bit of a slob but it's not malicious, not making a point or anything. I just don't notice.'

'Wow,' I say. 'What's brought on apology o'clock?'

Mark turns his head in Charlie's direction. 'Can this wait until tomorrow?'

'The thing is,' Charlie continues, 'it's a confusing time to be a guy. We're supposed to be strong and macho, fix cars, build sheds, cook on a barbecue –'

'You don't do any of those things,' I say.

'Charlie, we're in the middle of something.'

'– smoke Marlboros and chat up chicks, but also be cool with hairy armpits and doing the dishes. And be good looking.'

Mark and I laugh. He moves his hand to where the thin sheet covers my leg.

'But I'll get with the program. Won't leave the thongs lying around. I've read *The Female Eunuch*.'

'You have?' I say.

'I'm going to.'

'Charlie,' Mark says, smiling. 'Piss off, mate.'

I slip out of bed before sunrise, careful not to wake Mark, go to my jewellery box and remove my mother's ring. I fold my hand over it, feeling the metal warm instantly. I tiptoe to the kitchen and open the sliding door as quietly as I can, slowly, releasing my held breath once I'm outside.

The possums quit their carry-on and scuttle up the trees when they register my presence. I see their eyes glinting, watching me. A tawny frogmouth issues a gentle 'hoom'. A full moon shines on glossy monstera leaves. The grass is cool and tickly under-foot. Woof plods outside to greet me, wagging slowly, glad of company so early in the morning.

I hold the ring up to the moon, so the light can shine through the ruby. The gem is the colour of claret, deep and rich, but when the light strikes it the colour lifts and brightens. It's beautiful. I understand why Mum treasured it so much.

Woof rests against me as he sits. I bend down to stroke his back, letting my other hand cradle the ring. As the night-time animals prepare to sleep, and the sky begins to lighten, Mark's question repeats in my ears: What is it that I want? What is it that I need to do?

CHAPTER THIRTY

Tuesday 4 March 1975

Abby

'I have to go to the farm,' Charlie says.

'Why would he let you in if he won't even talk on the phone?' I ask.

'I don't know. Gives him the chance to thump me again.' Charlie sits on the couch, smoking, while I fold laundry on the coffee table. A breeze comes in through the open veranda doors.

'Your kookaburra is here,' I say, nodding my head at the bird sitting on the railing, waiting patiently for its daily meat scraps.

'Not mine,' Charlie says, then follows me into the kitchen and continues speaking while I tear strips of cold ham onto a paper towel to give to the bird. 'I'll yell at Dad through the windows until he listens. As soon as he knows Beau is here I guarantee he'll talk to me.'

I walk back to the veranda and place the ham a respectful distance from the bird, who once again hops backwards on the railing in anticipation of trouble. Dad did want Beau out of the commune and in my home, but I'm not sure he still regards this as a safe haven, now that he's decided his children are murderous and deceitful. He's always respected Mark but he's hanging up on him, too. 'It's a risk, Charlie. You could drive all the way there, get shouted at, and then have to drive all the way back.'

'Wouldn't be the worst day of my life if that's how it panned out. And one way or another, at least he'll know Beau is here.'

Inside, I throw a clean t-shirt at him. 'This one's yours. You'll want to borrow my car to get there, I guess.'

'Feels necessary,' he says, pushing the shirt off his lap onto the couch.

I stop folding. 'This is the first time you'll have driven since the crash.'

'That's occurred to me.'

'Maybe Mark should drive. If you freak out when you drive past . . .'

'I won't. I'm okay.'

'You're not, but if you can promise not to destroy my car that'd be great.' I look at my watch. 'Do me a favour and go get the kids before dinner? They rode their bikes down to the creek.'

He clicks his tongue and winks in a way that I take to mean yes. Since his promise to do his bit around the house, Charlie has stepped up. He's even made a pot of lamb curry for tonight's dinner. And though I know the kids won't eat it (and so I have,

298

in anticipation, bought supplies for a separate meal), I see his effort for what it is.

While I'm setting the table, Mark calls out that Petey has no clean pyjamas, although of course he does. Petey runs naked down the hallway, squealing in delight. At this sound of fun, Woof bounds towards him, thundering through Sarah's doll party, scattering the smiling lovelies across the floor. Sarah screams in outrage, alarming Beau, who darts into the kitchen to sit next to Joanne at the kitchen bench in time to hear her moan to me again that she is hungry, 'sooo hungry, Mum'. Charlie raises his voice over the noise to ask me if he can borrow some cash until his next dole cheque arrives. And for reasons I can't quite explain, none of this bothers me terribly much. I see it, hear it, and decide that I'm not going to address any of it other than Joanne's hunger. I kiss the top of her head as I walk past her.

As predicted, once we're seated at the table, the kids deem the curry disgusting.

'It looks like Woof's dinner,' Sarah says.

'Hey,' Charlie says.

Sarah laughs. 'Like dog food!'

I stand up to make the Plan B meal but Charlie gestures for me to sit back down. 'I'll do it.' He looks at Sarah. 'And you'll help. You're old enough to cook.'

'There are sausages,' I say. 'Frozen peas, corn –'

'We've got this,' Charlie says, and begins telling Sarah a story about Bali as they head into the kitchen together. The other children, having for the first time in history decided that making dinner might be fun, follow them, Woof at the rear.

Which means that Mark and I are, blissfully, left alone at the table to eat and drink. We lift our glasses and clink in recognition of this.

I hear laughter coming from the kitchen, and then music. Charlie has moved the radio dial away from the news. Sarah recognises the song and loudly sings the words she knows. 'This is a good curry,' Mark says, and I agree.

We're talking, and there's music. And while I'm loving this moment, I know it will move on. Something will be dropped or broken. Someone will be offended or bored. Mark could look at me and, despite himself, see the cold-hearted woman who drove away from a crash. I could watch him take his next mouthful and want to slap the lips that kissed Lou. Or we could reach across the table and hold hands. Charlie might come dancing out of the kitchen, the children in a happy conga line behind him. Who knows? The trick, I suppose, is to bend and move with as much of it as you can, without losing your own shape. To know that your life is this one night, this group of people, and also more than this. Also the people who aren't in the room . . . Also the things you haven't yet done.

After dinner, in the backyard, Sarah explains the rules of tunnel ball to Beau, Petey and Joanne, since that was the highlight of her school day. She uses a plastic ball, fished out of the pool, in lieu of the heavier medicine ball they'd used at school.

'Nobody knows why it's called a medicine ball. One of life's mysteries,' Charlie says to Petey as Sarah slaps her brother on the legs to stand wider.

Mark laughs. 'Do not listen to your uncle.'

'Ever,' I say.

'It's called a medicine ball because the ancient Greeks encouraged their patients to throw and roll heavy balls for medicinal purposes. They thought exercise cured sickness,' Mark says.

'Huh,' Charlie says.

'Does it?' Beau asks.

'Some.' Then, after quick consideration of who asked the question, Mark adds, 'But a doctor is the best bet if you ever feel sick. Do you feel sick?'

Beau shakes his head. 'Do you?' he asks Mark, genuinely concerned.

'I'm good, buddy.'

Mark, standing next to me, reaches out and takes my hand. This boy melts us. I hadn't anticipated how immediately, ferociously protective we would be, how possessive. We've talked through the practicalities of adding him to our brood (challenging, expensive, but not impossible) and decided what to say should the police show up. Our main concern now is what to do if Finn returns.

Because we're not giving Beau back. He's only been here for two nights, but we've already decided he needs us. We worry at his unfamiliarity with so many things our children take for granted. The ring of a telephone makes him jump, the TV was bewildering and now far too enticing, the word 'lunchbox' meant nothing until I explained it. And his knowingness with adult behaviour brought out the judgemental streak in both of us.

'What type of six-year-old knows how to help someone pierce their ears?' I'd asked Mark after a particularly alarming conversation when I was putting Beau to bed.

'That doesn't bother me as much as him saying that when an adult is screaming you're supposed to hold their hand. I mean –' He shook his head.

'Did they train them to do that because the adults are tripping?'

'I guess so. Have to hope the kids weren't given any drugs.'

Tunnel ball mastered, the kids have moved on to simply throwing the ball about. Mark watches as Beau helps Joanne with her clumsy catch.

'Great hand-eye coordination,' he says to me. 'Incredible. Might take him down to the nets.'

I smile, but my mind has gone elsewhere. Tomorrow, I decide, I will go to the library to read about how adoption works and what grounds qualify a child to be removed from his father.

At bedtime, I steer the children towards Sarah's room.

'But who owns it?' Sarah asks me again.

'It belongs to all of us,' I say.

'Whose room will it stay in?'

'Yours and Beau's.'

'Mine, you mean. My room,' she says. She's happy to play with Beau, but not at all happy at having a boy sleep on a camp bed in her room. Especially one who, she tells me, cries when she's trying to sleep.

'Our room,' says Joanne.

'I haven't read a single page yet. Why do you care whose room it lives in?'

'Because you said it's good,' Sarah replies.

'That's enough. Get on the bed, all of you. Leave space for me in the middle.'

The four children line themselves up on Sarah's bed with their backs resting against the wall, jockeying for more space, lobbying for their preferred configuration and the right to hold certain soft toys on their lap.

'I need to wee.' Petey scuttles off the bed.

'Is it a girls' book or a boys' book?' Joanne asks. I stroke her long shiny hair.

'It's both. This was my favourite book when I was a little girl but there are lots of poems in here for boys, too.'

'Poems?' Sarah slumps down the wall until she's lying across the bed, her t-shirt ruching up around her neck and exposing her belly, willing to tolerate discomfort to make a statement. 'You didn't say it was poems.'

'Can I see the cover?' Joanne asks, and I pass her our new copy of *A Child's Garden of Verses*. The cover is different from that of my childhood copy, but still lovely – two girls and a boy sit in a meadow, circled by poppies, daisies and woodland creatures. Bluebirds hover above them. The boy holds an open book from which a cast of characters fly off the page: a king and queen, a witch, a winged horse.

Joanne passes the book back to me, sceptical it will offer anything pleasing. Petey runs back into the room and bellyflops onto the bed, causing another round of laughing, outrage and wriggling. Only Beau stays composed. He reaches across my lap and taps Petey on the leg and Petey becomes quiet. When Beau sits back, Joanne rests her head on his shoulder.

I whisper into Beau's ear, 'Please teach me how to do that.'

After a few pages, Joanne and Sarah drop onto the floor to play marbles. Petey wanders off to do who knows what. And I read Beau a poem called 'At the Seaside'. He shows me the pictures he likes best: a parade of Arabian royalty and African animals, children building a ship from cushions and chairs, a boy making a sandcastle.

'Can we go to the beach one day?' he asks.

I close the book and lay it on my lap. 'You like the beach?'

'Dad said my mum used to take me to the beach when we lived in Cairns. I don't remember though.'

'We'll go then. I'll arrange it.'

I lift a soft curl off his forehead. He looks up at me and smiles.

CHAPTER THIRTY-ONE

Saturday 8 March 1975

Charlie

He isn't happy. He doesn't even show much surprise, offers a humph of displeasure at the first sight of me. Had I been in a sarcastic mood rather than just wrecked from tiredness, I'd have opened with: 'Don't worry, Dad, we're all okay. No need for alarm. Just drove five and a half hours because you won't take a bloody phone call.' My body aches from so much sitting, my hands sore from gripping a steering wheel that shuddered and tugged on the bumpy, potholed road.

My dry mouth makes an unwanted smacking noise when I say hi. Dad says nothing in reply. He glowers at me from behind the grey flywire mesh. I speak fast in case he's about to slam the door. 'Beau,' I say. I'd thought about this opener. Not elegant, but it was the only word that mattered right now and I knew it would get his attention.

'What about him?' he says. And with that, we're talking. I fight to ignore my body's aches, hunger and thirst, and concentrate on whether I should say more on the doorstep or use my father's interest to get inside. He scans my face, clearly deliberating on whether to send me away or show how interested he is (I've seen him smother this before: curiosity, eagerness), to speak or maintain the upper hand. Ryan is right – cynical, but right: people are locked in an eternal battle to be top dog. Every conversation, every silent interaction, we're vying for dominance. Withholding affection then dangling a taste of it (Sal), having sex with your best friend's man to punish a neglectful husband (Lou), the strategic trading of fact and anecdote to show you're in the centre of the storm (Mark), being frenetically busy, loudly competent (Abby), letting your sister, your mate and your father deal with life's responsibilities so that you can stay adolescent (me). Right now, my father is in control of whether or not I can step onto his turf, but I have information that we both know he wants.

'It's important,' I say. 'Let me in.' I throw down the gauntlet, done with the games.

But my father won't back down to his son – he's too proud for that. 'It's unlocked,' he says. 'Nothing stopping you.' And he turns his back on me and walks to his living room. I let myself in, follow him like a child.

Once we're in the living room, both seated, no drinks on offer, after I've made a U-turn to his bathroom, taken way longer than necessary in there, my father thumps the button on his armchair that flicks up his footrest and stares at me – arms folded across his middle, legs outstretched, king of his domain. 'Go on then,' he says. Jesus. No wonder the world is constantly at war.

I don't have it in me to keep up our stand-off. So I tell him about Abby and Mark, Maria and Beau. Everything. To the mundane and rhythmic sounds of my turkey friend Lenny scratching up leaves outside the open window, a magpie warbling, and the washing machine chugging.

Dad doesn't respond the way I'd imagined he would. He doesn't want to come to Brisbane to see Beau. 'What for? It was my job to get him out of that hellhole but I'm not going to mother the boy. Abby will do that.' He shrugs off Beau's bumpy entry into suburban life.

'Abby had to lie to the principal to get him into the local school,' I tell him. 'They asked where he'd come from and she said he'd been home-schooled. On his first day there Beau cracked it about the guinea pigs being in a cage. Then kept wandering away from his desk. Normal life freaks him out.'

'He'll adapt,' Dad says. Even the issue of Finn's potential return meets with a clipped reply: 'I'm sure Mark and Abby will sort something out. Mark's a clever fellow.'

His stubborn insistence on treating our conversation like a news report, one in which he has no vested interest, is infuriating. He cares. At least, I think he does. But once I've answered his few questions, we fall silent. I know what's coming next, though.

'If you think driving up here to tell me this, or your sister taking Beau in, redeems you, you'd better think again. You're lucky I let you in. You're a murderer. Your sister's a scheming liar.'

I lean forward and speak as calmly as I can. 'Dad, we are genuinely sorry, but insulting me –'

'Insulting you? You bloody baby,' he shouts. In an instant, his forced composure vanishes. His voice is shrill, wounded. His face is red.

I want to get up and leave. But I force myself to stay and take his stream of vitriol. Because my visit to the farm has two goals: tell Dad about Beau; man up and fix what's broken. So here goes.

I still don't know the chick version of man up. Maybe it's just what they do all the time. But it doesn't matter, since on this occasion we're both men. Point is, I need to offer Dad space to let rip at me, to say everything he needs to, and then own that I caused his pain. Me, not Abby. Me, not Finn.

And he does let rip. 'Have you or your sister given a moment's thought to what you've stolen from me? I've buried two women I loved. Your drunken childishness means the rest of my life will now be empty, lonely, meaningless. You took Skye, took our future, our child. And you're sitting here feeling sorry for yourself because I called you a name? What did I do to end up with a son like you?'

The act of hurling abuse at me, and of putting his pain into words, quickly exhausts him. I stay quiet and listen. When he's run out of things to say he sits panting, as if he's run a marathon. I know better than to try to lighten this moment. No jokes, no switching to more comfortable topics. I agree with him that everything he's said is true, tell him again that I'm sorry, and wait for him to break the silence.

'You can sleep here tonight, then I want you gone.'

*

Late afternoon I realise that if I'm going to stay we'll need food. I've looked in his fridge – eggs from his chickens, the heels of a loaf of white bread, milk, some wrinkly carrots. Not sure what he thought he was going to eat for dinner but this is not enough for two people. I have a carton of beer in the boot of Abby's car – an ill-considered peace offering – but it truly didn't occur to me to bring food.

I find Dad in the laundry, angrily shoving another load into the washer as if he hates the machine and everything he's putting in it. I tell him I'm going to Chinchilla to get dinner supplies.

'What, cornflakes?' he says. I'm going to have to take blow after blow until he softens. Which might be never. And my only adult choice is to do nothing, let it wash over me.

'I'll buy some chops, vegetables, some bread. Anything else you want while I'm there?'

He turns around and huffs. 'You'll never find the super-market. And I don't want you on the road. You're a menace.' Ignoring the fact I drove to him from Brisbane. 'I'll drive.' He waves a sock at me. 'But you're paying.'

'Not a problem. I'll cook, too,' I say.

He throws the sock in the machine and turns it on. 'You don't know how to cook.' Then leaves the room.

The Chinchilla supermarket is small but our needs are basic. I push the wobbly trolley along the scuffed lino to the tune of 'hurry up' and 'where are you going?', with a brief break from the droning personal criticism while Dad vents his spleen on the kid stacking shelves: 'Sold out of it every time I'm here.' Dad decides on chops, green beans and mash for dinner and, since I'm paying, adds shampoo, laundry soap, insect spray . . . I don't care. I take two tins of tomato soup, a box of Weet-Bix and a jar of honey from the wooden shelves and put them in the trolley, trying to think ahead for Dad, channelling Abby's forward planning, and remain quietly proud of myself even when Dad notices and says, 'Your money.'

The fluorescent lights seem to glow brighter as the sky outside darkens. A storm is on its way. We were lucky to make it inside before the rain came. Through the plate-glass windows I watch a beer-bellied man in overalls make a surprisingly graceful dash across the road from the feed store to the chemist.

As I force my trolley to turn into the next aisle, I hear Dad – who's stomped off ahead of me – speaking.

Roberts looks genuinely surprised to see me, but so did Finn in the RE beer garden. This encounter isn't as suspicious as that one since I know Roberts lives in Chinchilla and the town has a population of about three, but still . . . Are the cops and their crooks following me? That sort of thing happens. They could've even bugged Dad's farm, Abby's house. I walk towards them with the trolley.

'Or do you prefer to be called by your Christian name when you're off-duty?' Dad asks, his voice awkwardly formal. 'I imagine as with other jobs that –'

'Eric. I'm Eric when I'm off-duty.'

We stand in a circle. There are no other customers. At the end of the aisle I can see the checkout chick in profile – sixteen at most – arms folded across her blue apron, skinny ponytail, watching the rain fall in sheets from the gutter onto the footpath. The bagger, another rangy, sloped-shouldered teenager, glances our way before he returns his gaze to the girl.

310

'Eric, I'm glad we ran into you because it's been several weeks since I had any updates from you or your sergeant,' Dad says. 'I hope you're still giving your full attention to investigating Skye's accident.'

Roberts doesn't strike me as the scoffing kind, but he scoffs. 'I would if I could. Sergeant Doyle has declared this a closed case – car trouble. Which leaves me with nothing to investigate. He did tell you that, didn't he?' He frowns in confusion.

Dad has no idea about the deal Doyle struck with Abby and me. But I did think Doyle would've told him the case was closed, come up with some lie about why. Whether it's an oversight or deliberate, I can see on Dad's face that this is a blow. There's no longer any mystery he needs explained by the cops, but the fact they've stopped investigating must suggest to him the case is not important, that Skye's death deserves no more man hours.

It's obvious that Dad asked Roberts about the case because it's all they have to discuss, and he did it aggressively because he goes on the offensive to feel in control. It's like Abby with her lists. But with this unexpected turn in the conversation the three of us are floundering. Dad's winded, unable to figure out how to navigate this encounter without losing face. Off-duty Roberts has unwittingly broken news and must be wondering why. And I just want to get food and leave this place.

'Your sergeant needs to communicate a little better,' Dad says. 'That's something I should've been told. I –'

'Okay,' Roberts says, eyes shooting from Dad to me and back again. 'What if we drop this charade? We're all adults. John, you know, don't you?'

Dad straightens up. 'I know you lot are acting like Keystone Cops. It's been three months and –'

'And we know what happened. We know your son and daughter were driving to your farm and ran a car off the road, killing the driver –'

'Hey, whoa!' I say.

'That is an absolutely outrageous –' Dad is loud, but neither of us can stop Roberts from forging ahead.

'They crossed the bridge. Your son told the publican and three customers at the Chinchilla Pub that they crossed the bridge that night. They were driving away from your farm, not towards it. They had wet hair and clothes because they'd been in the rain, in the ditch with your fiancée. They lied about the times. They lied to you about everything. John, I know the who and when and I can guess at the how, but I can't answer any of the whys.'

'Come on, Dad, let's go. You don't need to listen to this.'

Dad ignores me, keeps his focus on Roberts. 'I don't think you know a single thing, son, or you'd have charged someone by now. I think you're hoping to provoke me or Charlie into saying what you want to hear. But that's not going to happen.'

Roberts glares at me. 'Your father was engaged to her. How can you cause her death and then shop for . . . Weet-Bix . . . with him? How can you lie to him?' Then returns his attention to my father. 'John, you know what I'm saying is true, don't you? That's why you left your daughter's house and came back to the farm, isn't it?'

'The farm is my home. I never intended to stay with my daughter forever.'

'Why on earth aren't you speaking up? You loved her. I've interviewed every person who ever saw you two together and they all say you were in love. She was carrying your child! Why are you letting them get away with it?'

'They're not getting away with anything,' Dad says, and in a strange way that's true.

I walk to the checkout, Dad and Roberts following me, and pile one item after another in front of the checkout chick as fast as I can. Her badge says Tansy but I don't think that's a name. 'Tansy,' I say. 'We're in a real hurry. How quickly can you guys get this stuff in a bag?'

'You didn't know right away, did you?' Roberts says to Dad. 'I saw how you greeted them, how your daughter baulked at the word fiancée. You didn't know then what they'd done, but you do now.'

I turn my head around. 'Man, this is harassment. You need to stop. You're not even on duty.'

He ignores me. 'Don't you want justice? Let me do my job.'

'You can't bring her back,' Dad says. 'And that's the only thing that I want.'

'Am I missing something?' Roberts says. 'Tell me, sir, *please*. Because for the life of me I can't imagine why a man would take this. How much can a father forgive? Surely not this.'

Outside the supermarket, the squall is gathering strength. Wind batters at the windows, slanted rain hits the panes. On the road, cars have slowed to a crawl, heads down against the waves of water. Thunder rumbles and lightning cracks across the sky. For an instant, the power fails in the supermarket and the lights go off, then flicker back to life. The checkout girl and bagger gawp at us shamelessly, ignoring everything else.

I take out my wallet and ask Tansy how much I owe. She looks at me like I'm mental. 'I haven't rung anything up yet.'

'Why?' Roberts stands behind my father. 'Why stay quiet?' He's staring at Dad with hunting-dog concentration.

'How much?' I say to the girl. 'Roughly?'

'You want me to make up a number?'

'Yeah, do that. How much?'

She picks up a tin of soup and slowly rings it up on the clunky register. She doesn't want this conversation to leave the store.

'Jesus, forget it.' I grab the meat, green beans, throw down more than enough cash to pay for them. 'Dad, we're going.' In an instant we've switched roles: I've taken charge, speedy with adrenaline. 'Now.'

I open the supermarket door to hot wet air, walk into the wind for a half-dozen steps or so, before realising that Dad is not behind me. Then I see him lurch out the door with Roberts still talking at him.

'They've committed a crime. It's not an option to ignore it.'

Dad raises his forefinger. 'You are an officer of the law. You know better than to make accusations without evidence, in or out of uniform. You should be ashamed of yourself.' He stops. I can hardly hear his voice over the rain. 'How do you not understand? They're all I've got left.'

'Oh no. Dad.' I jog back to where he stands, grab his arm and pull him towards the car. 'Don't.'

'That's not how things work,' Roberts says, following us. 'People commit a crime and they go to jail. You can't decide when laws apply to you.'

314

Dad pushes my hand off him. 'What good would come of locking up a young mother, leaving her husband to raise a family on his own? What good would come of jailing my son, destroying his life and mine?'

'Dad, stop talking.'

'Don't you want justice for Skye?'

'No, I don't,' Dad says. 'I've lost a fiancée and a baby. I want them back. And if you lock up a hundred people that's never going to happen. The one you'll hurt most if you send them to jail is me.'

We stand under the cover of a sagging canvas, rain pooling above our heads.

Roberts glares at me. 'One day you'll need me. Or someone like me. I'm the type of cop you want on the force. A cop who cares about the truth.'

'You're right,' I say. 'You're right about everything.'

'Charlie, no,' Dad says.

'It's okay, Dad.' I hadn't anticipated my manning-up would extend to a confession to the cops, but lately life is throwing all kinds of curve balls. 'There's no evidence and Doyle has shut the case. But if you need to hear it – and you seem to – you're right. I was driving. I fell asleep. Abby tried to get Skye up to the car but she couldn't. It was too late anyway . . . It's on me, the whole thing. And I'll be sorry till the day I die. You good now, man? We're done?'

'Oh, Charlie.' Dad shakes his head slowly.

'Let's go home,' I say.

We're walking towards the car when Roberts calls out. 'Wait.'

'Ignore him, Dad. There's nothing else to say.'

315

'You proposed that night.'

Dad stops at this, turns, as Roberts moves closer. 'Leave it alone, son. He's told you what you wanted to hear.'

'But she wasn't wearing a ring. I've seen her list of belongings a hundred times: wallet, birthing bag, silver chain – no ring. You would've given her a ring, wouldn't you? When you proposed?'

Dad frowns at him, suddenly indignant. 'I want that back. I assumed she – that it was on her hand when she was buried. If one of your men so much as –'

'There was no ring,' Roberts says.

'I want it back.'

'Dad, let's go.' I glare at him. Surely he knows Abby wouldn't have left Mum's ring with Skye?

'What did it look like?'

'A ruby in a gold band, the word "love" inscribed on it. You won't find another one like it in Australia. I had it brought in from Paris. You lot have no right –'

'Dad, stop! What is wrong with you?'

He seems confused, then shocked. 'Well, I want it back. That ring belonged to your mother.'

'Where's the ring?' Roberts asks me.

The car is ten feet away. 'Keys, Dad, give me the keys.'

'Your sister will want that ring. She always has.'

'Dad, *fuck*, get in the car!'

While he's hours away from Abby's house, it'll only take Roberts a few minutes to find a telephone and get some Brisbane cops out to her place – where she keeps Mum's ring, in her goddamn jewellery box. And he knows he's onto something now. I push Dad towards the car, swearing as he resists. Roberts takes off in the other direction.

As we drive away, I scan the rainy streets for a public phone box, but by the time the main strip runs out I still haven't seen one. I put my foot to the floor, despite Dad's shouts to slow down, and fang it back to his house.

CHAPTER THIRTY-TWO

Saturday 8 March 1975

Abby

I've taken the transistor radio into the front yard with me in case there's more news about the fire that started near Eumundi a few hours ago. It has to be the commune, but none of the news reports is using any word similar to that. There's no talk of teepees, kombis, naked kids, guns or dope fields. The flames have engulfed vast areas of bushland near Cooroy Mountain, and firefighters are trying to contain the spread. The newsreader has said some roads are blocked by fallen trees, and warned people to stay out of the area. I wonder whether the people at the commune lit the fire to cover their tracks, or if the police did it. Or someone else. And where did everyone go? What about the drugs? I have so many questions but can't talk to Mark about this until tomorrow. He knew better than to invite me on a fishing trip, and he and Geoff are perfectly capable of handling the kids for one night, but now I wish he was here.

I place the radio on the step near the front door and turn up the volume. I'll start my garden redux, by cutting back the boronia that's spread across the path.

As I kneel on the grass to begin, I hear the cough of an old muffler and watch a dusty brown Holden swing around the corner. The driver parks on a slant across the bottom of our driveway, about twenty feet away from me. A man gets out of the car, pushes his sunglasses up onto his mop of hair and takes a few steps in my direction. I know who he is. Finn is exactly as my father and Charlie have described him, though they'd both neglected to say how good looking he is. He's wearing khaki shorts, no shirt, no shoes, a leather strap around his neck. He smiles at me.

'Hey there. I'm Finn.'

I stiffen. 'What do you want?'

'Pleasure to meet you, too.' He walks up the driveway towards me as I slowly stand up, his eyes roaming over my dress, my legs. The grass will have made crisscross red marks across my knees. I shouldn't care, but I do. 'Beau here?'

I speak slowly, as if I'm untroubled by his presence. 'Why do you ask?'

He lifts his eyes to mine in a way that's almost coquettish. 'Now, normally I wouldn't mind a little to and fro with you but I don't have a lot of time today. So how about you go get my son so we can be on our way.'

At first I think 'we' is him and Beau, but there's a flash of movement in the car and I see that someone else is in there. Sal leans across the driver's seat and gives me a small wave, her silver bracelets jingling. 'Hey Abby, long time.' She offers me a half-smile, the smile of someone who knows how beautiful she is, how elegant and desirable, and feels a little bit sorry for you being you. 'How's Charlie?' she calls out. 'Haven't seen him since New Year's.'

'Fine. He's fine. Are you going somewhere with Finn? I'm not sure I understand what's going on.'

'Enough with the small talk, ladies,' Finn says, and Sal pulls back into the shade of the car. 'Abby, princess, go get Beau. We've got a long drive ahead of us.'

I pause. 'I don't think that's a good idea.' I could tell Finn the truth – that Beau isn't here, that no one is here but me – but I don't want him to know I'm alone. I'm unsure of my choice even as I dive headlong into it. 'Beau is so happy here. He's settled in really well. And the kids love him. I mean, we all do. He's –'

Finn walks closer. I clutch the secateurs. There's no trace of friendliness in his face. He's near enough that I can smell his sweat, his beery breath. 'Glad to hear he's happy. Now stop fucking around and go get him.'

'No.'

'Wasn't a request.'

On the radio behind me Helen Reddy is singing about strength in numbers and unity, but there is no one here to help me. Sal sits immobile and uncaring in the car. The street in front of me is empty. I could scream, I suppose, but what would I say he's done?

'Please don't do this to him.'

'I'll do what I want. I'm his father.' He is standing too close. 'And what are you to him? Nothing. The woman who killed his

320

mother.' I'm unable to hide my shock. 'Yeah, I know. But does Beau? You think he'll like you so much when he does?'

I feel my knees weaken. 'Please don't hurt him to get to me. I know what we did was wrong but he's already lost so much and he's such a sweet –'

'You know, I've had enough talking. I'll let myself in.'

I walk after him, unsteady, shaking. 'There's no one in there. Go in if you want to, but he's not here.'

He turns and scowls at me. 'So what was your song-and-dance routine about? Where is he?'

I have no idea what to say. If I tell him the truth, he might come back again tomorrow. And if he got here early, Mark would be ambushed, with no idea of what he was coming home to. Finn looks stronger than him, able to scoop Beau up even if we both resisted. And how awful for Beau to go through that tussle. But what lie will work?

It seems he doesn't believe me anyway. Finn goes inside the house and closes the door behind him. I hear the phone ringing. I run to the door but Finn has locked it. I hope one of my neighbours is witnessing this, can tell it's hostile and calls the police. But I don't see anyone out in their garden, or peering through their curtains.

After a few minutes, Finn walks outside and stands in front of me. 'I reckon you've misunderstood me. I'm not here to take Beau back – we're on the move. Won't work for a kid. I'm here to say goodbye. But now I guess you'll have to do that for me.'

And with the slam of a car door and a squeal of tyres, they're gone.

I drop onto the grass, my legs jelly, my throat tight. I should feel relieved that Finn is gone and nothing bad happened.

I should feel glad that he doesn't want to take Beau. But, instead, I feel a gut punch of sadness. Beau has been abandoned. His father has driven away without him, as though he was nothing and no one. How can I ever explain this to him?

The phone rings again, and this time I run inside and answer it.

'Not now, Abby.' Charlie cuts me off the moment I speak, launching into the story of his supermarket encounter before I can get to the word 'Finn'.

'You need to get rid of the ring. Right now. Brisbane cops will be on their way to your house. I'm sure of it. If Roberts finds it, he has evidence we were at the accident and we're cooked. No matter what Doyle wants.'

I run to the jewellery box, wrap the ring in a thick layer of tissues and hide it in my cleavage, well covered by my shirt.

I don't have a car. A taxi could take any amount of time. The back garden, the creek, the bottom of the rubbish bin could all fail me. Will they bring sniffer dogs?

I walk quickly to Lou's house. I hop about on her doormat, waiting for her to answer my loud knocking. 'Be home, be home, be home,' I mutter.

'Abby.' She's surprised, and then, in an instant, anxious. It's been more than two months since we last spoke. She sees how flustered I am. 'Do you want to come in?' She steps to one side but I don't move from the doormat.

'I need a favour.' I put my hand down my shirt and pull out the wad of tissue. 'Mind this. Hide it somewhere safe and don't tell anyone – not Andrew, not *anyone* – that you have it.' I give the tissue bundle a gentle press, reassuring it and me, then pass it to Lou.

She looks down at the tissues. 'Can I ask what it is?'

'It's a ring.' She glances at my wedding finger. 'And it's none of your business. I need you to take care of it and not ask any questions. This is important. Okay?'

She nods earnestly, brows furrowed. 'All right. I can do that. Are we – friends again?'

'I don't know.' I look over my shoulder back at my house and then at the road, but I don't see a police car. 'I'm trusting you with this. Don't let me down.'

She holds the tissue bundle close to her. 'I'll guard it with my life.'

The police showed up a few hours after Charlie called, which was a blessing and a curse. I'd wondered if they'd come on Sunday, in which case Mark and the children might be back. I hadn't wanted to explain to the kids what they were searching for, nor explain to the police why Beau was here (well-rehearsed script or not). But when Mark told me, later, that I'd had the right to ask if they had a search warrant and then refuse them entry – they couldn't have obtained a warrant in that amount of time, and on a weekend – I wished he'd been there.

They found nothing because, of course, there was nothing to find. And they had no dogs with them to sniff my track from my home to Lou's, if dogs can do such a thing. So while the whole encounter felt awkward and shameful, they'd left empty-handed and I'd rushed to the phone to tell Charlie. Then stared at the wall until my shoulders shook and tears ran down my cheeks.

PART THREE

CHAPTER THIRTY-THREE

Thursday 27 March 1975

Abby

We're at the Happy Valley campground in Caloundra, with the northern tip of Bribie Island in sight across a sparkling sapphire inlet and a white-sand beach a dozen feet away from our car. Because we've arrived a day before the Easter holidays begin, we have the place to ourselves and pick the best spot – close to the beach, far enough from the road that all we hear is the whoosh and crash of waves, surrounded by pandanus pines, casuarinas and a strip of green grass, kookaburras and rainbow lorikeets in the branches above us.

The four kids help unload the car then whine their way through a few tasks until Mark frees them to go exploring with Woof. Beau offers to stay with us, and proves unnervingly competent with tent ropes and pegs. When he sees the fire pit, though, he stops in his tracks. Noticing this, Mark says, 'We're good, mate. Why don't you go find the others?'

Mark and I work companionably to set up an area where we can store the food and fold-out table. I feel certain that getting away from the house will be a balm for all of us. And this place is perfect. No TV, no phone, no work or school, and no chance Finn will show up unannounced. It's a place where we can start to replace Beau's bad memories with good ones, as much as that's possible.

'Charlie decide if he's joining us?' Mark asks as we lay the kids' tent flat on the ground. I kneel close to him. The sandy soil is hot on the surface, cool just an inch below.

'I'm not sure. Hope so. But if he does it'll only be for a few nights. He and Ryan are keen to push ahead with their shop plans.' I pass lengths of metal rod to Mark one at a time and he assembles the supports that will hold up the tent's thick canvas sides. 'They want to open in June.'

'It's not a terrible idea,' he says, and flicks a fly away from his mouth. 'People are obsessed with Bali, and since they know someone who can arrange the exporting –'

'Ketut.'

'Ketut. I reckon they can make a go of it.'

'Ryan's dad's still furious. Charlie said he yelled that Ryan had become a *merchant*.'

Mark laughs. 'My God, not a *merchant*!'

'I know,' I say. 'The shame of it.'

We stand and pull the tent up one section at a time. I push each roped peg into the dirt with the heel of my thong then Mark hammers them down further with the mallet.

328

'Well, I guess you can reassure Ryan that working in a law firm isn't everyone's path in life.'

'At least he has a path,' I say.

'You'll find yours.' He smiles at me, points to a stray peg near my feet, which I hand to him. 'And once you do we'll be your cheer squad.'

A salty breeze wafts over us. It'll be cold tonight. I've brought sweatshirts for the kids, and had thought we'd sit around the fire roasting marshmallows. I'm not sure about that now. I never know what will trigger a memory for Beau, but I'm kicking myself for not thinking that the commune would've had an open fire. Of course they would. Maybe Beau helped Finn make the campfires. Or sat on logs squashed between his friends, laughing and nudging, singing songs. I decide to assume his memories of fires are happy ones.

Over the past few weeks, I've looked for opportunities to ask Beau about his life, tentatively, pulling back and changing the topic if he showed any discomfort. I've asked if he'd ever had anyone check his teeth, then explained what a dentist is, asked if the kids ever had red spots that weren't from mosquitoes, if he was used to sleeping in the same bed every night. I'm drawing a deer into a clearing, murmuring encouragement, offering treats.

And comforting. Late last night, Beau and I sat on the couch in the dark, after Sarah had come to our room complaining that he was crying again. My arm around his shoulder, I told him that when I was young I'd lost my mother, too, but that sometimes I could feel her with me. He'd let his eyes roam the living room, lit by a full moon beaming through the glass veranda doors.

329

'I don't think she's here now,' I said. 'But when she does show up I'll let you know. She'll like you a lot.' He'd nestled into my side. Woof joined us on the couch, sprawled across Beau's lap for a tummy rub, and made us both laugh. 'Maybe your mum will visit you,' I'd said, then held him until he fell asleep, laid him gently on the couch next to Woof and woken Mark to carry him to bed. I wish Maria had told us more.

I ask Mark if we should give up on the campfire idea. He understands why I'm asking, and says he'll think about it. A few days ago, Mark met with Jim's brother, a psychologist, to ask how to help Beau adjust to his new life. But I'm not convinced that we need someone with experience in easing adults out of cults. The adoption lawyer will, I think, be a more useful ally.

Once we're finished setting up, Mark and I sit in our fold-out chairs and face the waves. From here, we can see the kids noodling about on the beach: Petey, Beau and Woof are crouched next to a shallow pool made by the low tide, all three heads down as if staring into a well, Joanne is dragging a long branch behind her and making wavy lines in the sand, and Sarah follows, rubbing them out with her foot.

Mark turns on the transistor, 'just for the news bulletin, I promise', because he's convinced another storm is about to come.

I point up at the clear blue sky.

'Not that kind of storm,' he says.

Even as I roll my eyes, I feel the wind blow sharp sand against my legs.

After lunch, we put on our bathers, collect towels, a bat, tennis ball, zinc cream and other items deemed essential, and regroup on the beach. Mark, Petey and Beau play cricket on the wet sand. The girls make a sandcastle.

Mark's not feeling great about this beach and has suggested we move tomorrow morning. 'It's too rough,' he tells me after he's had a swim. 'We're too close to where the tide comes in.' I sigh, but I can see he's right. The stretch of water to the north looks infinitely better. This will do for one day, though.

Sarah calls out to Mark to come watch her do cartwheels, jealous, I suspect, of him being so openly impressed by Beau's cricketing skills. The other children paddle about in the shallow water. I lie back on my towel, oiled in Coppertone, dozing, reading, listening to the screech of seagulls and the crashing waves.

I wake up when I feel water drip onto my belly. Beau is standing over me, a hand outstretched.

'I think this one has an animal inside,' he says, kneeling down beside me, holding a striped cone shell on his open palm. He watches the shell intently but the small creature is not tricked into peeking out. 'Can you mind it for me?'

'Sure,' I say. 'Maybe it'll pop its head out later. When it thinks we're not looking.' I prop myself up on my elbows. 'Where's everyone else?'

He points to Sarah, plopped down on the sand, her back to the sea, digging, and tells me that Mark took the twins back to the tents because they were hungry again. 'Who could've predicted that?' I say. And we share a smile.

'Are you going to swim?' he asks.

'Sure, yes. You go ahead. I'll join you in a sec.'

I watch him walk down to the water, skinny, arms like twigs, knock-kneed but striding. I feel a stab in my stomach at how vulnerable he is, and know that it's our job now – mine and

Mark's – to keep this boy safe and happy. I fold the corner of my towel over Beau's shell. The wind has picked up and I worry it might get blown away.

I follow Beau out into the sea, ploughing forward as the water deepens, holding my balance against the current, which is stronger than I'd expected. I look out at the inlet, the boundless expanse of sea, out to where the whitecaps are spaced far apart. I rise and fall on the ocean's breath, lifted slowly then lowered.

There is nothing but ocean around us, water so clear the sunlight marbles my thighs and I can see the red nail polish on my toes. The swell raises my arms up. 'Wave,' Beau calls. He points at the water rising behind him. He's excited, not scared. I give him a thumbs-up. He disappears under the churning water to come up on the other side. I marvel at how he knew to do that. He flicks wet hair from his face and we grin at one another. I turn and watch the wave melt to a spill as it touches the beach.

But something isn't right. I feel sudden panic as Beau grows smaller right before my eyes. This current is dangerously strong. I should've noticed the rip. I call out to him, trying to hide the worry in my voice. He's moving away from me quickly. There are no whitecaps where he is now. The water is darker. 'Swim to the sand,' I yell, but he's not in control of where he's going.

'Sarah, *Sarah*.' I want her to run for Mark, but she can't hear me. We're already too far out.

I tread water in my safe spot outside the rip while I figure out how I can get to Beau. There's no easy way. I need to swim a large arc around the edge of the current then cut into it and allow it to pull me to him. Summoning my muscles and resolve,

I remind myself I'm good at this, that the water was once my second home. 'I'm coming,' I shout to him.

I push through the water, strong arms and breath powering me. I pause, check I'm on track, adjust, then swim again. Once I'm close enough to feel the tug, I give over to the current and it flings me, like a slingshot, towards Beau. When I can, I reach out and grab his arm. He's scared, panting.

We're in the slipstream, being pulled out to deep water. But I know what to do, and that I can do it. And that he can, too. I nod to where the current swoops close to the shore. 'We let the water take us there. Then swim diagonal to the beach.' I draw a line in the air to show what I mean. 'Breaking waves go to the sand.' Entrusting ourselves to the waves. 'We'll be okay.'

With his arms tight around me, my eyes fixed on the shore, with full lungs and a strong heart, I swim.

ACKNOWLEDGEMENTS

My gratitude and love go to my partner Dave and older son Liam. But I've dedicated this book to my younger son, Milo, for bravery, kindness and wisdom in the face of adversity. The human body is both astonishing and ridiculous, and the number of ways it can cause pain seems to be limitless. I'm sorry you've had to experience the challenges you have. I'm in awe of you. And I love you.

Thank you to my agent, Jacinta di Mase, for your years of patience in guiding this story to a good home.

Thank you to PEN America for shortlisting an early version of this story for the Bellwether Prize. Your encouragement was life-changing.

Thank you to Canadian novelist Alissa York for sage feedback on the manuscript during my too-brief stay at the Banff Centre for Creativity; and to the talented, thoughtful group of writers I was blessed to meet while there.

Alissa only had time to walk me a certain way down the road. I am grateful (though wish there was a word bigger than this) for the more recent editorial guidance of Penguin Random House publisher Beverley Cousins and editor Tom Langshaw. You each offered advice that has made this story immeasurably better than it was. Thank you for your care and intelligence. And Beverley, thank you for taking a risk on me.

Thank you, Christa Moffitt, for your beautiful cover design. I dip my lid and am grateful.

Thank you to my brother Kevin Alexander, sisters-in-law Wendy Alexander and Kelly King, and nephews Joshua and Eli Alexander. You've been so supportive and encouraging. I want this book to succeed mostly so I don't embarrass you!

Thank you to my Melbourne friends and neighbours for being patient with me. I know how annoying it is that I cancel dates and take forever to reply to messages. You mean the world to me, even though I'm garbage at showing that.

Thank you to the city of Brisbane. Anyone who grew up in Brisbane understands how complicated a relationship with a city can be. I love the place and couldn't wait to get away from it, and I'm not sure I fully understand either of those responses. The city shaped me. As did the fact I was born in San Francisco but grew up in a harsh tropical Australian city – but that's another story. Thank you to every person I knew at school, Queensland University, 4ZZZ and beyond. Thank you to Susan Attewell and Tony Moore for being the best house-mates and friends through my youth, and the best humans I know. I say with deep respect that my Brisbane friends and family are more resilient, unflappable and astute than people I've met anywhere. One of the many things Brisbane taught me is to never judge a place by its elected officials. Sometimes you just don't have much to choose from.

And though I never met Andrew McGahan, I owe him my thanks, too. Until I read his novel *Last Drinks* I didn't know it was possible to write about my hometown and all its contradictions with honesty and affection. He was an incredible writer, gone too soon.

Kirsten Alexander was born in San Francisco, raised in Brisbane, and spent some years in London. She lives in Melbourne with her partner, two sons and two dogs. Her first novel was *Half Moon Lake*; this is her second.

Discover a
new favourite

Visit **penguin.com.au/readmore**